THE GOOD DAUGHTER

J. A. BAKER

Boldwood

First published in Great Britain in 2025 by Boldwood Books Ltd.

Copyright © J. A. Baker, 2025

Cover Design by Head Design Ltd

Cover Images: Alamy and iStock

The moral right of J. A. Baker to be identified as the author of this work has been asserted in accordance with the Copyright, Designs and Patents Act 1988.

All rights reserved. No part of this book may be reproduced in any form or by any electronic or mechanical means, including information storage and retrieval systems, without written permission from the author, except for the use of brief quotations in a book review. This book is a work of fiction and, except in the case of historical fact, any resemblance to actual persons, living or dead, is purely coincidental.

Every effort has been made to obtain the necessary permissions with reference to copyright material, both illustrative and quoted. We apologise for any omissions in this respect and will be pleased to make the appropriate acknowledgements in any future edition.

A CIP catalogue record for this book is available from the British Library.

Paperback ISBN 978-1-83561-188-3

Large Print ISBN 978-1-83561-187-6

Hardback ISBN 978-1-83561-186-9

Ebook ISBN 978-1-83561-189-0

Kindle ISBN 978-1-83561-190-6

Audio CD ISBN 978-1-83561-181-4

MP3 CD ISBN 978-1-83561-182-1

Digital audio download ISBN 978-1-83561-183-8

This book is printed on certified sustainable paper. Boldwood Books is dedicated to putting sustainability at the heart of our business. For more information please visit https://www.boldwoodbooks.com/about-us/sustainability/

Boldwood Books Ltd, 23 Bowerdean Street, London, SW6 3TN

www.boldwoodbooks.com

*For Mam and Dad, and Ellen and Jack
to see and speak
to you just one more time
would be so precious.*

Justic delayed is justice denied

— WILLIAM E. GLADSTONE

PROLOGUE

Her eyes snapped open. Something was awry. She could feel it in the air, her senses attuned to every movement, every tiny change in the atmosphere. She blinked and placed a trembling hand over her mouth, the fleshiness of her lips pressing against the ridge of her teeth.

He was here. After all those nocturnal visits, the times she had seen him standing outside her bedroom window, he had finally found a way inside the house. She could sense him, smell him even; the stranger in her room. The sour meaty tang of his body odour drifted her way, filling her nostrils, clinging to her skin. It was everywhere, the stench of his arrogance, the strength and power of his longing. It emanated from his pores, made her want to retch. Her stomach roiled, blood surged through her veins. And all the while she lay silently. Too frightened to do or say anything. Too terrified to move.

A shaft of moonlight filtering in through the bedroom curtains revealed his outline, the breadth of his shoulders, the angular cut of his jaw. The sheer heft and sturdiness of him. This wasn't a dream. She was awake, her nerve endings aflame, her skin rippling with disgust and dread. This was a living nightmare.

Lying motionless, she held her breath, a pocket of air suspended in her lungs, her body making no sound for fear of drawing attention to herself. He was sitting on the stool next to her grandma's old dressing table, legs spread wide as he watched her. Assessed her. His eyes were fixed on her body, on her frozen form as she continued to lie still beneath the bedsheets. No longer an ominous shadow outside her window, a figure observing her from afar, he was here inside her room, and this was real. How long had he been there? Observing her as she slept, dark sinister thoughts rumbling through his head. A minute? An hour? The darkness intensified as she feigned sleep. It was oppressive, the blackness of the room, closing in, pooling around her, swallowing her whole.

She couldn't move or cry out even if she wanted to, sheer panic anchoring her to the mattress. With limbs that were infused with iron, she was locked in place, her head too heavy for her body, her tongue glued to the roof of her mouth. This was it; she felt sure of it. This was how she was going to die, her demise a clear-cut image in her mind; a knife thrust deep into her abdomen. Or maybe a firm hand clasped tightly around her throat stopping any air from getting in. She wanted to scream for help but knew that crying out would bring about a rapid death, her pleas for assistance resulting in her throat being cut or her head being caved in with a blunt instrument. She just wanted more time. Time to think. To plan. To work out what to do next.

Seconds passed. Minutes perhaps. No, not minutes. Fear was warping her ability to measure time with any accuracy. A strange lightness took hold in her mind, a sudden clarity of thought as she wondered what his weapon of choice would be when he finally made his move; she guessed at a blade, something long and serrated. Something horrifically painful and deadly. She could almost visualise it in his hands, his huge strong fingers clasped around the handle as he sat close by, his long legs stretched out, his body relaxed and supple, biding his time as if this were some kind of sick game, waiting for the moment when he would strike. Enjoying it even. She had to be careful, not do anything rash or anything at all that would rile him. The longer she left it, the more prepared she would be. That was her plan, the only weapon in her own armoury.

Logic and a small amount of time pitted against a six-foot monster. It wasn't a fair match but there was nothing else at hand.

Perhaps he would leave if she continued to simulate sleep. Tired of waiting, maybe he would slip away into the night. So she waited in silence, the covers hitched up to her chin, eyes slowly and carefully scouring the darkness of the room for something weighty and substantial. Anything she could use to protect herself. He was heavier and stronger than she was, muscles bulging beneath his clothes. Using her nails would be futile. A kick between his legs would fell him momentarily, but she needed more than that. An image of the knife he may be carrying loomed large in her mind, the glint of the blade making her queasy. A baseball bat or a cricket bat, that would be enough. One good swing at his head to knock him out. She would make sure she hit her target, a strength she didn't know she possessed giving her extra momentum. Fear driving her on. Striking him would give her a chance to escape at least, or to get to the phone. Except the baseball bat wasn't close by, but in her brother's room at the other end of the house. The phone was downstairs. She had nothing. She was alone in this.

And yet, she couldn't just let this happen. She had to do something. Lying there inert and rigid was the wrong thing to do. He would see her as weak, a victim. Easy pickings.

The lack of noise in the house was deafening, her family all asleep; outside in the vast rural terrain, the birds and wildlife slumbered. Even the usual hooting of the owls was absent, as if his presence had shocked them into silence. Any movements she made would be heard; every breath, every rustle of fabric heightened and detected. And yet she had to do something. Whatever he had planned, whatever atrocity he had in mind for her, she would go down fighting.

Her mouth was dry as she let out an inadvertent whimper, barbed wired cutting into the soft flesh of her throat, ripping and shredding her windpipe. She sucked in her breath, aware he would hear. Then out of nowhere, her limbs sprang into action, her body suddenly free of the paralysis that had kept her locked in place. Slowly, so very slowly as if in a dream, she inched her way off the mattress, legs first, hands placed squarely on the floor before slithering under the wooden bedframe, praying he hadn't heard the rustle of the bedsheets or the dull thump of the floorboards as she clambered into the small space, and at the same time, knowing that he had.

'Come out, come out, wherever you are...'

It was a dry whisper, the voice that rang around the room, followed by a low burst of laughter; the demented giggling of the unhinged. He knew. He had been studying her, had seen her vain attempt at hiding, his pupils boring through the darkness like a pick through solid ice. He had sat and watched, amused at her clumsy endeavours as she slid under the bed for protection, her body heavy, her co-ordination lumbering and ungainly. And now he was just sitting there. Watching and waiting. Scheming. It was too dark to see his face but she recognised that voice. She knew who it was, the sound of it like a punch to the gut. No more shadowy figures. No more standing outside in the darkness, his identity concealed by a velvety black sky.

'Don't hide. I'll find you wherever you go, you do know that, don't you?' The timbre of his voice forced bile up into her throat. The clunk of her swallow, the rush of her blood, the thud of her heartbeat all echoed in her head, a clashing discordant sound.

Outlandish notions punched their way into her brain, things she could do to make him leave. Screaming, rattling at the bed frame. Clambering out of her hidey-hole and running at him, teeth bared, nails at the ready. But this was a large house, noises muffled by solid walls and heavy oak doors. Her bedroom was on the other side of the farmhouse, far from the other rooms. She'd chosen it, wanting privacy. And this was the result. Facing her terror, alone and unsupported.

Fear vibrated through her body. She closed her eyes, counted, thought of other things – praying he would leave. It had happened before. Like the time she had crouched behind the curtains, waiting until her fear receded, watching as he made his retreat before she slipped back into bed, her limbs watery with fear. But that time was very different. That time he was outside, a brick wall and locked doors separating them. This time he was here, in the house. In her room. And she knew, she just *knew* deep down in her gut, that this time he wasn't going to leave. He was here to stay. To do something terrible. Something unthinkable. His previous visits had been a warm up. This one was the real deal.

She brought up her knees to her chest as if to protect herself, a foetal curling of her young soft body. Then came a movement, his slow ragged breathing, the snap of his belt and the sharp rustle of his clothing; wild manic echoes that filled her head with fire, flickering flames searing at her skin.

And next, slow footsteps and shuffling methodical movements. She curled up tighter under the bed, squirming and twitching, her limbs struggling to remain still, her fingers reaching out for a means of escape and finding nothing. He was beside her. He was behind her. He was everywhere. There was no way out.

Large hands, pulling at her ankles, dragging her out from under the bed. Her mouth opened and the scream that had been frozen in place by terror forced its way up her throat. A hand was clasped over her face, trapping the sound before it could emerge. Trapping *her*. This was it. This was the end. The end of her life as she knew it.

Would her mother believe her now? The person who had rejected and ignored her claims. Would she take notice now? Not dismiss her as a fantasist. A freak. A fake.

Suddenly, he was upon her, her airways constricted by his hands and the sheer heft of his body. She thought of other things, filled her head with anything other than him. School. Family. How long it would take for her to die.

Tears burned behind her eyelids. A lump rose in her throat, a large jagged rock jammed at an awkward painful angle as he pulled down her underwear and forced her legs apart with his knee. Cold air, alien and sinister, wrapped itself around the most private parts of her body. She tried to swallow down her fear, to scream for help, but it was hopeless, his vice-like grip forcing her mouth closed. The weight of his body keeping her motionless. He had won. He had come into her room, the place where she should have been safe, and he was doing whatever he wanted. Treating her like a piece of dirt. An inconsequential speck of dust.

An arrow of pain, sharp and relentless, shot through her lower body as he pushed himself inside her. His face was close to hers, his breath hot and rancid, a mist of spittle spraying over her skin. She closed her eyes, using the darkness as a shield. A barrier between her sanity and his actions. Between her and his filthy invasive thrusting.

A grunt. A whimper. A slight jerking of his lower body. And then it was over. He rolled off her onto the floor with a dull thud leaving her flesh cold and exposed, like a slab of raw meat. Her stomach and lower body trembled. Dampness leaked from between her legs, the revulsion of what had just taken place making her gag. Fingers worried at fabric as she pulled down her nightdress, shame blooming in her veins. She listened to the scramble of his limbs as he clambered up off the floor and crept out of the room. Then the creak of the floorboards as he descended the stairs, followed by a prolonged silence, everybody sleeping soundly in other rooms, unaware of what had just taken place. She was too weak to shout, too shocked to move. Too humiliated to wake them and beg for help. The tears that had built behind her eyes ran down her face, streaking over her skin, their salty wetness cooling her burning flesh.

Her mattress, usually soft and welcoming, was now a bed of stones and rubble; each limb, each part of her body, aching and bruised as she climbed in and pulled the duvet tight around herself. A warm downy shield to help blot out the horror of what had just taken place. All those ideas of how she would fight him off, how she would scream and yell and kick and scratch, and in the end she did nothing, sheer terror rendering her immobile. Her body moored and pinioned to the floor while he did whatever he wanted to her.

This would never leave her, this night of horror. This night of unutterable dread. His actions, how he had defiled her, robbed her of her confidence, would be there always. Fear would follow her, perching on her shoulder, whispering in her ear. It would pass, this event. Life would go on. She would tell no-one, the shame and humiliation she felt at what he had done too great to share with others. It would remain buried deep within her. She would make it through each day, but she knew that at some point, somehow, she would find a way to prove to the world how despicable he was. She was young, inexperienced, and not so well versed in the intricacies and workings of the world around her. But she was patient. She would wait. And one day – she didn't know when – her time would come. She only hoped that when it arrived, that day of reckoning, that she would catch him unawares. Make him realise that he had sullied and degraded the wrong person. A person who would never forgive. A person who would never ever forget.

1

PENNY

Day 1

I feel like I've dodged a bullet, relief blossoming in my chest as I watch everyone gather at the far end of the room. Ten weeks. Such a long time to be holed up in a room with a crowd of strangers, everyone herded together like cattle and forced into a confined space, their lives put on hold as they decide the fate of a perfect stranger. All that formality and those baffling legal processes. Rows and rows of seats filled with staring eyes and rigid spines, jurors sitting stiff-lipped and resentful at the injustice of their forced captivity. And then the defendant staring at them, willing each and every person on that bench to find them not guilty. I inhale deeply, cold air rushing into my lungs. There have been cases where defendants have threatened members of the jury, attempting to coerce them into passing a not guilty verdict.

I shiver, relieved to have been passed over, relieved to still be sitting here. Perhaps I won't be needed, the court clerk informing me at some point during the morning that there aren't any more cases for this week. I will get sent home, given a thank you for my time and be back in my house by lunchtime.

'I hope I don't get called up for this one.' The lady seated next to me feverishly bites at her nails, her jaw pulsing rhythmically as she nibbles and gnaws, her movements rapid and rodent-like. 'I don't have childcare for that length of time.'

Jocelyn Jacobs
David Marshall
Paul Oswald

I hear her gasp, see her eyes widen as she stands and marches over to join the throng. The list is being read out alphabetically. I'm off the hook. I'm going to be okay. Everything is going to be just fine. My balled fists ache, my nails digging into the soft flesh of my palms. I can't afford to take ten weeks off work. I'm self-employed and it would be catastrophic. The possible undoing of my recently formed business. Expenses paid by the court wouldn't be anywhere near enough to cover my costs.

'Apparently a lack of childcare doesn't get taken into account.' A female I guess to be in her fifties sitting opposite me shakes her head and purses her lips. 'Illness. That's the one. If you're a full-time carer for someone who is disabled or ill, they'll let you off with cases that are likely to drag on and on.'

I think of my mother, how I could use her condition to squirm my way out of a long drawn-out case, and I feel shame burrow beneath my skin. I've heard people complain about such get-out clauses, saying how we should all do our civic duty. A week, possibly two. That's all it will be, then I can leave this place and get on with my life. Forget any of it ever happened.

'They're going through the names alphabetically. What's yours?' A silver-haired man nods, leaning forwards, his gaze sweeping across the room before landing on me.

I want to tell him that I already know this, that I've got it all worked out, but instead I give him a watery smile and clear my throat before speaking.

'Collins,' I say. 'Penny Collins.' My tongue lodges in the crevices of my mouth as I sweep it around my gums, trying to alleviate the dryness. My throat is like sandpaper, my eyes sore and gritty. I suppress a yawn, wishing I had brought a bottle of water with me. Already the overhead strip lighting is giving me a headache. I rummage in my bag for a couple of painkillers and swallow them down dry.

'Looks like you'll be okay.'

Aqsa Rahib

Samuel Sanderson

'That's me,' he says to nobody in particular, his voice a crack of ice in our small circle. 'Ten weeks out of my life. Wish me luck.' He pats his knees and sighs before standing and walking towards a multitude of people gathered near the double doors.

'Why so many?' I turn to the lady next to me, casting my eye over the crowd of what looks to be at least thirty murmuring individuals. 'I thought it was fifteen that then got whittled down to twelve?'

'Because it's going to be a long trial, they need to work out who can do it and who can't. My husband has got advanced cancer and I'm his main carer. I wouldn't be able to leave him for that length of time. If they call me, I'll have to tell them. I can't leave him for that long. I just can't.' She purses her lips, craning her neck to get a better view of the crowd.

I nod and watch the hustle and bustle of the disgruntled mass, thankful I'm not amongst them. I think of Damien, my husband, and our dog, Freda. Then I think of my mum in her house that's adjoined to ours. I don't have time to sit through a ten-week trial. I don't *want* to sit through a ten-week trial. Every fibre of my being wants to walk away from this, to simply turn and flee. But I can't. I could lie and tell them that I'm Mum's official carer, even though I'm not and her dementia is still in its early stages. She has good days and bad days, and on the good days she can function fairly well, but on the bad days she has rages which are, frankly, quite terrifying. But right now, Mum's rages hold more appeal than this place, with its demands and constraints that are damaging my business and eating away at my time.

The clerk's voice cuts through my musings, calling for the attention of the crowd who shift about as one large flock, their dark clothing and sour expressions putting me in mind of a huge cockroach. Feet shuffling and tapping on the tiled floor, they are led out of the waiting area and through the double doors, disappearing into the unknown. The sense of liberation among the remaining individuals is palpable. They scroll through phones or pick up books and read, a collective sense of smugness and relief crackling in the air around us.

I barely have time to open my magazine before the voice over the loudspeaker once again calls for our attention, asking for the following people to stand and wait with the court clerk.

Alison Bainbridge

David Braithwaite

Penny Collins

My stomach tightens. It's happening.

'Here we go,' I say to the woman seated next to me, praying this isn't going to be a case that goes on forever.

She offers me a thin-lipped smile, her eyes a crinkle of sympathy, then returns to her phone, her gaze locked onto the screen.

The voice on the loudspeaker blurs in my head while I mentally go through what will happen next. Will this be a long case? I suspect not. The last group of potential jurors were given advance warning. Dread is a clenched fist at the base of my gut, the knuckles digging deep into my flesh. I want to go home, to immerse myself in my business. To be anywhere but here.

The final name is called. I stand waiting, and after a few seconds, fifteen of us are led down a corridor into a smaller waiting area where twelve of us are summoned. The remaining three people heave a sigh of relief as we, the final dozen, are led into the courtroom in single file.

'The order you're in now must stay that way for the duration of the case,' the clerk tells us with a wink and a smile, as if to soften the command.

We each glance at the people ahead and behind us, casting their faces to memory. I'm second in line. Easy to remember. A diminutive lady in her sixties is ahead of me. She turns, eyebrows raised, and salutes in mock servitude.

'At least our place is easy for us to remember, eh? We're the leaders.'

'The leaders,' I say, parroting her words.

We are welcomed by a kindly faced judge. He sits higher than everyone else, his formal red gown and long wig in sharp contrast to our ordinary clothing. We stand as he greets us, reminding everyone to report any conflict of interest that may arise with the defendant and witnesses. A remarkably shabby piece of paper that contains a list of names and places is given to each person.

'Of course,' he says softly, 'this is a local courtroom that deals with local cases and you have all been selected from the local electoral register, so knowing the town doesn't necessarily count as a conflict. What we are asking is if you are well acquainted with the exact address where the crime took place. For instance, if you live next door or over the road from any of the witnesses or the defendant, or even the victim in this case, then please let the clerk know as soon as you can. And if you recognise any of the names written down there, we also need to be informed.'

I glance down and as instructed, read both the name and the location. The floor tilts and sways beneath me. The throbbing that takes hold in my head is immediate, like a hammer busily tapping at my skull. It can't be. This is wrong. A terrible coincidence. My vision is hazy, the words distorted when I read them again, the name of the defendant and the location branding themselves into my brain. I have no idea how to react, what to say. So I say nothing. Instead I blithely hand the paper back, the moment to declare any conflict of interest already over.

'If at any point you recognise any of the witnesses or the defendant once you are sworn in, then please pass a piece of paper to the court clerk and we will take necessary action.'

My heart thrums in my chest. Nobody makes a sound. I attempt a smile but my face is frozen, my jaw aching with the effort of attempting to look impassive and fearless when all the while my insides are roiling. Every second that passes puts a greater distance between being honest and being deceitful. I should declare. Honesty has always been important to me. I have prided myself on living a good life. A decent honest life. Until now. Because despite the fear that is pulsing through my veins, despite the fire that is raging in my chest and the fact I'm finding it hard to breathe properly, I know that I'm not going to speak up.

We are each handed another slip of paper and asked to read it aloud. It's an oath. We are being sworn in. This is it. The lady next to me reads hers and I follow, each of us saying it out loud until the final juror finishes and hands the paper back to the clerk.

'If you could all please step back outside while the defendant is led in.' More smiling from the judge. It's clear he is doing his best to make us feel relaxed and comfortable. It isn't working. My thoughts drift to my mother, wondering how she is also coping while I'm not there. More importantly, how she and Damien are getting on. They're amiable with each other, Damien a supportive son-in-law, but my mother's demands are increasing with each passing day. Our working arrangements – me in my office at the bottom of the garden and Damien in his study – are an easy and accessible way of making sure she comes to no harm. Only last week, she knocked at our door asking for milk, repeating the process five times in one afternoon. Half a dozen pints were already lined up in her fridge. Every day brings a new drama and an added layer of apprehension that things are about to get a whole lot worse.

We sit in the waiting area outside the courtroom, a cramped space that doesn't resemble a waiting area at all. It's a dumping ground for unwanted office furniture. Chairs are piled high around us, small occasional tables stacked up in the far corner. High windows ensure we can't see what is going on outside. I remind myself that we're the innocent ones here. The unwilling captives. So why do I feel like a prisoner?

His name continues to tap away in my brain. The name of the defendant. I wipe away a layer of perspiration from my top lip, my skin hot and clammy even though deep inside I feel shivery and cold.

It's not him. It can't be.

And yet I know that it is. Somehow, I always knew this day would come.

Small talk and pleasantries begin, whispers soon escalating into a loud buzz. Myriad voices escalate, different threads of conversations overlapping. The usher who is standing by the door presses a slim finger to his lips and makes a shushing sound. He winks and smiles, his informal manner enough to quieten us momentarily. His austere garb and dark eyes rove around the room, making sure we comply.

Whispers soon start up again, a stream of disembodied voices, low and inaudible. I say nothing to the people sitting either side of me. My tongue feels too big for my mouth, my throat and gums lacking in moisture.

'They can hear everything in there.' The usher nods towards the courtroom, his brows knitted together as he peers through the glass panel of the door.

He slips inside like a breeze curling its way through the tiniest of gaps and appears a few seconds later, beckoning us to go back into the courtroom. Lining up like dutiful schoolchildren, we form a queue in our designated places and file in, sitting on a long wooden bench once we are all inside. The defendant is standing in the dock to the right of us. I make a point of not looking at him. He is a figure in my peripheral vision, his very existence in the room a disquieting presence. I keep my eyes lowered, focusing on my hands that I've placed on my lap. My fingers are locked together to stop the tremble before I am able to pluck up enough courage to look his way. I expect to see a monster of sorts, a character who fits the stereotypical image of a criminal. That's how I remember him, the form he has taken in my mind for all these decades. I feel my bodyweight lighten when all I can see is his lowered head. My legs and innards turn to liquid all the same. His presence in the room is enough to terrify me, stealing all the air from my lungs in a hot rush. I try to control my breathing, to stem the panic that is crawling crab-like up my throat, but my heart is pounding, a huge metronome that relentlessly knocks at my sternum. I can't see his face yet. He keeps his head lowered as he stares down at his feet. I hope he feels ashamed and frightened and everything I felt when he did what he did to me all those years ago. I was a young teenager. A child, for God's sake.

You thought you were allowed to forget that period of your life, didn't you?

I ignore the voice in my head that is screaming at me to declare my knowledge of him, pushing it back into that dark dusty corner of my brain. His eyes continue to sweep the floor, unable or unwilling to look our way. I wait, trying to keep hold of my terror, to not come undone when I see his face. I will deny all knowledge should he recognise me. He won't. It was a long time ago. I've changed, physically and emotionally. I'm a different person. More mature. Wiser. I keep my cracks and fissures hidden deep within me. My damage dwells in the darkest shadows in the farthest reaches of my soul.

And then, finally, he looks up. Once again, the room begins to move, the walls leaning in at drunken angles. He hasn't changed that much. Older, with thinning hair, but still that sallow complexion. Those dark bottomless eyes. That confident gait. And a smirk, arrogance evident in his steady unmoving features.

Heat burns my face, my skin sizzling and vibrating. Sweat pearls around my hairline and my neck, gathering in my clavicle and blooming under my arms. His gaze passes over me, his eyes assessing the jury. He doesn't recognise me. I was a nobody to him, a nuisance. A child. And yet, *his* face is emblazoned in my brain. Images and memories of him fire off in all directions in my head, their strength and potency making me nauseated and woozy. I sit up straight as if to show him I'm not scared when what I actually want to do is fall to the floor and weep. Every muscle, every sinew in my body, is slack with terror. I feel sick, a hundred insects hungrily nibbling at my skin, and yet there he stands with his lopsided sneer, as if his appearance in this courtroom is an everyday occurrence. As if what he did to me all those years ago didn't happen or didn't matter.

I thought I had finally managed to repress that memory, that period of my life. I hadn't. It's still there. It will always be there. I will remember every detail about him until the day I die because standing there in the dock, waiting to be tried, is the man who almost ruined my life.

2

THE HOUSE

She hated it. Perhaps hate was too strong a word. She disliked it, always had, but was now being forced to tolerate it, to call it home, be happy living there. Hallshead Farmhouse was an oversized ancient building, difficult to heat and impossible to keep clean. But it was free. An unwanted inheritance. Eric's family had lived in the place for generations and now it was their turn. Could she really afford to say no? Probably not. It would be ungrateful and churlish to turn down such a gift. Besides, this place meant a lot to Eric. Whether she liked it or not, she was now going to have to make it mean a lot to her.

Connie draped her hand across the bare brick wall of the monstrously long hallway, her fingers catching and snagging on the rough, ragged surface. How many people had walked this route before her, she wondered. How many sets of feet had padded along this floor, across these worn yet remarkably solid flagstones? Silent invisible bodies paraded past. She could almost hear their whispers, feel their stares. Touch their grey, haunted faces. A century of family members, watching her. Waiting to pass judgement on her plans and renovations for their crumbling home.

She and Eric were already in the process of attempting to sell their modern house and move somewhere bigger when Hallshead Farmhouse became abruptly and unexpectedly vacant. They needed somewhere that was more suited to a growing family, but everything was either too small, too rundown or too expensive. Nothing was right. Large living room, tiny outside space. Recently refitted kitchen, too few bedrooms. Large garden, dilapidated bathroom and kitchen. Everywhere they looked, all the houses failed to match up to their requirements or their meagre budget. They despaired, thinking nothing would ever come up. And then it did. But not in the way they'd imagined or hoped. A family tragedy. Their lives ripped apart while simultaneously handing them a place so large they could get lost in it.

'We'll have enough money to renovate,' Eric said on seeing her face as she sloped around the farmhouse, her disdain evident in the downward curve of her mouth and tapered eyes as she examined the dated décor, the layers of dust and dead flies that peppered the windowsills. The peeling wallpaper and mould that crept spider-like across the ceiling.

She moved in silence from room to room, saying nothing, her crestfallen features betraying her innermost emotions. Her despair. The horror she felt at the thought of living there. Eric deserved to have this old place, she knew that. Aside from his sister, it was all that remained of his family. His memories, his childhood; they were embedded into every corner and crevice. She knew how important the house was to him and wasn't cruel enough to deny him his inheritance and access to his past. And yet, already she missed their old home, their too-small modern house that shrank around them once the children were born; the walls closing in, squashing them into a tiny huddle. Hallshead Farmhouse had all the space they required and more. It was dated, isolated, its rundown state an ever-open mouth that would probably strip them of their savings. And now it was theirs. The possibilities swam before her eyes, as did the problems, a mountain of them piling up, breaking apart, toppling and crushing her.

Connie nodded at Eric, swallowing down the lump that bobbed about in her throat. What he was saying about having enough cash to renovate was true. His words made perfect sense. The equity from their old house was more than enough to spruce up their new home. In truth, she didn't know what it was that was dampening her fervour. Dust could be cleaned, old fixtures and fittings replaced. Memories perhaps? Maybe they were nudging their way in. And guilt. That was the overriding emotion that stamped out all others, obliterating the glimmers of happiness that twinkled at the edges of her thoughts. Guilt was a powerful emotion. Easy to bend under its weight. Harder to shake off its greedy powerful clutches.

Connie and Eric had been sitting having lunch when the phone call came. She recalled with startling clarity her husband's face as he snatched up the handset and listened. His slack-jawed appearance, how he had stumbled on weakened legs, hanging on to the kitchen countertop for balance before sliding down onto the floor. Then her race to scoop him up, to ask over and over what had happened. And soon after, the dreadful sinking and furling of her stomach as she listened to the voice at the other end, the words leaving a lasting imprint on their lives. A gaping wound that would never heal. She had taken the phone from him, one hand pressing the receiver against her ear, the other resting on her husband's shoulder.

'Hello?' Her voice was croaky, anxiety and apprehension choking her airway.

'Connie, it's me.' Eric's sister, Rita, spoke, her voice low, almost a whisper, firing off a stilted collection of words that brought their world as they knew it crashing down around them.

Rita and Eric's parents and their brother. An accident in the car. Plunged into the river. No survivors.

The words took a few seconds to filter into Connie's brain. She had swallowed and run her fingers through her hair because she didn't know what else to do.

'All of them? Sam as well?'

'All of them.'

And then Rita began to cry, her composure crumbling as the reality of what she had just said kicked in. Her parents and her brother, gone. All dead. Swallowed up by the freezing river and carried downstream in their car, unable to get out. Each of them watching as the water grew higher and higher around them, trapping them in its icy watery depths.

An accident. Just an awful unforeseen accident. The police were firm on that score, ruling out foul play, blaming the weather. Heavy rain had swollen the river to record levels. Sam had been driving, his parents the passengers. They had been to town. Nothing special. Just a regular visit to buy food and other essentials. The dent on the rear bumper was caused by Sam hitting the stone handrail of the bridge as he had attempted to reverse away from the floods to find an alternative route. Their unheard cries haunted Connie's dreams for weeks afterwards, their panicked expressions as they attempted to claw their way out of the car, waking her at night, her chest damp with perspiration. Much as she tried, she couldn't shake the image of those bulging eyes and gaping mouths, their features twisted with fear as their vehicle sank below the surface and disappeared out of sight.

And now, almost a year later, she and Eric were here at the home of her deceased in-laws and there was no going back. An interloper; that was who she was. She had profited from their deaths, inherited a house borne out of tragedy, and it didn't sit well with her. Feelings of discomfort and shame regularly coiled in her veins, chiselling down into the marrow of her bones until she felt hollow with grief and guilt.

'You take the house,' Rita had said without an ounce of bitterness once the funerals had been conducted and the will read and digested. 'I don't need it. I have enough money and space here.'

It was true, she didn't need it, her wealth already extensive after setting up her own art and antiques dealership in York. Rita had an eye for such things, and if Eric and his parents were to be believed, she had once sold a rare painting for over £150,000 after finding it in a house clearance for pennies.

Eric suggested that his sister take whatever cash her parents had left in the bank, money they had salted away for possible care for Sam after their death, and Rita agreed. Sam was the only offspring who had stayed at the farmhouse, happy to keep his circle small, his shyness and lack of social skills a barrier between him and the outside world. And in the end, it was his undoing.

The kitchen was the most dilapidated part of the house, the units old and dusty, the appliances fit for a museum. Or a scrapyard. Eric's parents shunned modern living. Connie recalled their stricken expressions, their laughter and the shaking of heads as she and Eric bought new rugs and blinds, doing what they could to soften the edges of their own modern home, attempting to disguise its sharp angles and dark corners with scatter cushions and subdued lighting.

You're warm and dry. What more do you need?

Already she could hear their voices, filled with disbelief and horror as she mentally planned a new kitchen, wondering how long it would take to dismantle the old units that had been there for as long as Eric and Rita could remember.

Good solid units, those. No need to get rid. You'll rue the day if you get one of those new-fangled kitchens. It'll drop to bits before you know it.

Did she want to be the one who storm-trooped through this old house that hadn't been altered for decades, ripping it apart and erasing the memory of his family? Connie's sense of unease grew, her eyes travelling over the heavy oak beams and uninsulated uneven walls. She shivered. Even in the dead of summer, this place was freezing. It would also need a rewire. How they hadn't all fried before now was a mystery to her.

'It can be a sympathetic renovation,' Eric said from behind.

Time and time again, he was able to read her mind, unpicking her nuanced thinking with such aplomb, it would often catch her unawares. And yet already she was wondering how sympathetic? Eric, like his parents, was often averse to change, but even he knew that they couldn't live in Hallshead Farmhouse as it was. Connie's approach would have to be measured and thoughtful, compromises made. Conversations held that required careful negotiation.

She nodded and sighed, briefly closing her eyes against the tide of apprehension that regularly threatened to swamp her. She was drowning in an ocean of discomfort and anxiety. They had a long road ahead of them but surely it couldn't be any worse than what they had already endured? The house and the land around it were both a gift and a hindrance. The bulk of the farmland had been sold off many years back by Eric's grandparents, but there were still five acres to tend. Eric was right; they would have to tread carefully with the interior of this old farmhouse, not ruin the legacy of his family by knocking down walls and ripping out original features. And yet, she could not, and would not, live here unless they made plans to update and modernise it. Mould that crept up walls and an ancient boiler that didn't provide enough hot water to fill a bath puckered her skin and made her scalp crinkle with horror.

'One room at a time,' she said quietly, as if the dead were watching, picking apart her every word and thought, scrutinising the contents of her head and finding her notions and ideas wanting. 'One room at a time.'

3
PENNY

Day 1

The urge to declare my knowledge of the defendant is strong, but tempered with something dark and forceful, overpowering even. It is a fetid desire that won't exit my brain, and that desire is the overriding compulsion I feel to seek vengeance for what he did to me. I want to see him suffer. I'm breaking the law, standing here saying nothing, I know that. Do I really want to take such a dangerous and lawless route? The answer to that is no. I'm an upstanding citizen, a law-abiding individual who is fearful of authoritative figures that have the power to take away my liberties. And yet still I stand, all my contradictory notions and ideas tightly held in place in my head. Bound with an iron clasp. Already, even though my thoughts are jumbled and in no semblance of order, *already* I know that I am going to keep my silence. I owe it to my family. I owe it to myself. He doesn't recognise me. That was the defining moment, the thing that set me on this path. Had he shown any signs of recognition then I would have had no choice than to step down. But he didn't. And so here I am, about to break the law in order to restore some stability into my life. To reset a balance in my existence that has been askew for far too long. I have nothing to lose and everything to gain.

A loud drum bangs against my ribcage, my heart a frenetic thrashing object that pounds and pounds against my sternum, making me light-headed and marginally giddy. I take a shaky breath and try to appear unmoved by my surroundings. This is my time, this moment a gift. God knows I've waited long enough. Almost thirty years. There he stands, and here I am, the sturdier one; the scales of power finally tipped in my direction. He may look unperturbed by his current predicament but I'm not the one in the dock facing a possible prison sentence. That's his fate. I'm free to go home every evening while he will be led away to a cold cell until the verdict is announced. As long as I hold my secret close, that is. As long as I don't inadvertently tell anybody that I know him. *Used* to know him. We weren't friends. I would never befriend such a vile monster, but at one point, he established himself as somebody of note on the periphery of my life, forcing himself into my home. Forcing himself on me. He appeared uninvited and stripped away my dignity and confidence. He stole so much from me. It's time to take it back.

I was so young, so immature back then, thinking I knew everything when I knew nothing about anything. I felt sure I could handle whatever life threw at me. I was so wrong. For so many years, that man, that *entity*, lived in my head, the memory of him a large looming presence with long oily tentacles that draped over every corner of my brain, poisoning me, his toxic waste seeping into my veins and travelling around my body at lightning speed. There were days when I could barely get out of bed because of what he did to me. It took years to shake him off, to peel away layer after layer of dirt and grime. To shed those residual memories, and scrub away that trauma. To feel whole and wholesome again. I was so scared of him. Terrified. He took hold in my brain, his shape a monstrous thing that grew bigger and stronger with each passing day. And now he is here, a weak specimen of an individual. His life, his entire future, is in my hands. I have the power to inflict on him the same level of suffering and helplessness that he imposed on me. I suppress a smile, my feelings of superiority clawing to be set free. I know little of the legal system in this country but I do know that even the most robust of cases can fail at the slightest hitch. A nervous witness. A flimsy piece of evidence that is taken apart by the defence team. An ill-willed rogue juror.

Small bolts of electricity needle my skin, the tingle jolting me back to the present. The judge is speaking, his voice a distant hum in my head. I correct my posture, paint on a mask of attentiveness and tune back in to his instructions, picking up on the last few directives about not discussing the case to anybody outside of the courtroom, even the other jurors. We must all hold our silence even though we will sit side by side, listening to the same evidence for the next week.

We are led outside once again, back into the small waiting-room-cum-storage area.

'There'll be lots of this, I'm afraid,' says the usher as we perch ourselves on the spread of badly arranged seats. 'Every time a new witness is called, the judge will ask you to leave until they're in place in the courtroom and then you'll get called back in.'

'I can't take my eyes off his wig,' says a young red-haired female, the shriek and pitch of her voice jangling my nerves.

Again, the usher places his finger to his lips. And just like last time, he winks to soften the gesture. She lowers her shoulders and giggles, falling silent before glancing around the room. Perhaps she is looking for allies, others who will join in with her inane chatter and bouts of girlish laughter. Already, I find myself disliking her. Perhaps it's her manner or screeching voice. Perhaps it's both. I try to shrug away that sentiment. Regardless of her immaturity, regardless of the differences in our natures, we all need to gel. A week. That's how long the judge expects the trial to last. That much I did tune in to. Just enough to keep me informed. Long enough to allow me to think about what to do next, how I can make sure things go my way and that man doesn't walk free.

We sit in a quiet huddle, a trail of murmurs floating around the room, heads cocked to one side as we listen to forbidden whispered words. We're a disparate-looking bunch – one muscle-bound man with tattoos, the red-haired female, a diminutive elderly lady who looks to be in her seventies. An eclectic mix of individuals. I curtail my silent attempts to assess them, knowing better than to judge. Diamond-bright eyes and a wide smile can mask the darkest of souls.

He can't hurt you any more. But you can hurt him. This is your chance.

'I didn't realise it would be like this,' says a thin middle-aged lady.

Her voice is deliberately low. A hoarse whisper. Her eyes dart between me and the usher for fear of being reprimanded. 'I thought the wigs and long black coats were just for show on TV.'

The usher looks over at us and smiles, readjusting his own gown, pulling it over his shoulders and setting it properly on his neck. 'It's the latest fashion. I wear mine down at the local pub. Keeps the troublemakers in line.'

A few titters from the group. I smile, not wanting to appear dour. A laugh feels like a step too far. I'm unable to see the humour in any of this. It's this setting, the person in the dock. Grotesque memories are needling me, puncturing my skin. Drawing blood.

There's a movement of air to my left as the usher slips through the double doors into the courtroom, reappearing seconds later, bidding us all to file back inside. We line up, glancing ahead and behind to ensure we're in the correct order. The usher's head bobs about over us, nodding fervently like a Victorian schoolmaster conducting a thorough headcount of his charges.

The lady in front turns and grins at me. 'Here we go again, eh? This is it.'

There's no time to reply as we are led back inside to the bench where we sit in silence. The judge explains what is expected of us, what the case is about and an outline of the legal process, then tells us that court is adjourned until 9 a.m. tomorrow morning when the prosecution will offer their evidence and present their witnesses for questioning. The words *rape* and *assault* cut into my brain, settling there, leaving me dazed and disorientated. I am neither surprised nor shocked at this revelation. If I had to guess what his crime was going to be, that particular misdemeanour would have been top of the list. Nothing has the power to surprise me any more. Disgust and repulse, for sure. But what he did to me when I was no more than a child made me realise how depraved and cunning people can be in order to get what they want.

We file out again, this routine already an irritant. I feel out of sorts; underwhelmed by the whole process. It's barely lunchtime and we're making our way back into the main waiting area where instructions will be given to us on tomorrow's proceedings.

It's empty when we get there, save for a handful of people gathered around a small table, reading their phones or engaged in casual chat with the person next to them.

'You can either order your lunch at the main desk or bring something in, but you'll get an allowance regardless. Remember to bring in your receipts for travel and car parking. If you hand them to Stacey at the desk and show her your jurors' paperwork, she'll reimburse you. Make sure you've filled it all in properly with your bank details. Don't want anybody going short, do we?' A few titters, mainly borne out of a sense of relief. 'I'll lead you out down the back corridor and show you the entrance you need to use for the rest of the week. No more coming in the front door.'

And before we have a chance to protest or say anything in return, the usher bustles ahead of us and we're led out through countless doors and corridors I feel sure I won't remember in the morning.

I blink, craning my neck, trying to cast to memory every door and direction as we make our way out. The lady next to me nudges my arm. 'Follow the little black arrows on the wall.'

I glance to my left, catching sight of the line of small roughly made pointers that lead back to the door we have just exited.

'Thanks. It's all a bit—'

'I know,' she says, tapping my hand and shuffling along beside me. 'I know.'

I'm a bewildered child. A helpless soul in need of guidance. I need to sharpen up, not be so in awe of these surroundings, my senses dulled by anxiety and images of the past. If I don't keep a clear head, listen closely to every word that's being said, I am in danger of missing this opportunity. And it's the only one I will ever get. This is my time. A chance to right a terrible wrong. When he crept into my room all those years ago and assaulted me, I vowed that somehow, no matter how long it took, I would prove to everyone what he had done. To pass up on this opportunity, this moment that has been handed to me on a silver platter, because I am nervous and unprepared, my past stirring up old fears and deadening my responses and lucidity, would be a tragedy.

At the bottom of the stairs, a security guard sits on a wooden chair, boredom etched into his expression. He stands and opens the door, a blast of air catching the back of my throat as we exit. The wind hisses around the courtyard, buffeting us as we make our way over the stretch of tarmac to the large wrought-iron gates. Another security guard watches us from his little sentry hut. I feel the burn of his stare and look his way, giving him a weak smile before lowering my eyes. He nods in return and we all filter out into the street and head towards the car park and train station.

I think about the instructions we were given back in the courtroom.

No discussing the case with other jurors until it is over and a verdict has been reached. No chatting to each other about any of it.

The judge was adamant. No speaking at all to anybody until it's all over. I'm not allowed to say a single word to another living soul until that bastard is locked away.

My legs are made of rubber, my insides a slosh of water as we all head in the same direction, desperate to get home. Desperate to rest and ready ourselves for tomorrow when the hard part of this sickening case will begin.

4

PENNY

Day 1

The house exudes a calm energy, its softness and near silence a tonic for my frayed nerves. Damien messaged to say he has already walked Freda, our Border Collie, and made both himself and Mum some lunch. Even more remarkably, she has eaten it without a fuss. No rages or refusals. I left home this morning expecting mayhem and fury by lunchtime, and instead I'm here, floating into a sea of tranquillity, the choppy waters that are usually present due to Mum's deteriorating behaviour and illness a millpond.

'You're early?' Damien is standing at the kitchen window, his hair a halo of golden brown as clouds shift and part, the room suddenly flooded with natural light. We are bathed in warmth, the sun an iridescent orb that shimmers and is full of promise. Before I can reply, a mass of clouds the colour of gunmetal sweep across the sky, plunging us back into near darkness. I exhale, the memory of the morning's events stamped into my brain, the shock of seeing him after all these years like having an electrical probe pushed deep into my pores. The walk to the car park, the drive home, they were carried out on autopilot, my reflexes guiding me home. He is all I can think about – his face, his hands, his depraved behaviour all those years ago.

'We got sworn in, told the rules by the judge, and the case starts tomorrow morning. It will last to the end of the week apparently.'

Freda clambers out of her basket and sidles up next to me, her soft white fur pressing against my leg. I lean down and ruffle her coat. She responds by licking my hand, her affection and eagerness to please such a stark contrast to the formality of the courtroom. I need this, these normal everyday family occurrences, to help smooth out the difficulties that lie ahead. Yin and yang. Darkness and light. Whatever it takes to restore some balance into my life for the next five days. How I will cope if he is found not guilty is a notion that gives me pause for thought, obliterating the small glow of positivity afforded to me by an affectionate pet and a brief snatch of sunlight and warmth.

I swallow and try to look calm, unruffled, continuing to fuss Freda, doing what I can to banish all thoughts of that man. He is a persistent presence, taking up space in my brain. A headache threatens. My skin feels hot and cold simultaneously, my blood bubbling inside my veins.

'Everything okay? You look tired.' Damien's head is tilted to one side. He is observing me, like a parent keeping watch over an errant child.

I nod. 'It's a rape case so it's going to be a stressful experience, but we're not allowed to speak to anybody about it until it's over and he's been convicted.'

He raises his eyebrows, his face crooked with a half-smile. 'A little premature, aren't you? He might be found not guilty.'

Fire rages in my abdomen; gravel fills my throat. I try to look nonchalant, unmoved by his comment. I widen my eyes, nodding and sighing to try and express my admission of error.

'You sure you're okay?' he says quietly. 'You look a bit peaky.'

'I'm fine. I'll be fine.'

I'm not fine. I won't be fine until this is all over. We are plunged into a sudden frosty silence, my past a barrier between us. It's always been there, it's just that Damien doesn't know it. I've done what I can to forge ahead with my life, be a good wife and accommodating lover. Becoming parents was something that never happened for us. But we have each other, and that was always enough. And now my past is back, my damaged history lurking behind me like a phantom ready to strike, and Damien has absolutely no idea why I currently look out of sorts or why ice and fire are fighting for space in my veins. I haven't ever been able to find the words to speak to him about it. I've hidden it, pushed that event, that harrowing time, deep down inside of me, hoping it would go away. And for a while it did. I married a good, kind man who never questioned my erratic moods, why I sometimes turned my back on him when he attempted to hold me close at night. But now it's back. *He* is back. Wreaking more havoc in my life. But not for long. One week and it will all be over. He will be found guilty and I can finally put it all behind me. I'll make sure of it.

Damien breaks the moment, his voice conveying lightness and warmth. 'Your mum has been really quiet today,' he says, wiping his hands on the tea towel. 'Really good, actually. She ate her lunch and when I went back, she had even washed the dishes ready for me to collect.'

I smile and heave a sigh of relief. A swift stream of sour air is expelled from my guts and hangs in the air in front of my face. The last of the toxins I was forced to inhale in his presence. I'm tempted to go next door, see how Mum is doing, but I don't want to disrupt the moment, the brief peaceful environment we have here. It's a fragile thing, this level of calm, as delicate as a butterfly's wing and just as easily broken. Mum has eaten her lunch without upending the plate, without accusing us of trying to poison her. Why break a golden moment of peace? Besides, she's probably napping. No wandering around the garden or banging on our door asking for more milk. In a few days, it might change to butter or soap or even toothpaste, which is actually rather comical given that she wears dentures. Every week brings a new demand. With each passing day, she descends lower and lower into an abyss; that lonely desolate place from which there is no return. And this is the early stages of dementia. God help us when the disease gets a proper hold of her and she becomes totally incapacitated. I don't want to think about that, about what our next step will be, how she will have to move in with us or be taken into a care home.

'She was asking after you, though.'

Guilt is a serrated blade in my chest. 'I'll go and peek through her window. If she's sleeping, I'll leave her be, call in later after she's had a nap.'

Mum is always better when she is rested, her mind sharper. Her temper easier to bear.

'Right. Well, I'm off to my study. Got a stack of work to get through.' He steps towards me and plants a kiss on my cheek, his touch as soft as silk. 'See you at five o'clock.'

Freda senses that the gathering is over and slinks back to her basket, her eyes fluttering wildly before drooping and then snapping shut. Within seconds she is asleep, her quiet cadenced snores another reminder of how fortunate I am to have the life that I now have. Another reminder of how easily a decent peaceful life can be snatched away and shattered beyond repair.

Not wanting to disturb her, I keep my movements light, tiptoeing to the back door and heading outside into the garden before opening the gate that connects our house to Mum's.

'I don't want a gate. What if people get in and spy on me?'

'Mum, the only people who can use it are me and Damien.'

'What about the other side? What if somebody decides to spy on me from that end of the house?'

'Mum, they would have to climb over a seven-foot fence and a row of hawthorn bushes to get to your house. Nobody is going to spy on you.'

Her resistance was a solid blockade, and she treated our idea as an infringement on her privacy and rights. It took many weeks and a huge amount of patience to bend her will and allow us to pay a joiner to fit a new gate between our two gardens so we could come and go with ease.

At least she is close by. I cannot imagine having to drive miles and miles to check up on her every morning before I start work. I have Damien to thank for that, for pushing for our current living arrangements. He was instrumental in persuading Mum to move next door, encouraging both her and me to actively consider it as soon as our previous neighbours put up the for sale sign. Mum refuses to have strangers in the house and neither Damien nor I could afford to give up work to look after her. So far, she has managed well enough, but as close as I am to her, both physically and emotionally, even I can now see how the disease is taking its toll. It's not just her memory – the misnomer that dementia is simply memory loss really grinds my gears – it's the seismic shift in her personality. Unlike the adverts on television where a sweet old lady sips at her tea, tipping her head to one side and sighing dramatically because she has forgotten where she keeps the biscuit tin, Mum often flies into rages and breaks things. Not because she has misplaced items or can't locate basic foodstuffs, but simply because that's how dementia has got her. She is trapped inside her own head with no means of escape. A prisoner in her own mind. And she knows it. She still has a degree of insight into her own thoughts and behaviour and that is a torturous and painful thing to observe; seeing the realisation in her eyes, the fact that she knows what she has become and is unable to do anything about it.

I keep myself concealed behind a large pot plant and peer through her patio doors. She is lying curled up on the sofa, her legs tucked up into her chest. Everything about her is childlike, from her diminutive frame and foetal sleeping position to her actions and reasoning skills. Once a strong minded, well-built woman, she has now been reduced to—

The sudden slam of her body against the glass sends me reeling. I stumble backwards, falling into the plant pot. It shatters into a hundred pieces, shards of porcelain and soil tumbling around me, littering the patio area.

I dip my head, pockets of air catching in my throat. Small vibrations pulse beneath my flesh. It took her only a second or two to wake and fling herself towards me. From a deep sleep to full blown rage in less than five seconds.

I take a deep shuddering breath, too afraid to look at the patio doors, frightened of what I'll see there. In these type of situations, it's the shock and the dread that rattles my nerves, the not knowing of what will come next. Every day, every hour, even from minute to minute, we are confronted with a deluge of challenging behaviours, her conduct too difficult to gauge and comprehend. Will she seethe and rage for the next hour or will she slump, exhausted and terrified at her own mental decline and physical capabilities? Every day, I wonder how much further she will fall. But then she often surprises us, holding prolonged conversations, her reasoning skills as sharp as ever. On a good day, strangers would struggle to marry the eloquent woman before them to the diagnosis she has been given.

But not this afternoon. Damien was fortunate. This morning he interacted with a contented Connie. The darkness has since crept into her brain like a stealthy assassin and I am now confronted with a different person. I am faced with a difficult, unpredictable Connie. I count to three, unable to ignore the banging, then take a scared glance, a rapid side-eyed view at the patio doors, too frightened to meet her wild stare full on. Mum is standing there her body pressed against the pane, white-hot anger evident in her contorted features. Her teeth are bared and she is glaring at me, her expression rucking my flesh. I neither know nor recognise the person behind that glass. I am certain, however, that the growling misshapen creature standing there isn't my mother. Not the mother I know and love. My mother was a confident individual, full of kindness and compassion, and like most other people also brimming with impatience and exasperation. But not any more. A ferocious beast has taken her hostage and is holding her prisoner against her will. It's eating at her brain, tearing away every memory and thought she has ever had, and replacing them with terror and rage. Dementia isn't just a disease, it's a prison sentence. A grotesque twisting of reality. It squeezes every last drop of joy out of a person's life, wringing it dry like a discarded old sponge until there is nothing left but grains of dust and sand. I try to focus on the good days. The days when she is sweet and happy, not days like this when this hideous disease slowly ravages her mind.

I swallow, running my fingers through my hair, giving myself just enough time to still my hammering heart and allow my spiking blood pressure to right itself. Then I move forward and place my fingers around the handle of the patio doors, turning it, not surprised to find it locked. As it should be. Once she begins unlocking doors and windows, leaving herself exposed to possible intruders, then it's time to consider looking for suitable care homes.

Old memories nudge at my brain.

Intruders. Unwanted visitors.

No. I shove those thoughts aside.

Deal with the present. Don't let the past push you off course.

I walk along the garden path and unlock the kitchen door then head inside, my neck still pulsing, the steady beat of it making me nauseated and dizzy. Mum hasn't physically assaulted me yet, but there's still time. Her body may have shrunk but her inner core of strength is still present. I forget that at my peril.

'Mum, it's me. Just popped in to see if you're okay?' A singsong voice, non-threatening. Experience has taught me to keep my approach light and airy.

By the time I get to the living room, she is lying on the sofa again, her previous position resumed with such accuracy, I wonder if I imagined the sight of her furious squirming form pressed against the glass. Except I didn't. I know what I saw.

'Mum, I know you're awake. I saw you through the patio doors. Would you like a cup of tea?'

'Yes, that'll be right, love. Milky tea, three sugars.' She sits up and stares straight ahead, her eyes pools of confusion, an emptiness there that frightens me. She is neither hostile nor contented, her body present, her mind wandering into the vast yonder. 'Milky, milky, milky. Who's the milkman today then, eh?'

Her posture is rigid, her spine a rod of iron. I wait, willing the moment to pass, for my mum to come back to me, for recognition to brighten her eyes and tighten her slackened features. Her hair is plastered to one side where she has lain on it, her complexion the colour of ash. 'Come out, come out wherever you are...' Her voice cuts through the silence and I feel myself wilt with terror. Those words. It's a coincidence, has to be. It's been years since we spoke about what took place. One conversation, that's all it was, something I blurted out after a particularly difficult week at work. I had counselled a lady who had been sexually assaulted by her son-in-law and it was a trying session for both of us. It's impossible Mum has remembered that conversation, not with her failing memory. Not with her being the way she is.

She turns to face me and I can see then that she is back, her pre-dementia disposition restored, her cloudy eyes clear once again. Relief floods through me, respite from this tense moment sliding over my skin like a welcome cool breeze.

'Tea?' she says, a tremble evident in her tone.

Her eyes are glassy with unshed tears, her mouth lolling open as she struggles to control the quiver that has taken hold. A thin line of saliva runs from the corner of her lip, gathering in the cleft of her chin. She shakes her head and wipes it away, a flush creeping up her neck. She is painfully aware of her own mental decline. I blink back tears of my own. This situation, seeing her like this, fills me with horror, my helplessness and inability to support her like having a knife driven into my heart. I feel horribly ill-equipped to deal with it – her sudden recognition. The humiliation of her knowing that I know.

A pain lodges behind my eyes. It's been a day and although still only early afternoon, I'm exhausted. The fear and formality of the court setting coupled with seeing him standing there has left me feeling hollowed out. And now this. I love my mother dearly, but there will always be *this* to contend with every time I call round to see her.

She won't be able to live alone for much longer. I know that now. Part of me wishes we had formally applied to be her carers, informed Mum's doctor or the local authority and filled out the relevant paperwork. It would have been the perfect reason to excuse me from jury duty.

But then, you wouldn't be able to secure a conviction for the man who did that awful thing to you all those years ago, would you?

'You get yourself comfortable, Mum, and I'll make a cup of tea.' I try to empty my head of him. One problem at a time.

The kitchen is clean, the sink and counter tops recently tidied with pots stacked up, albeit haphazardly. I'm not about to complain. At least she's made an effort. I've found them inside the oven or piled up in the bath before now. It's wise to pick one's arguments, especially when fatigue is this overwhelming. I straighten the crockery and make the tea, placing a piece of cake on a plate.

'Here you go, Mum. Chocolate cake and tea from a china cup.'

She slurps her way through it, shovelling lumps of sponge into her mouth like a woman who hasn't eaten for months, then stops, a lone tear rolling down her cheek. The cup and plate rattle when she places them down on the coffee table, the sudden clunk of porcelain meeting wood, jarring my nerves.

A fist pummels at my heart, pressing it flat against my ribs. I take a sharp breath, lean forward, and envelop Mum in my arms.

Her voice forces all the air out of my lungs as her words pour into my chest, her mouth saying things I don't want to hear. It's as if she knows my current predicament, my plans to change the direction of a trial to suit my own agenda. And yet she can't. Nobody knows. This is my problem. My secret.

'I'm scared,' she wails as I comfort and shush her, my fingers stroking her tufts of soft dry hair. 'I'm scared of the man. And what about my boy, Penny?' she says, her voice rattling against my neck. 'Look what happened to him. He's burning. My house is on fire and my poor boy is burning.'

5

THE HOUSE

Less than a month. That was all it took for the torturous slide into madness to begin. Connie often looked back on those first few weeks with mixed emotions; a combination of relief at having moved in without too much trauma, and then dread as she recalled the day when she found him standing there at her door. Her instincts sprang to life, blazing like a wildfire, telling her there and then that something was horribly awry. The way he watched her as he stood silently, his bulky frame casting long shadows over the floor. How he swept his eyes over her, wordlessly assessing her, passing judgement and finding her wanting. She pushed back her shoulders, able to see past his wily ways and faux charm. His expensive clothes and leather riding boots. Connie had met his type before, could see inside his head, was able to rummage in the darkest corners of his brain. An iron fist in a velvet glove, that was her first thought when he gave her a lopsided smirk and asked if he could come in for a chat.

'It will only take a couple of minutes to sort this thing out.'

And before she could refuse, he pushed past her and strode along the hallway into the living room as if it were his own home. A prescient notion, she thought later that day after he had left, given the conversation they were about to have.

She followed, acutely aware she was alone in the house with him. Just the two of them, the rest of the family at work and school. Connie pulled her cardigan tighter around her shoulders, the flimsy fabric doing little to ward off any possible blows. She swept her hand out in front of her, indicating for him to take a seat, his towering height putting her at a disadvantage and filling her with a deep sense of unease. Standing with him on the doorstep was one thing, something she could handle with ease, but having him here in her home gave her a feeling of vulnerability. Acerbic words she could deal with. A possible assault was another matter.

'What can I do for you?' No polite introductions. He forfeited that right when he pushed his way past her into her home without being invited to do so. She neither wanted nor requested his company. The sooner he left, the better. A delicate lilt of birdsong filtered through the open window, sweet and gentle, incongruous against his dark heavy tweed clothing and vacuous scowl.

The stranger sat, legs splayed, head cocked to one side. She watched as his gaze swept around the room, taking in the general decay of the place, eyeing up the many unpacked boxes that were stacked in the corner of the room. The high dirty floor littered with debris. The cobwebbed ceilings splattered with black mould. Eventually he spoke, his voice filling the void of silence between them, his words cutting through the veil of dead air.

'Looks like you've got your work cut out here, eh?'

A pain slid across her forehead, coming to rest behind her eyes. Anger and resentment crashed and collided in her stomach, exploding into her veins.

'We'll manage. And you are?'

The recesses of her brain proffered shadowy notions of his identity. She thought that perhaps she knew him or knew *of* him, but needed confirmation. His thick jacket and waistcoat stretched across his midriff as he leaned forwards and spoke, buttons and fabric pulling and twisting in resistance against his paunch.

'Oh,' he said quietly, his words drawn out, whispered hoarsely for effect, every syllable enunciated through gritted teeth, 'let's not play games here. I think you know who I am. I'm a very busy man. I don't have time for petulance and denial.'

Silence. Only the relentless *thump thump* of Connie's heartbeat and the hiss of her anger as it bounced around her head, echoing in her ears.

'I think you need to leave.' She stood, her eyes flicking to the telephone in the far corner. She was closer to it than he was should she need to make *that* call. 'I too am a busy woman and have no time for your bullying behaviour.'

No movement. He continued to sit, mouth wide with fake outrage, hands clapped over his knees, then as if pushed by an invisible force, he pulled himself upright, face ashen, his eyes now bulging with barely suppressed rage.

'You know, I came here without any preconceptions. I was prepared to have an open and frank discussion with you. I wanted to sort out your taking up residence here, and you have refused. Surely you want to hear about the contract I had with your father-in-law regarding this property before you dismiss me and send me on my way? You are aware, aren't you, that this house and the land on which it stands actually belongs to me?'

The heat of exploding fireworks in her gut didn't stop Connie from doing what she needed to do. She stood, arm outstretched towards the front door, trying to keep her limbs rigid, to stop the tremble in her fingers from travelling up her limbs and rocking her entire body. She shook her head, fearing the vibration of it would send her tumbling to the ground. 'There was no contract – *is* no contract. This house and the land around it belongs to me and my husband. Now please leave.'

He took a step closer, his shoes squeaking on the flagstones as he approached Connie's comparatively diminutive frame. 'You'll live to regret this, Mrs McLeod. Don't ever say I didn't try to negotiate with you. Or warn you. You're living in my house. This place belongs to me. I hoped for a little more respect.'

With his final words pulsing in her ears, Connie leaned against the wall, a veil of tears misting her vision as he marched along the hallway, pulled at the door latch and let himself out. Limbs trembling, stomach churning, she slumped into the nearest chair. The local nuisance. The stereotypical landed gentry, that was all he was. She pawed at her eyes and sat for a few seconds trying to think. Trying to summon up enough energy to locate long-forgotten thoughts and foggy images. A blurry memory of her in-laws speaking of him gradually slithered into her brain, his presence in their lives more of an irritant than somebody who was to be feared. Eric's parents were old school, unruffled by life's perils, dismissing with a shake of their heads and clicking of tongues events and problems that would fell lesser folk. He came here to mark his territory, like a dog pissing on its patch, that was all it was. And yet his words continued to boom in her head.

You're living in my house. This place belongs to me.

Anger and frustration pulsed in her neck, a smattering of fear at the possible truth of his words forcing her head back onto the chair and draining her of energy. Eyes heavy, she sat immersed in her own thoughts until the ticking of the old clock propelled her up, its steady rhythmic beat strengthening her resolve. She refused to allow a stranger to dictate her ideas, beliefs and movements. Resilience was her middle name. She wasn't about to kowtow to a pompous bully, regardless of how wealthy or powerful he purportedly was. Connie had never understood the mindset of those who doffed their caps to the upper classes, bowing and scraping like a peasant because somebody happened to be prosperous and lucky enough to live in opulence. It was a notion she refused to entertain.

The living room came first. Armed with a feather duster and a yard brush, Connie cleaned and scrubbed, removing a mesh of sticky silvery cobwebs from the four corners of the room, the rough bristles of the wire brush digging into the farthest angles of every crevice. She continued unabated until her energy levels waned and she could do no more. Back sore, knees aching, she stood and surveyed her efforts, disappointed at the barely noticeable dent her hour-long cleaning regime had made.

Undeterred, she moved to the kitchen, sweeping, scouring, discarding unused under-sink items and replacing them with bottles of detergent before stopping, sweat speckling her brow and blooming under her arms. All that effort, the muscle-burning intense burst of energy that forced her on, and still the image of him burned bright in her mind. His size. His arrogance. The way he strode into her home barking out commands, each word like a knife being inserted deep into her abdomen, its blade twisting and jabbing at her organs, doing its damnedest to puncture and maim. This place wasn't yet her home, but she would make it so. She would put her heart and soul into making it desirable, a place people would admire and envy. A secure safe environment for her and her family. That man, that repulsive, egotistical individual could go fuck himself. She would speak to Eric later this evening, find out what he meant when he spoke of a contract about Hallshead Farmhouse. Living in close proximity to such an arrogant individual would rattle her nerves and rob her of sleep. This issue had to be discussed and resolved. Leaving an open wound to fester would only end one way.

Connie tried to think back, to recall the conversations she'd had with her in-laws regarding his presence in their lives, but came up with only snippets of long since forgotten tales of an annoying neighbour they'd batted away like one would with a fly; an irritating presence but only ever on the periphery of their day-to-day existence.

They were hardy folk, her deceased in-laws. Had lived through many winters out here in the wilds of North Yorkshire and asked for nothing, using only an old stove and an open fire for warmth even through the darkest days and the most brutal of Januarys. Freezing fog continued to swirl in these parts until late May, when elsewhere, spring had already made an appearance, taking tentative steps across the icy sodden ground. Connie would have to be as they were, grow a second skin and become inured to threats and inclement weather. She could do that. She wasn't soft in the middle like many of her friends back in town. And she certainly wasn't about to bend, willow-like, to an ignorant man who lacked manners and common decency. He'd entered her home uninvited. He threatened her. He lied and bullied his way through the conversation. She would fight long and hard. She would resist and refuse to give in to his demands, but without all the available facts, she was fighting blind. Hallshead Farmhouse was once set in acres and acres of land – land that had gradually been sold off over the decades; that much she did know. The building was situated way back from the road and a mile from the closest village. The remaining plot had been sorely neglected, field after field now a tangle of weeds and shrubbery, her in-laws too weak to tend it, their ageing limbs and joints a physical barrier between them and toiling on the land. And then there was Sam, her brother-in-law, his needs too great to ever have the capability to take care of anything except ferrying his parents around and cooking the odd meal. After the accident, Connie contemplated whether he should have been granted a driving licence in the first place, but to take away the only bit of freedom he ever had would have been cruel. The police deemed it an accident, the inclement weather a major contributing factor. If that was their ruling then who was she to question their findings?

With instincts like sharpened talons, Connie wandered from room to room, locking doors, ensuring every window was properly closed, the latches jammed in place. He wasn't a burglar or a vandal. He wasn't going to do something unthinkable to her home, but it reinforced her feelings of safety. She had hoped for better, thinking neighbours would welcome them with open arms to this house after such a tragedy had befallen their family. Perhaps even bringing small hampers, and a few words of comfort. Instead she had received veiled threats from a man who claimed this house belonged to him.

Eric would know more about it. Be able to give her some history on the family, possibly know of any historical agreements or contracts that would give her a clue to his motives, help her discover the meaning behind this purported agreement regarding the house. And what to do and say to him if he ever decided to come back.

6

PENNY

Day 2

I sip at my coffee while I wait for the other jurors to arrive. Tendrils of steam curl up from the cup, misting my skin. My head feels heavy, my limbs leaden and wieldy. Last night, I lay awake, going over everything in my head. Mum's words coupled with seeing him standing there in the dock earlier in the day catapulted me back to that time, that place, and no matter how hard I tried, I couldn't shake the images that seeped into my brain like poison. By the time I finally fell asleep, it was 3 a.m. The alarm was set for 6.30. Today is going to be a long one.

It's overly warm in here. Sweat clings to my chest and midriff. I wipe at my top lip, brushing away orbs of perspiration, then glance at the large window, thinking of the cool breeze that lapped at my face on the walk from the car park, longing for it to sneak beneath the window frames and spread over my burning body. Outside, in the main square below, people pass by, their expressions frozen, bodies stiff as they make their way to work in the office block opposite the law courts building. They're the lucky ones, their lives continuing as normal while mine is on hold, the past resurrected, the cracks I spent so long attempting to stitch together now splintering and coming apart. Which is exactly why I have to do what I'm about to do, why I won't admit to a conflict of interest; it's to shake off those dark memories that cling like lichen. And already, it feels like an arduous undertaking. What I'm doing is illegal. But that doesn't matter. I've weathered worse storms. A week and it will all be over. I need justice.

Perhaps you dreamed it?

It was dark. You couldn't be sure who it was.

My mother's claims that I had imagined seeing that figure outside my bedroom window night after night cut deep at the time. And yet I refuse to stay angry. What's done is done and cannot be undone. She was battling her own demons at the time, doing what she could to hold our family together. But I've now been given this chance to right a huge wrong. To readjust the balance. It's time to settle old scores. I've spent so many years living in the shadows and dodging the many monsters that regularly haunted my dreams. Time to step out into the light and be the person I always wanted to be. The person I *could* have been had it not been for him and what he did to me all those years ago.

'Morning. You ready for today's action, then?'

The voice drags me out of my dark thoughts, catching me by surprise. An older man is standing over me, a cup of coffee in hand. I recognise him from yesterday.

'I think so. Looks like we're early.' My eyes sweep around at the near-empty room.

'They'll all arrive soon enough. The roads were chronic yesterday so I set off extra early just in case and have ended up getting here before anybody else.'

'I'm Penny, by the way,' I say apropos of nothing.

'Bob,' he replies, giving me a quick nod before lowering himself into the chair opposite.

The room fills up after only a few seconds, noise spreading around us. We're enveloped by the chatter of newcomers, the occasional burst of laughter. The rustle of fabric as people remove coats and scarves, slinging them over the backs of chairs.

Already, small cliques have formed, people huddled together, conspiratorial whispers circling. I take out my phone and glance at the screen. No messages. Mum is still coping in my absence. Yesterday's outburst was short-lived. This morning, she ate breakfast and settled on the sofa to watch TV. She was normal, if I dare use such a word. She was who she used to be. A healthy functioning adult; cognisant and rational. For now.

'What did you make of the defendant yesterday?' One of the female jurors has planted herself next to me and is watching me intently, her dark eyes fixed on mine. Not the redhead. She has yet to make an appearance. This lady is mid-thirties, short blonde hair. My skin burns. I wonder why she is asking, why she has chosen me out of all the other jurors. Was it obvious in my expression that I knew him? Are my thoughts really that transparent?

I shrug and act nonchalant and untroubled by her question even though my heart is crawling up my neck. 'Not sure really. Just another defendant who will protest his innocence, I guess.'

'So you already think he's guilty?'

I shake my head so vigorously, it hurts. 'No, of course not. But everyone always protests their innocence, don't they? Otherwise we wouldn't be here. Us jurors, I mean. If he had pleaded guilty, there wouldn't be any need for a court appearance, would there? It would go straight to sentencing.'

She nods, her bottom lip jutting out as if giving silent approval to my words. Then she speaks, her voice loud, her posture self-assured. 'I just thought he looked as if he didn't belong in the dock. He looked really confident, like this whole scenario was just something he had to go through before walking free.'

I have no reply at the ready, no pre-planned words to nudge aside her first impressions and tell her the truth about the man in the dock who is a master at manipulating others and twisting reality to suit his own agenda, so instead, I give her a half-smile and stare off over her shoulder. My teeth are clamped together, my jaw aching with the effort. She grows bored of my non-committal responses and heads off to find gossip elsewhere. I need to keep my own counsel, not get dragged into situations where I could be accused of doing or saying anything untoward that could see me in the dock alongside him. And yet I do need to do something. *Say* something to sow seeds of doubt in the minds of the other jurors. It's still too soon. We need to hear the evidence, see how the victim bears up under intense scrutiny of the barrister's questions. Only then will I be able to slowly get them on my side, to use subtle nuanced ways of turning them against him. Trying to sway somebody before any of that happens will be seen as an obvious ploy.

The noise in the waiting area grows, more people gradually filtering in, grumbling about the amount of traffic, a lack of parking spaces, late overcrowded trains and slow buses. The red-headed lady appears at the edge of my vision. She makes her way in my general direction, dropping her bag on the chair next to mine.

'Anybody sitting here?'

I look up and force a smile, the pain in my jaw now a prolonged dull ache. 'No, go right ahead.'

She is oblivious to my brusque tone or the stiffening of my spine, slumping down on the chair next to me regardless. I try harder and give her a bland smile, keen to get her on side. It's imperative I make her like me. I need every ear I can bend if I am to be successful in my attempts to find him guilty. My prickly demeanour is a barrier to forging friendships with these people. I'm going to have to work harder at this team-building business, be more relaxed and easier in my own skin when all the while I am crawling with apprehension as old memories worm their way into my pores and score at my bones, scratching with such intensity I find myself shuffling about in my chair.

'Everything okay?' Red-headed woman is watching me, her small eyes narrowed into dark slits.

'Yes, thanks. Just aching. I didn't sleep too well last night.'

She nods as if she understands my plight. She doesn't. She can't. None of these people have any idea of what that man did to me and what I am about to do.

'Yeah, I was the same.'

Were you? I doubt it.

'It's a bit nerve-wracking, isn't it?' I murmur, my voice a near whisper.

'Nerve-wracking? I think it's great. I'm really looking forward to it. Can't wait to get my teeth stuck into this case.'

I suppress a heavy sigh and stare out of the window. Sometimes people baffle me. But most of the time, they simply disgust me.

'What about the victim?' My voice is hoarse as I try to evoke some pity and empathy from this woman.

'Well, yeah. Of course I feel sorry for them. I mean, that's why we're here, right? To get justice for them.' A crimson flush creeps up her neck, a splash of pink pasted across her throat and chest.

'Exactly. Justice where it's due.'

Our conversation is interrupted by the arrival of more jurors, hair ruffled and windswept. Red-headed lady moves away from me, gravitating towards the burly guy with the tattoos. He smiles and they sit together, heads bowed, their conversation hurried and animated. The blonde lady has already turned her attention elsewhere, speaking to the person next to her, her staccato voice and rapid eye movements irritating me more than they should. So many diverse opinions to shape. So many attitudes and beliefs to mould and bend.

I suddenly realise that I can't do this alone. It's too big a job. Too difficult an undertaking. I glance around, trying to determine who the lynchpin is amongst us, the one person who will hold influence over the others. It's not me. I'm too gruff and unwelcoming. I'm not a shrinking violet but neither am I loud or strident. I couldn't control and direct a group of eleven perfect strangers, but I think he can, the man from this morning. Bob. I watch him as he speaks to people, moving around the circle of chairs, putting everyone at ease. Working the group. He's the one – the guy I need to befriend. The juror who will help me put my rapist behind bars. I don't care if the defendant isn't guilty of this particular crime. He is guilty of *a* crime. The crime that snatched away my early years and plunged me into a cold void of misery and darkness. I have less than a week. Four full days in which to make sure he doesn't walk free. And I need Bob to help me.

My throat is tight as I turn and stare out of the window, steeling myself for the week ahead. Thinking of ways in which I can convince the others that we have all the evidence we need to convict him. Even if we don't. I need to summon up just enough poise and self-assurance to catch their attention but not so much that I'm considered overbearing.

Which is why I need *him* on my side – Bob. He's got the knack, a special way of interacting with everyone. I continue watching him as he sails seamlessly from person to person, his smile, his easy manner, a thing of beauty. I'm not envious of his ability to hold court, but I am in awe of it. He has presence. I need that presence and certainty of mind. I need him.

He looks over at me and comes and sits down.

'You ready for this case then, Penny?'

I nod and clear my throat before speaking. 'I think so. It's not going to be easy, is it? Listening to all the details, I mean, but I guess if we do the right thing by both parties, that's all anyone can ask, isn't it?'

'You are absolutely right there. Fairness and justice. That's what's important. It cuts both ways.'

He smiles at me and I feel a rush of euphoria swell and flower in my veins. I'm making headway here, playing the game. It's not as difficult as I imagined, being cunning and deceitful. In fact, I think I might actually be rather good at it.

The voice over the loudspeaker calls us to the courtroom and we all stand. 'Here we go, Bob,' I say quietly, my heart keeping up an easy comfortable rhythm in my chest. 'This is where it all begins.'

We stand and shuffle towards the usher, my earlier fears dissolving like snowflakes at the first sign of spring.

7
THE HOUSE

'He's just the local wealthy landowner. All bluff and bluster. Best ignored if you ask me.' Eric scooped up the remainder of his mashed potato, pushing it onto his fork and squaring it up with his knife as if making a pat of butter before shovelling it into his mouth.

'Easy for you to say. You weren't the one here having to deal with him.' Cold air curled around Connie when she swivelled her body away from the table. She didn't want to look at her husband, was enraged by his less than enthusiastic response to her query. The dull drum of fingers tap tapping on the wooden surface echoed around them, the muted thudding noise heightening her slow growing fury and frustration. 'So, who is he exactly?' She turned back to observe Eric's expression, her body angled towards his. 'And I don't mean as a neighbour. I recall your parents talking about having some problems with him from time to time. What I mean is, what's his name and background and what exactly does he want from us? What is this so-called agreement or contract that he mentioned?'

Eric sighed, the dropping of his cutlery onto his plate a dramatic tactic that Connie recognised as frustration at having his meal disturbed. He leaned back in his chair. 'It's nothing more than a stupid flimsy gentlemen's agreement that goes back years. Before I was even born. A gentlemen's agreement isn't worth anything.'

She waited, her eyes burning into his flesh.

More sighing. Then, 'This house and land, according to his claims, used to belong to his family and he said that there was an agreement in place that once my parents passed away, he could have it back.'

An uncomfortable buzzing sensation crept beneath Connie's skin, prickling her scalp, making her hot and uncomfortable. 'Belonged to or still belongs?'

Eric shrugged. 'Well, it clearly doesn't belong to him, does it? It belongs to us. We've seen the deeds. We heard the will being read out. This place is ours.' He continued eating, finishing his meal and watching Connie intently.

'And I take it he lives in the big house beyond the hill? Fairbridge House?'

Eric nodded and let out a deep sigh, his cutlery rattling against his plate as he stood and carried his dishes to the sink. He turned and spoke again. 'You've already said you recalled my parents talking about him from time to time. It's no big deal, honestly.'

'I recall them speaking about an annoying neighbour, but I didn't realise he would come here making threats. It feels like quite a big deal to me. This is a step-up from petty squabbles about unkempt land and dilapidated barns spoiling his view. He didn't even say what he really wanted. He just strode in here acting like the big man, doling out threats.'

'That's just how he operates. Never had to do a day's work in his life so he spends his time strolling round these parts lording over people.' Eric stretched, his shirt sleeves rising, exposing a bronzed forearm. Years of working outside on building sites had weathered his skin, giving him a year-round tan. Every now and again, Connie would snatch a glance of the young man he once was, the handsome hardworking youth who came along and swept her off her feet with bunches of flowers and promises of eternal happiness together.

'What's his name again?' Connie's brow knitted together as she waited for his reply. She could feel the thrum of her own heart nestled deep in the cavity of her chest, its rhythmic pulsing a reminder that she was strong enough to fight this battle.

'Douglas. Douglas Fairbridge.'

'I want chains or bolts on all the doors. Preferably both.'

She gave a look from beneath her lashes, her piercing blue eyes sweeping over his face; it was enough to silence Eric's laughter. Connie's eyes met his, her glare precise and chilling enough to cut glass. Sometimes a look said more than a thousand words ever could.

'Okay, okay! I'll sort it at the weekend. In the meantime, don't answer the door to him if he frightens you that much. And keep all the doors and windows closed and locked while you're in the house on your own.'

The metallic taste of blood pooled in the recess of Connie's gums as she tugged at a loose piece of skin, the sharp bite of pain forcing her to stop. Her fears had just been batted away with a few throwaway comments and a bellow of mordant laughter. Acid swilled in her gut, boiling and bubbling like magma.

'Who frightens you? And why do we need chains and bolts on the doors?' Penny stepped out of the long shadowy hallway into the kitchen, her appearance stunting their conversation.

Connie waved her hand in her daughter's direction, her forced smile a grimace. 'It's nothing to worry about. Have you finished your homework?'

Penny rolled her eyes. Inane pedestrian questions always had the same effect on her daughter. Connie had seen that look before, been subject to it many times should she ever dare to ask about schoolwork or friends or any number of subjects that her teenage daughter deemed trivial or private.

'I'm fourteen years old. You don't need to keep checking up on me, you know. And yes,' she said, her sigh deliberately protracted, 'before you ask again, it's done. Did it as soon as I got in.'

The apple in her palm, a burnished glow of russet, was in sharp contrast to the griminess of the room. With her fingers clutched around it, Penny bit into the soft flesh, the sound of her teeth breaking the skin an explosive crunch in the strained artificial silence. Juice ran down her chin, tiny golden rivulets that she wiped away with the back of her hand. 'So who or what frightens you?'

'Your ability to creep around the house unnoticed, eavesdropping on our conversations. That's what frightens us.' The damp cloth from the sink that Eric threw across the room caught Penny on the side of the face.

'Hey!' Her gentle tinkling laughter was a breath of fresh air amidst the growing tension.

The ensuing scene softened the atmosphere, the frolics of father and daughter painting a picture of gentle amusement and controlled mayhem. Connie observed it all, a rush of endorphins whistling through her system, swelling in her chest. Penny's attentions had been shifted elsewhere, her laughter reverberating around the kitchen. Moving here hadn't been easy for either of their children. They were miles away from their friends and school. Miles away from everybody and everything.

Except him – Douglas Fairbridge. Their neighbour from the big house on the hill, a near stranger and already an enemy. Somebody to be feared and avoided. He wasn't going anywhere, but then neither was she. Connie was tenacious and persistent, her beliefs and ethics sound and inflexible. Right was right and wrong was wrong. And Douglas Fairbridge was wrong. She was sure of it. This rambling old house may not have been her first choice, given to them as it was in the most dreadful and shocking of circumstances, but it was her home now, and she wasn't about to give it up without a fight. If Fairbridge was hoping she would collapse like a deck of cards, then he had picked on the wrong woman. She would prove just how persistent and resilient she could be.

'Fucking hell, it's like a scene from one of those shitty Carry On movies in here.' Aaron appeared in the doorway, his limbs and body lean and willowy as he slalomed his way around Connie and his sister to get to the sink. Water gushed into the porcelain while he waited to fill his glass, glugging it back in one long slurp and quickly wiping his mouth with a savage swipe on the back of his hand.

'Language, Aaron!' Eric's roar filled the kitchen, its thunderous pitch bringing the laughter to an abrupt end, curtailing their brief spell of joy in an otherwise drab environment. Bare brick walls, dangling wires, rubble-covered dusty floors all added to the feeling of gloom. Connie held in her sigh. Peace and tranquillity was a fragile thing, hard to conjure and easily broken.

'You both swear. I've heard you.'

'We're adults. Cut it out.'

'And I'm fifteen, going on sixteen.'

Eric's brown-eyed glare sliced into the smirk on Aaron's face, cutting it dead. Connie willed the moment to be over. Arguments she could do without. This house, its depressing state and location, and now threats from wealthy neighbours who had the power to inflict misery, and the financial means to wreak havoc with their security and well-being, was about as much as she could stand. Any more and she feared she may open her mouth to scream until there wasn't any air left in her lungs.

'Enough.' She held up her hand and attempted a smile. Always, she endeavoured to create a sense of harmony with her family, no matter how brittle or volatile the mood. No matter how low she felt. That was her job as a wife and a mother. Brought up by a woman who had lived through two world wars and given birth to six children, enduring more hardship in her life than many could ever imagine, Connie had learned well from her own mother and took note early on in her life to count her blessings and focus on the positives, but everyone had their tipping point. Creating a distraction to all possible looming conflicts was key. 'You can all give me a hand with opening some of these boxes. Come on, let's get to it.' She snapped her fingers, combining the abrupt action with a smile to lessen its intensity.

The collective groan of dismay prickled her scalp. Enough with the prevaricating. It was time to start tackling this old place. She had to push all thoughts of disgruntled neighbours out of her mind and make a solid start on settling into this house. For the past couple of weeks, they had danced around boxes that were stacked high to the ceiling. They had stumbled over debris that littered the floor and staggered across containers that should have been unpacked a long time ago. It was time to put an end to it, time for her to be the positive role model her own mother had been all those years back, not an over-anxious husk of a woman who fell at the first hurdle. Hallshead Farmhouse was theirs now. No longer a shell of a house. It was time to start turning it into a home.

Threats voiced by Douglas Fairbridge of snatching it away from her hung in her brain like ivy, clinging and growing, but she did what she could to bat them way, picking off each leaf and stubborn length of vine and discarding them with as much strength as she could muster.

'Aaron, take that box up into your room. It's got your stuff in it. And Penny, you can sort out that little lot over in the corner. God knows where it's going to go but your rooms are big enough to house whatever's inside those boxes. Once we get the place painted and decorated, you'll both be getting new bedroom furniture but even as it is, you've got enough room to swing a thousand cats, so unpack, find a space for your stuff and get cracking.'

'We've only been here for a few weeks. And it's not as if this place is a palace,' Aaron moaned, his footsteps loud and heavy as he trudged past her, his arms loaded with a large cardboard box, its sides bulging and splitting.

Connie bustled past him, opening doors and turning on lights. 'Exactly. Almost a month and we're still living out of boxes. I'd like some normality back please.'

There was a creak of wood and the shuffle of feet against worn carpet as one by one they did as instructed, huffing at the injustice of it, banging bedroom doors behind them in protest. The echoing and rattling of old door frames, reminding Connie of their current predicament. What they had done. Selling their other home and moving here into this desolate farmhouse. And then a lingering silence where once again, the enormity of what they had taken on hit home, slamming into her like a speeding truck, knocking her off balance and forcing her into a chair where she sat, dazed and disorientated. This place was a money pit. A decrepit crumbling old farmhouse in the middle of nowhere.

'It'll all come together. You'll see.' Eric watched her, his back against the kitchen wall, his dark eyes fixed on her face.

'It's just...'

'I know, I know. It's different. The polar opposite to what we're used to. You've never much liked this place, I do realise that. And as for Douglas Fairbridge – don't let that big-mouthed charlatan frighten you. He's full of shit. One strong puff of wind would knock him right over.'

She was trying, God knows, she was trying with all her might to dispel the creeping feelings of discontent that were snaking their way in, but the smile she readily displayed in front of the children to cajole and comfort was waning. Difficult to maintain. She wanted her old house back, with its tiny rooms and box-like design. Her old house with its sparkling new windows and smooth walls and shiny modern fireplace. The same house that contracted around them with alarming speed as their family grew now held such appeal. Every evening since getting here, she would lie in bed, close her eyes and imagine herself back in their old bedroom with its white fitted wardrobes and full-length mirror, and then the next morning she would stumble out of bed, stubbing her toes on unopened suitcases, her nose wrinkling at the stench of damp and old rugs that had captured the smell of every person who ever lived here since the dawn of time, and she found herself fighting back tears. Where had Connie the stalwart gone? The woman who tackled problems head on? This place, its history and location, was squashing her usual zeal into a tight dark corner, compressing it into an uncomfortable ill-fitting part of her that she neither recognised nor liked.

'I want to believe that, Eric, I really do. I want to believe that this Douglas guy is a harmless old eccentric who likes scaring people, but there was something about his manner, the way he pushed past me. He was brusque and he was rude and the sooner we put in some sort of security to stop him doing anything like that again, the better.'

Plans for refurbishing Hallshead Farmhouse hadn't even begun to take shape and already Connie was exhausted, the weight of what they had taken on bearing down on her. This house, this area, their new neighbours; it all felt too much. She placed the heel of her hands into her eye sockets, rested her head on her knees and let out a long lingering sigh.

8

PENNY

Day 2

'So, are you denying that you had sexual intercourse with Ms Albright on the night in question?'

'No. Of course not. We had sex and it was consensual.'

I want to scream and pull at my hair until it comes out in clumps. It's a monumental effort to contain it, to disguise my thoughts and not weaken and reveal what is really going on inside my head. I'm doing what I can to keep my expression and body language impassive and controlled while wanting to shriek at everyone in the room that he is a liar and a sexual deviant. He thinks he can fool the judge and the rest of the jury with his cut-glass accent and immaculate appearance. And the problem is, he might just do it. Already some of them are smiling and tipping their heads to one side, listening to him with rapt expressions, their eyes shiny with undisguised admiration every time he looks their way and affords them a humble smile. It's an act he has perfected for so many years that it almost looks real. Almost, but not quite. Not if you know him as I once did. He's a perfect liar for sure and now he is also a perjurer.

'Can you tell the jury why Ms Albright had bruises on her chest and neck after the sexual intercourse took place?' The prosecution barrister briefly looks our way before turning her attention back to him. 'Because the fact you had sexual relations with Ms Albright isn't the issue here. It's whether she consented that is at the heart of this case.'

Another smug lopsided grin. He thinks he's going to pull this off. I'm here to make sure he doesn't.

'Well, what can I say except that Ms Albright likes it rough?'

There's a titter from a jury member quickly disguised as throat clearing. I'm willing to bet it's red-headed lady. Or the other woman in her thirties with the short blonde hair. He glances her way and widens his eyes before looking at the barrister, who is waiting for his attention, her eyes locked on his. She reminds me of a Victorian school ma'am, her wig perfectly placed on her head, her glasses perched at the end of her nose. Her accent is also cut-glass, her pitch and projection enough to scare the hardest of criminals. It clearly doesn't scare him. He is accustomed to such people, his life of privilege making him well versed in how to deal with figures of authority who dare to question his credentials and integrity.

'You beat her up whilst having sexual intercourse? Is that what you're saying? That you used her as a punchbag whilst penetrating her?'

A sigh, as if such a question is beneath him and unworthy of a proper explanation. 'No. I'm saying that she asked me to treat her roughly while we were having sex.' Once again, he glances at the jury then back to the prosecution barrister, who is beginning to look weary of his little game. 'So I did. And she liked it too.'

This time, it's a gasp from the jury. He bows his head slightly, aware he has overstepped that invisible boundary. It's a fine balancing act, keeping everyone onside, keeping them entertained whilst making sure not to repulse and horrify them. He will have to backtrack now, work his way out of the hole he has dug for himself. I hope he sinks even lower, his feet stuck in a filthy quagmire, his fingernails clinging on to dirt as he attempts to haul himself back up whilst slipping even farther into that dark cavernous pit of deception and outright lies that he has created.

My own nails cut into my palms. I pray he makes plenty more mistakes like this, that he brings about his own demise with his loose mouth and slack morals. If he carries on in this vein, his arrogance and towering confidence putting him in an unstable position, it will make my job a whole lot easier. He can dig his own grave. All I will need to do is give him a slight shove to push him in and make sure he stays there.

The prosecution fires more questions his way.

Why do you think Ms Albright reported you to the police immediately after the purported consensual sexual intercourse took place?

Why do you think she was so anxious and distressed afterwards?

Do you recall her trying to push you away?

His mask slips, the smile sliding off his face as he answers each question. He barks out his final reply with a snap, his crooked grin morphing into an angry sneer.

'No, I don't recall her pushing me away because that never happened.' He glances at the jury and straightens his tie, his shoulders rotating like a boxer preparing for the next round of a match. 'In fact, if my memory serves me correctly, she actually asked for more.'

Another collective gasp from the jury. I focus on his defence barrister, who lowers his head, despondency and despair radiating from him. I want to laugh and jump to my feet whilst punching the air triumphantly. Who needs an effective prosecution barrister when the defendant is doing the job for her, constantly tripping himself up with obvious fabrications and hostile behaviour.

'Can the defendant please stick to answering the questions in a more direct manner and not elaborate.' The judge eyes him with a terse expression, riled by this show of superiority and conceit.

He isn't doing it deliberately! I want to shout it across the courtroom, that this is just how he is. He doesn't know how to be humble or kind or how to adhere to the rules that the rest of us abide by day in and day out. For so long now, he has set his own boundaries and danced to his own tune with few if any repercussions. And now this. For the first time in his warped, privileged little life, he is out of his depth. The strict regulations put in place by the law of the land must be a mystery to him. A completely alien concept.

His body is still rigid, his posture displaying not one ounce of regret or shame. His eyes shine brightly and his mouth is now curved into a half-smile. Dear God. He's actually *enjoying* this.

The prosecution launches more questions his way but his line remains the same. *It was consensual.*

And therein lies the rub. He knows how this works. He might not understand how to align himself to rules and regulations, but he is clever enough to know that this is a case of *he said, she said.*

We break for lunch and my earlier hopes of him being hoist with his own petard begin to diminish. Everyone files back to the main waiting area, a small clutch of them heading into town to buy a sandwich. Already they have formed friendship groups, their conduct reminding me of children in the playground. Red-headed lady is with a huddle of people in the corner, as is the bulky tattoo guy. Bob collects his sandwich from the area at the back of the long room and sits next to me. The urge to speak about the case, to tell him how revolting that man is, is overwhelming. I remain tight-lipped. Too soon to start speaking so openly. I'll lose his confidence and right now I need his friendship and respect to move forward with what I have planned.

'What do you think of him, then?' Bob's question catches me unawares.

That whole session was a punch to the gut, like watching a game show host on television, a man used to winning. He put on a display and we were the audience. Every second of it sickened me.

I unwrap my sandwich and take a bite, giving myself some time to think of my answer. One that won't send him scurrying away but engaging enough to keep him here by my side. Exactly where I want him.

'Too early to tell. I know we're not supposed to discuss it, but he appears to be switched on so I guess we'll just have to wait and see.'

Bob nods, seemingly happy with my bland response. Even though we're virtually alone and nobody can hear us discussing the case, I change the subject to something else, talking about what was on the TV last night and how grim the weather is lately. By the time the conversation dries up and we have eaten our lunch, people have begun to filter back in, sitting in the empty chairs nearby.

'I can't stop staring at the judge's wig! He looks so calm and yet still quite scary, don't you think?'

I don't need to look to see who's speaking. It's red-headed lady. Again. She suppresses a giggle, her hand covering her mouth. I hear a sigh from somebody close by and then an awkward silence descends, broken only by the sound of the loudspeaker, calling for another group of jurors to go to court 6.

'How long does lunchtime last, does anybody know?' The diminutive lady who sits next to me in the courtroom looks around the group for an answer.

'I would imagine it'll be an hour,' I say to her, thinking it's about time I established myself as a person who has all the answers even though my insides are squirming like eels at the idea of what I need to do to make sure that man doesn't walk free.

Small talk ensues until the voice over the loudspeaker calls for us to line up.

'Here we go again,' Bob says to the rest of the jurors. 'Back into the lion's den.'

His voice is authoritative with a sprinkling of humour. Exactly what I want. I need everyone to sit up and take notice of him. I have a week to bend his ear. Less than a week. It's Tuesday lunchtime. I've got my work cut out. That is, if my rapist doesn't do my work for me with his haughtiness and inability to read the room. All I need is a few more faux pas comments from him and he will lose everyone, the jurors turning against him, repulsed by his arrogance and lack of remorse. Even a twinkle in his eye and a winning smile won't be enough to get them back on his side. Nobody likes a smart arse.

We file back into the courtroom, our new formation already feeling like an established familiar routine. I press my hands onto my knees, praying he further damages his character with his runaway mouth. I pray his elaborate lies and duplicitous behaviour reveal him for who he really is.

Once we are seated, the judge explains that we are going to hear from Ms Albright via a videolink. The footage has been pre-recorded due to her age and vulnerability. I feel a surge of positivity, its presence lighting up deadened parts of me that he extinguished all those decades ago. If she is young and vulnerable, then this has to be a clear-cut case and I won't have to try and manipulate those around me. Her character and tender years will hopefully be enough to sway them.

The clerk turns on the screen and we all watch. I wait to see what she is like; this fledgling female he assaulted, the young victim who suffered the same fate I did all those years ago. My fingers are locked together, my knuckles a taut waxy ridge. Every muscle in my body tenses in readiness as I prepare to be transported back in time, to listen to her account of what that monster did to her while she lay there helpless and terrified. I take a deep breath, close my eyes and wait.

9

THE HOUSE

She could feel his eyes on her, sense his lingering gaze following her every move. Uncomfortable with his constant leering, Penny headed into the kitchen and sat at the large oak table. An hour, that was all she had to stomach, and then hopefully he would be gone. She would be free from his crooked sneer and those chilling eyes that travelled over her body, resting on her T-shirt and midriff. It wasn't her clothes; they were neither tight nor revealing. It was him; it was just how he was. A lecherous individual incapable of conducting himself in a decent manner when he was in somebody else's house. Later, she would speak with her parents, see if they could get somebody else to do the job. A different architect who was just as capable of producing some half-decent plans for this ramshackle old house. If this was how it was going to be for the next few months with him calling around every few days on the pretext of requiring more measurements, then she wasn't sure she could stand it.

'I think I'm almost done here.'

Thank God. Not before time.

She spun around, startled by his voice, by the strength and proximity of it. How he enunciated every word, his accent crisp and clear. He was close – too close – his breath misting on her neck. Somehow, he had crept up behind her, catching her unexpectedly. Not only was it unnerving and creepy, it was also unprofessional. Her parents were paying this man to do a job. He was in somebody else's house and he needed to learn how to respect their boundaries, not tiptoe behind her, catching her unawares. It was tantamount to stalking, and she hated it. She hated *him*. She wiped at the back of her neck, rubbing away the dampness of his breath, the noxious mist that clung to her flesh.

'Right, well, you'll probably need to contact my parents for the next set of instructions. They'll be back any minute.'

Penny shuddered. Tucked her revulsion away out of sight. That was a complete lie. She wanted to let him know that they weren't alone together in the house for much longer, that he had better be on his guard. That it wasn't just him and her. Even though it was. Aaron was supposed to be here but had taken himself off to a friend's house in the next village. She had followed him to the hallway as he was getting ready to leave and begged him to stay but he had refused, claiming she was overreacting and being hysterical. Aaron had left, a sarcastic grin plastered on his face. Penny had wanted to slap him, just stopping short of pulling him back in and begging him to stay. That had been the instructions left by their parents – to both remain in the house until the architect had finished while they went out to choose wall tiles. She hoped her brother had slipped and fallen in cow dung on the way to his friend's house. It was a two-mile walk, most of it down narrow country lanes and over fields. Maybe he had been stung by a crop of high nettles or chased by a swarm of angry wasps. It would serve him right, leaving her alone here with this man whose eyes were everywhere but where they should be.

'Okay, well, I can wait.'

The long drawn-out silence made her skin crawl. She filled the kettle simply because she didn't know what else to do to break this ghastly stream of nothingness that seemed to go on and on and on.

'Ooh, white with one sugar if you're making coffee?' His voice echoed around the kitchen, the strength of his diction making her bristle with anger.

He had enough confidence to make up for the fear she felt in his presence. She was used to her father's gruff voice, his northern accent and gravelly timbre. This man was different. He exuded a level of sureness that left her feeling out of sorts. His projection and accent was like salt on a wound. He was everywhere in the house, his voice, whether speaking to her parents about designs and plans or to himself, taking measurements and wandering from room to room, ringing out klaxon like. He was a stranger in their midst who had quickly – too quickly – made himself at home, running his large hands over walls and staring up at beams before patting them fondly while smiling as if meeting up with a long-forgotten friend.

The scrape of the chair on the flagstones reverberated in her head. He was sitting down, making himself comfortable, as if he lived here. Soundlessly, she made his coffee and handed it over, the faded chipped mug a symbol of the loathing she felt towards him. A pocket of dead air sat between them until eventually he broke the silence.

'So, your parents have big plans for this place, then?'

Penny shrugged. She wasn't going to get drawn into a conversation with this man; a person she barely knew and yet already disliked. What were her parents thinking, leaving her children with this creepy guy? She bit at the inside of her mouth, giving him a sideways glance. He was looking around the room, assessing it. Mentally sizing up walls and beams and doors. For once, he wasn't looking at her.

You're imagining it. This is all in your head.

Guilt slithered beneath her skin. *Was* she overreacting, misinterpreting his words and sly glances? She didn't think so but just lately it was hard to think straight. They had lost Sam and Nan and Grandad so unexpectedly and tragically, and then, before any of them had had a chance to properly grieve, for them to find a comfortable space for it in their heads, they had been uprooted and brought to this place, leaving behind their friends and having to get two buses to school. And now there were strangers wandering around the house. Everything felt out of kilter, her usual routine and life blurred and disjointed. Frightening even. The nights were the worst. That large bedroom, the faded peeling wallpaper. The darkness. God, the darkness was intense, like being buried alive beneath thick mud and slime, the weight of the heavy loam pressing down on her. Some evenings she would wake, a choking sensation in her throat, the opaqueness of the room more than she could bear.

She swallowed, thinking about the past year, the trauma of it. This was her issue. It had to be her. She had mistaken his behaviour, made things about her when they weren't. She wasn't thinking straight.

Penny attempted a smile, hoping to dispel the frosty vibes that emanated from her whenever he was around. She took a trembling breath and drummed her fingernails on the wooden table, suddenly stuck for words.

'What's your favourite subject at school, then?'

She suppressed a snarl, and instead gave him a limp half-hearted smile. Such a bland predictable question. Was he really so old that he felt the need to come out with a well-worn trope about schoolwork? Maybe he was simply struggling with making conversation, unsure what to say to her now that he had her full attention. Now that she had remonstrated with herself and decided to wipe the slate clean and start again, she did what she could to appear polite and interested.

'English. And history.'

He nodded and sipped at his coffee. 'You're into the humanities then? No maths or science for you?'

Penny shrugged, her bottom lip jutting out. God, he sounded just like her dad. He had also tried to steer her into subjects that held no interest for her, claiming she was bright enough to go down the science route.

That's where the money is.

She told him she wasn't interested in making money. Like many people, she wanted enough to get by but was more enamoured with the idea of being happy and fulfilled in her chosen career. Money couldn't buy happiness, she had said. The world was filled with miserable rich people.

At least they're miserable in comfort.

Her father's words had sounded hollow to her ears.

'I would quite like a job in the publishing industry,' she had said, knowing her dad didn't think of such occupations as real jobs. If you didn't make or produce anything then how could it be called a proper profession?

He had walked away, having no answer or comeback to her reply. What did he know anyway? He had spent all his adult life working on a building site, starting off as a hod carrier after leaving school and eventually working his way up to site manager. He wasn't a scientist, had no or few qualifications and yet regularly nagged at her to work harder, change subjects, be somebody she didn't want to be.

'Nope. I prefer language to numbers,' she now said softly, her reply laced with a streak of determination. Just enough to deter any further questions. 'That's how my brain works.'

The architect nodded and drained his coffee, then stood up and walked past her to the sink, placing his palm on her shoulder as he did so. Penny froze, the weight of his hand, the strangeness of his touch, the *heat* and nearness of him making her skin ripple with trepidation. She was wearing a strappy shirt. His fingers had touched her bare flesh.

'Tell your parents I'll be in touch with my latest designs.'

Her head buzzed. A gurgle of protestation was trapped in her throat. Did she imagine it? Was she overreacting? Aaron had said so. Was he right or had this man deliberately trailed his fingers over her body, inching his way ever closer to doing something awful?

He rinsed his mug in the sink – another over-familiar action – and walked behind her, his legs brushing against the back of her chair as he squeezed past. Instinctively, her fingers clasped at its wooden legs, dragging it farther under the table until her midriff was pressed up hard against the oak rim. She could feel her heart battering against her ribcage, was able to detect her pulse as it crept up her throat and banged in her neck, the steady thud of it increasing her anxiety and making her woozy.

Any words she wanted to say became stuck in her throat. Unable to bid goodbye or make any sound, she sat immobile, her muscles finally loosening once she heard the slamming of the front door. Penny stood, her legs weak, her insides a gurgle of anxiety, and stared around the room, trying to piece together the last few minutes. Were his actions accidental or were they deliberate, a sly way of initiating contact in readiness for something more intimate? His fingers didn't linger on her bare shoulder, but he did touch her. Would her father ever do such a thing to a young girl? Would he sidle up to somebody half his age and allow his hands to brush against their bare flesh? The answer was a definite no. Perhaps this architect whose name she couldn't and didn't want to remember felt he had a right, given the fact he was roaming freely around her house. If that was his mode of thought, then he needed to think again because he was wrong. It was a peculiar and overly familiar thing to do. They were virtually strangers. He had been to the house only three or four times, his ease in her company increasing with each consecutive visit.

It would be another half hour before her parents returned, perhaps even longer. What if he came back? What would she do then? She could ignore his knocking, hide away in her bedroom, let him think she had left the house. Or she could risk the wrath of her parents by confronting him, allowing her unfettered thoughts to hit him square between the eyes. It would wreck their professional relationship. He would inform them of what she had said, tell them how their daughter had insulted him and made wild unsubstantiated accusations that could end his career. A thousand stars burst behind her eyes at the thought of it. They were under enough strain as it was. It had been a torrid year. Her father had lost his parents and his brother in an unimaginably tragic way. Her mother was living in an old house that she'd never much liked to begin with. Penny knew she wasn't the only one who was suffering. All she had to do was ignore his presence around the house until his services were no longer required. When would that be – a few more weeks perhaps? She could do that. Couldn't she? Whenever he came, she would salt herself away in her room, pretend he didn't exist. And in a few weeks, it would all be over, his leering expression and deliberate closeness to her bare flesh no more than a dim and distant memory.

An icy chill passed over her shoulders and neck, her skin puckering, the tiny hairs on her arms standing to attention. This was an old house, the heating and insulation inadequate. She recalled as a child how even in the height of summer, each room in this place remained cold. On the rare occasions she and Aaron slept over as children, they would clump together under a thick coarse blanket, cuddling each other for warmth, the distant hoots of the owls and the caustic caw of overhead crows all adding to the effect of being isolated and horribly homesick. They had grown up accustomed to hearing the idle chat of neighbours and the rumble of nearby traffic. Hallshead Farmhouse was miles from anywhere, their previous life already fading from her brain, smudged out by chaos and fear and the strain of living in a house that was akin to one of the building sites managed by her dad.

Penny marched into the hallway, grabbing a cardigan from a hook on the wall. The next time the architect visited, she would wear a high-necked sweater, lock herself in her room, go see a friend. Anything to stay away from him. And if anybody asked, she would explain how he made her feel uncomfortable, his roving eye always following her. She had been right all along, she was sure of it. That touch, dressed up as an accidental brush past, was deliberate. She wasn't imagining things. She wasn't being oversensitive or churlish or any number of insults that are hurled at teenagers should they dare to complain about people acting inappropriately in their presence. She was uneasy in his company and rightly so because his behaviour and his sinister conduct was questionable. And the time had come for it to all stop.

10

PENNY

Day 2

I sit, my eyes glued to the screen, my nerve endings on fire. I am unable to look away, focusing on her features, her body language, listening intently to every single word and slurred syllable that comes out of her mouth. She is only fifteen years old. A year older than I was when it happened to me. Bitter experience has taught me how words uttered at such a tender age can be misconstrued, taken apart by adults and shredded until they no longer hold any meaning. I watch her movements and posture, willing her to sit up straight, to fucking well *look* like a victim. Because another lesson I learned when I was younger was that strong young girls who refuse to be beaten down, who refuse to sit hunched and desperate looking, are viewed with suspicion and mistrust. Treated as if they are liars. Spoken about with derision and, sometimes, disgust. Even if what they are saying is true.

She nibbles at her nails, the young female on the video, shrugging when asked why she visited his house that night, why she didn't decline his offer when, by her own admission, she felt intimidated by him. Threatened even.

'Dunno. He asked me, didn't he?'

'I thought you said you felt scared of him when he had spoken to you the previous evening?'

'I did, sort of. He was older than me, wasn't he? Way older. So I thought if I went, it might put him off me, stop him asking again. If I didn't go, I thought he might come looking for me anyway, so I went along.' More nail nibbling then a definite sneer followed by a shrug of the shoulders.

I inwardly will her to shed the truculent teenager stance, to lose her aggressive tone and manner. And yet I know why she is doing it. It's fear. A need to remain private while your innermost thoughts and emotions are being stripped away by a team of strangers. Few youngsters have the ability to assess the contents of their own head, to sift through all those raging emotions and put them into some sort of coherent order that will impress adults. Because that's what this is – a showcase for this girl to see how she fares in front of an audience. An audience that has been specially selected to judge her performance. To assess and appraise her even though she isn't the one on trial here. Anybody would be forgiven for thinking otherwise given the huffing and puffing of certain jurors, their dislike of her already evident by their withering expressions and drawn-out groans and sighs.

I suck in a lungful of air. It lodges in my chest, a painful lump that hinders my breathing. I try to remain expressionless. It's imperative I am seen to be viewing this interview through impartial eyes. Not through the eyes of somebody who has walked in her shoes, thought her thoughts, and had that surly look about them when questioned.

'You met him at a party the previous evening, is that correct?'

'Yeah.'

'And that's when he asked if you wanted to go to his house?'

'Yeah.'

Elaborate, for fuck's sake! Sit up straight. Look upset and distressed. Play the bloody part of a distraught victim whose world has been torn apart.

My insides are a tight knot of despair, my mind a tangle of dark thoughts as I focus on how this young girl should conduct herself to glean as much sympathy as she can out of each member of the jury. It shouldn't be this way. This poor girl hasn't done anything wrong. And yet that is exactly how it feels. The smiles and head tilts that the jury afforded the defendant are woefully absent. In their place is a row of narrowed eyes and sour faces punctuated with the odd sigh and head shake that is clearly aimed at Melanie Albright's demeanour as the interviewer probes into her movements and intentions on the night of the assault.

'Tell me what you said when he sat next to you on the sofa in his house and put his arm around you.'

Another shrug of her shoulders. Then, 'I didn't say anything.'

'Okay, can you tell me what happened next?'

'He moved closer to me. I could feel his legs touching mine. And then he gave me a drink.'

'What was the drink?'

'Not sure. Coke, I think.'

'Did it have alcohol in it?'

A silence. She chews her nails and shakes her head. 'Don't think so.'

'Can you tell us what happened next? Take your time and feel free to pause if you need a break.'

'He leaned in and tried to kiss me after I finished my drink. I said I had to go. He was way older than me and it was like, you know, gross.'

A curl of her lip. Silence from the courtroom. I'm convinced everyone can hear the pounding of my heart and the steady thudding of my pulse as blood courses through my veins at lightning speed.

'And what happened when you told him you had to leave?'

She blinks, a lone tear rolling out of the corner of her eye, trailing down her cheek, leaving a silvery vertical line. She paws it away with an angry swipe, her bottom lip jutting out defiantly. I get her, I really do. I just hope the rest of the jury can see her pain. She is slowly revealing herself, peeling away her outer veneer bit by bit. Another layer gone. We're closer to who she really is now, closer to her discomfort. The humiliation and anger that sits at the core of her. It won't ever leave. I hope she knows that and is prepared for it. The heat of her burning fury will simmer down over the years but those furious flickering flames will never truly be extinguished. They will linger and smoulder, ready to combust at the slightest provocation.

'He pushed me back against the sofa, like, really hard. Angrily. I tried to stand up but he pushed me again.'

She stops, her head dipped, then stares at her hands, picking at her nails with a feverish agitated flick of her fingers.

'And then what happened?'

She shrugs again and briefly closes her eyes. 'He put his hands round my throat and held me in place. Then he pulled down my trousers, and then,' she says with a loud swallow, 'he raped me.'

On instinct, her hand flutters up to her neck, her fingers remaining there, tracing a line around her collarbone. I hope the other jurors notice it. I hope it sticks in their minds, her body language, her nervous mannerisms, telling them in loud clear gestures what that man, what that *monster*, did to her.

We watch for a few more minutes until the video finishes and we are left, sitting in silence. On my part, it's a stunned muteness. I concentrate on controlling my breathing, counting each breath in and out, keeping my spine rigid, my face straight and eyes lowered and vacant. I should have known how difficult this would be. I *did* know and yet it's still jarring to sit through her ordeal, to listen to what she was forced to go through. What she had to endure and will continue to endure for the rest of her life.

We're asked to leave the courtroom for a short while, and we shuffle out in a quiet line while the prosecution presents their witness for questioning.

Somehow, I end up sitting next to the red-headed lady in the waiting area even though we are at opposite ends of the jurors' bench. She lowers her voice and turns to me, her face flushed with what appears to be exhilaration. Her eyes have a definite excited sparkle to them as if this is some kind of reality TV show we're being forced to watch.

'I've already made up my mind.' She glances around to make sure nobody is looking our way or listening in. The outside burst of birdsong stops anybody else from overhearing her statement. 'What about you?'

My face burns even though my hands are as cold as ice, a wintry chill sitting in the very centre of me. 'Too early. We haven't heard all the evidence yet. We've got a few more days to go.'

The scream of frustration I feel rising inside of me stays in my throat, trapped in place by our surroundings and a need to remain polite and decorous. I sit on my hands, the urge to push her away so strong and overwhelming, it frightens me.

'I'll tell you my thoughts later. Are you parked in the long stay car park over by the bridge?'

I find myself nodding. This is what I want, isn't it? To get people on side, to try and push for a guilty verdict despite any opposing evidence.

'My name's Cheryl, by the way.'

She waits for me to reply. It takes a second or two for her words to sink in. I feel dazed by her enthusiasm. Appalled by her excitement.

'Penny,' I say quietly. 'My name is Penny.'

And that man also raped me.

We are called back in and sit in our usual order. Next to the judge's seat, in the witness box sits a female, young and terrified-looking. She is hidden behind a screen to ensure she can't see the defendant while she is asked questions. Before the interrogation has even begun, she starts to cry, her hand shaking as she wipes away a flood of tears. I hear a sigh from somewhere on the jurors' bench and wonder if it's out of sympathy or irritation. I hope it's the former but suspect it's the latter. Sympathy for the plight of distressed young females is sadly lacking. I should know. I recall the side-eye glances and looks of disdain and disbelief when I tried to tell my side of the story, to tell my family that I had been pursued, that somebody had been lying in wait outside my bedroom window. I was a nervous agitated teenager, crying out for help but treated as if I had an overactive imagination, told time and time again that it was all in my head. I was alone in my turmoil, completely and utterly alone, and so is she.

I attempt to meet her gaze, to give her a warm supportive smile. To let her know that I'm on her side and that if she just sticks to the truth, no embellishments, no emotional outbursts, which are also viewed with distrust and derision, then the rest of the jury might also feel the same way. She needs us, and I need her to evoke some pity and compassion from these people, these hard-nosed, insensitive individuals, many of whom are treating this as a form of entertainment, to make them realise that appearing as a witness for the prosecution at such a young age is terrifying. Almost as terrifying as witnessing how judgemental and harsh people can be, how little they listen, how quick they are to come to ill-informed conclusions, deaf to all the facts. Blind to the reality of how difficult life can be for young females. They are unaware of the number of psychopaths and predators who walk among us, oblivious to the danger that surrounds us on a daily basis.

My hands are balled into fists as I sit and wait for her to speak, hoping she manages to pull it off and convince these people that this assault actually happened. I want her to break hearts, to bat those large glassy eyes of hers and let these members of the jury see that beyond their safe little worlds, their easy uninterrupted little lives, lies danger, fear, and some of the most grotesque individuals who are capable of the worst of crimes, doing unspeakable things to their fellow man without even breaking a sweat.

She takes a shuddering breath, her shoulders vibrating with the effort, and from her sleeve she produces a tiny white handkerchief, dabbing at her eyes before sitting up and readying herself for what comes next.

11

THE HOUSE

The light pollution was zero. That had been one of the most alarming and difficult things for Connie to come to terms with since moving to Hallshead Farmhouse. Come sunset, that hazy amber orb would settle over the hills, its descent bringing a blazing lilac sky that slowly turned grey before plunging them into complete darkness; an inky swathe of nothingness, occasionally sprinkled with a constellation of stars. It was both breathtaking and disturbing as it hung over them, the sheer heft of it pushing down on her like a shroud. It served as a reminder of where she was. How isolated they were. No hazy yellow shafts of light from nearby properties, no snaking streetlights casting a welcome glow across the landscape. Nothing but an impenetrable spread of darkness that weighed heavily on her until morning arrived, at which point she would rise, the pressing need to escape the place lifting until the following evening when it would begin all over again. Every day, the pitiless darkness forced her further and further into the cold wet loam until she felt as if she were choking on it.

The sleeping tablets helped. Wrapping her in their solid dependable cocoon every night, they would help take her mind away from the house and its endless problems for a full eight hours before pulling her back into the light of day, her refreshed body and mind more able to cope with the demands of Hallshead Farmhouse and its endless problems. Every day brought a new drama, another layer of dread that ate at her insides like acid. Rewires that took twice as long as promised as electricians hammered at walls and chiselled through plaster, all the while shaking their heads and sucking their teeth in despair. A local planning department that dragged its feet, postponing meetings and requesting multiple copies of plans already submitted. Builders whose prices skyrocketed every time she picked up the phone. And an incalcitrant husband who disagreed with all of her ideas. She hadn't planned for such levels of outright stubbornness. Wasn't prepared for it. Eric had stated from the outset that he wanted a sympathetic renovation, which she now realised meant keeping everything the same aside from a lick of paint here and there. She had thought they were thinking along the same lines, but as each old fitting was removed, Eric became less and less able to deal with the changes, acting as if it was his own skin that was being stripped away. And then there was the usual everyday dramas; the stress of having to deal with two surly teenagers who had been rudely yanked away from their network of friends, resulting in them storming around the house with sour expressions, barking out curt exchanges that bounced off bare flaking walls.

Her eyes snapped open. It wasn't her daughter's presence in the doorway of her bedroom that had woken her. It was the nightmare. She was already awake when Penny spoke, her voice helping to clear the fog of fear that had filled Connie's brain after dreaming that the house was collapsing around them, trapping them in the rubble as she and Eric fought to free their children from the dust and bricks, and the piles and piles of concrete that wouldn't stop tumbling down on them.

'There's somebody outside.'

Connie sat up in bed, a tight band of pain wrapped around her skull. Her eyelids drooped, the tablets doing their damnedest to drag her back into that thick blanket of drug-induced sleep. Penny had also had a nightmare. That was the only logical explanation. That was why she was standing there, ghost-like. Silent and unmoving. Saying those words. They were in an old farmhouse miles away from anywhere and anyone. They were miles from the nearest village. There wasn't anybody outside.

The glare of the clock told her it was 2 a.m., its green glow making her eyes throb and her head ache.

'Mum?'

'Go back to bed. You must have been dreaming. There's nobody there.'

Reassuring her daughter at this hour felt like a step too far. She didn't have the energy. Tomorrow the electrician would be back to continue rewiring the older part of the house. They had a busy week ahead of them. A busy week, month, year. The list of jobs was endless.

'It wasn't a dream. I heard something and when I looked out of my bedroom window, there was someone standing next to the fence.'

Connie let out a prolonged shaky sigh. Ignoring the mesh of dark unforgiving thoughts that filled her mind, she swung her legs off the mattress and stood up. Every part of her ached. With bones as heavy as solid steel, she pulled on her dressing gown, yanking it tightly around her body to stave off the chill of the unheated house, and shuffled out of the bedroom, Penny following close behind. 'Right, come on,' she muttered, doing what she could to disguise her annoyance. 'Show me.'

The moon cast an eerie glow across the back lawn and beyond, silvering the crooked fence with a triangular slab of pale light.

'There was definitely somebody there. I saw them! They were standing in the moonlight, staring up at me.'

The expanse of emptiness, the dark rolling landscape highlighted by the crescent moon that hung in a velvet-textured black sky, did little to alleviate Penny's growing frustration, her claim seeming more outlandish by the second.

'Penny, it's the early hours. We're all tired. Whatever you thought you saw isn't there now. Can I suggest we both go back to bed and try to get some sleep? We've got a team of electricians coming first thing. Your dad and I need to be up for work and you need to be up early for school.'

Her daughter's fury was palpable. Connie could feel the hiss of it in the air, a heavy-bellied cloud of anger that hovered over them. It neither mattered nor worried her. Nothing was going to keep Connie from her bed. All the doors and windows were locked. Even if there *was* somebody out there, they would need a sledgehammer to get in. After

Douglas Fairbridge's visit a few days back, she'd made sure they were as secure as they could be. Nobody was getting inside this house without her permission. Nobody.

'It'll be him.'

Grit dug into Connie's eyes, small fragments scratching at her eyeballs. She suppressed another sigh and took the bait.

'Okay, Penny. Despite being completely shattered and feeling as if I could sleep for a hundred years and still wake up exhausted, I'll bite. It will be who, exactly?'

'That creepy architect guy. The one who keeps staring at me. He makes my skin crawl. I can't bear to be anywhere near him.'

Connie held up her hand, her temper unravelling. Life was difficult. Her daughter was making it even harder with her wild unfounded allegations. 'Enough! I have had enough of your stories.'

This again. Penny claiming only hours earlier that Duncan, their architect, had touched her while they were out. Their initial horror had soon turned to scepticism and disbelief once Penny had told her and Eric the full story, how he had briefly brushed past her shoulder whilst walking towards the sink. It was ludicrous. He was a capable, industrious and professional man, the only one who hadn't let them down after others had submitted ludicrous prices and cancelled meetings at the last minute, many of them not even turning up at all. She had no idea what was going on in her daughter's head at the moment, but common sense was definitely lacking.

'Look,' she said, turning away from the window and facing Penny, 'I don't know what your game is here, whether you're trying to punish me and your father for dragging you away from your friends, but this needs to stop. I've been in the house while you've been here with him and I haven't noticed anything inappropriate going on.'

Thoughts of a previous event kaleidoscoped around Connie's brain – an older boy at school. A throwaway comment that Penny had mistaken for lurid sarcasm. A comment that almost saw the boy expelled. He had mentioned Penny's figure, told her she resembled a top model. Many girls of her age would have taken it as a compliment, dining out on it for months on end. But not her daughter. She had spun on her heel, reported him for making her feel uncomfortable, said he had sexualised her and demeaned her as a person. It took an awful lot of negotiations with his parents and the headteacher to keep him in school. The poor lad had showed genuine contrition for something that required only a brief apology. He admitted making a comment about Penny's figure, and showed deep remorse. And now this; claims of strangers standing outside her window. Accusations against a man they regarded as highly professional.

It was too dark to see Penny's expression. Probably for the best. It was hard to think straight after taking those damn tablets every night. Connie sighed, guilt biting at her, nipping her skin at the way she so readily dismissed her daughter's claims, but in the end, fatigue, coupled with Penny's propensity for dramatising the simplest of situations, won over. Exhaustion plucked at her with its strong hot fingers, the sleeping tablets taking their toll. Staying and arguing with Penny wasn't an option. She had neither the strength nor the enthusiasm for it, turning and shuffling along the landing back to her own bed. Her eyes were leaden, her muscles knotted and tense. The mattress groaned when she turned over and pulled the duvet up under her chin.

She would deal with it in the morning when the world was a brighter place, her mind clear of the swirling fog that impaired her thinking and skewed her judgement. Everything was always much easier to bear after a night's sleep. Penny's head was full of anger lately, her body a surge of hormones. That's all it was. There was nothing to worry about. Nothing at all. Thoughts of Douglas Fairbridge and his threats ballooned in her mind before being pushed aside and ground underfoot by the heavy boots of lassitude.

* * *

She wasn't dreaming. Somebody had been standing next to the fence. She'd seen him. Could make out his outline, sharp as granite against the dark landscape, his silhouette bathed in the haze of the moonlight. He was there. It was *him*. Had to be. Who else would stand there in the dead of night, staring up at her bedroom window? Dread coiled in Penny's abdomen, twisting and turning. A sleeping serpent waiting to strike. What if he hung around until daylight? Followed her to school? Waited outside until she came back out again? What then? Would her mother believe her if he attacked her on the long route home?

Penny fought back hot tears, hurt at the rejection. Frustrated, after being dismissed and treated like a liar. An attention seeker.

'You think I'm saying these things because your focus is elsewhere lately? You really think I'm so egocentric and selfish that I'd make this shit up to switch the spotlight back onto me?' Her voice had been a near shriek when she had barked at her mother earlier in the day after being told she had an overactive imagination and that her parents believed an architect who was practically a stranger over their own daughter.

On instinct, Penny checked the window, making sure it was closed properly. No lock, but the glazier company was coming next week to measure up for new windows. In the meantime, she would remain vigilant, keep her distance from creepy architect man and be constantly looking over her shoulder.

It had been the same with the lad at school. Don McCarrick. His name had haunted her for months after the event. Every day she had to pass his sneering face in the corridor, his comment lodged in her brain. How he had tried to act innocent, playing down his words. Lying and manipulating his way out of it. Telling everyone he had made a simple comment about how beautiful Penny was and how she could become a model when in fact he had brushed against her, his hot breath on her neck, mentioning how he would like to fuck her, how she had the biggest tits in school. Too embarrassed to relay his actual comments, Penny had gone along with his sick little game and also played it down, sparing him from permanent expulsion. And she had been the one who was vilified for refusing to forgive him. She wasn't about to let that happen again. More experienced and now hypercautious and wary, she could now see those type of people for who they were – predators. McCarrick had done the same with plenty of girls in school but Penny was the only one brave enough to stand up to him, albeit in a half-hearted way.

She peered out once again, her eyes roving over the fields outside, everything now swathed in darkness as the moon slid behind a thick veil of clouds. He could be there right now, crouching or standing or doing whatever the fuck he wanted because without the aid of the moon, it was impossible to see anything out there. They were in the middle of nowhere, in a rundown old farmhouse in the middle of the North Yorkshire moors. She'd thought it might be an adventure when her parents had first spoken about moving here. How wrong she was. What it was was a nightmare. A great big fucking nightmare without end. No proper neighbours apart from the local landed gentry, no friends close by and no light pollution to help identify the person who had taken it upon themselves to stand below her bedroom window like a figure from a horror movie. It couldn't be McCarrick. He hadn't the means to get there. Which left the architect.

Penny shivered, pulling and tugging at the curtains until they closed, then climbed into bed, the cool sheets a welcome sensation against her burning limbs. Sleep would take a while to come. Only four hours and she would have to be up for school. She stared up at the ceiling before closing her eyes, thinking how much she hated this house and her new life and everybody in it.

12

PENNY

Day 2

The witness looks tiny behind the screen, her face pale, her spine curved like a small infant craving solace from its mother. It is apparent by her body language, the tremble of her limbs and her terrified expression, that if it were possible to do so, she would curl up inside herself and disappear.

'You were with Ms Albright on the evening before the alleged attack took place?'

Her chin quivers as she nods, her bottom lip jutting out in fear. She reminds me of a fawn, all wide-eyed and fragile-looking. She is a frightened prey seconds before the kill, somebody who is likely to bolt from the room at the slightest provocation. I suspect fear of the nearby authoritative figures is the only thing that is keeping her seated and upright. I imagine her later, after all of this is over, curling up on her bed with her eyes closed tight, doing what she can to block out the rest of the world.

'For the record, the witness is nodding.' The prosecution barrister smiles and glances down at her notes. 'If you could possibly speak a little louder, that would be tremendously helpful.' Another smile, her equine face and piercing gaze suddenly softer and calmer to try and encourage this young female, give her some support and let her know that she isn't completely alone in this undertaking.

I feel like jumping out of my seat and rushing over there, wrapping an arm around her shoulder and telling her that everything is going to be all right as long as she tells the truth and she doesn't buckle under the strain. I want to tell her that I am also on her side and she needs to do whatever she can to make sure that bastard gets locked up. A pain throbs at the base of my neck, its intensity threatening to travel up my head and clamp itself around my skull like a metal vice. I swallow and try to ignore it, keeping my focus on my surroundings. It's easy for an outsider looking in. Not so easy when you're up there in the witness box being interrogated. All those people watching you and waiting for you to crack, for your sanity to splinter. Seems easy as a bystander. All you need to do is tell the truth and answer a few questions. Not so easy an undertaking when you're caught in the eye of the storm, a whirling vortex that is doing its utmost to shred you to pieces, leaving you a wreck of your former self.

'Yeah, I was with her that night.'

'And did you see her speaking to anybody?'

'Yes, she was talking to an older man. They were standing together in the corner of the room.'

'This was at the party of your friend's sister who is more than ten years older than you and Ms Albright. Is that correct?'

'That's correct.'

'Did you speak to the man at all?'

She shakes her head then gives a trembling half-smile and replies, 'No.'

'And how did your friend, Ms Albright, look? Did she look happy and relaxed?'

The young woman swallows and wipes away a stream of tears. 'Sorry, I'm really anxious. I was scared to come here. This is all so…'

Her voice trails away and the judge nods sympathetically, his gentle-looking expression and avuncular manner enough to put anybody at ease, although I'm willing to bet that he has had to face some hardened criminals in his time. 'We totally understand. Just take your time. This is a new formal environment for you and it makes the most experienced of people nervous.'

She nods and bites at her lip, her tears and diminutive body like that of a primary-aged child rather than a female in her mid-teens. With her chalk-white skin, she is all eyes and quivering chin.

'Sorry. Yes, she seemed okay but maybe a bit on edge?'

'Could you perhaps explain what you mean?' The prosecution barrister's voice is so low it's almost a whisper.

The witness chews at a nail then pulls her hand away from her mouth and presses her palms together before sliding them under her legs. She is so very young; frightened and naïve, her limbs shuddering like a fledgling bird trying to pluck up enough courage to flee the nest and fly. I can understand why they put up the screen. Sitting staring at a man who may or may not have raped and assaulted your friend whilst you're being scrutinised by barristers, a judge and a dozen jurors must be a terrifying experience. I feel nervous for her and I'm only a bystander.

Don't cover up for him like I did because you are afraid of being told you're exaggerating. Don't be like me.

I want to scream those words at her, tell her to stick to her story, make sure she doesn't get pushed off course by disbelieving adults who are too busy with their own lives to take some time out to dig deeper for the real story, to scrape beneath the surface for the actual truth. Because the truth is rarely easily found. It conceals itself inside a sticky web of fear and complex emotions. And don't make frantic hollow accusations or lash out at others because you're scared and infuriated, convinced that all men have a secret ill-intentioned agenda. It's unfair to punish the innocent for the sins of those you're too frightened to confront. I would like to say that to Melanie Albright, to meet with her and guide her. This girl's vulnerability is evident. I wish I could subliminally send across my thoughts to her, to let her know that I'm behind her and am willing her to speak up and do the right thing.

She bites at her lip and briefly glances at the judge before elaborating. 'Well, it's just that, she kept looking over at me and widening her eyes, like she wanted to tell me something.'

'And did she? Tell you something, that is?' says the barrister, her voice flowing, still easy and as soft as silk.

'Erm, just that on the way home, she said something about him pestering her. Something like, "God, he was soo annoying and creepy. He wouldn't leave me alone."'

The barrister thanks the girl and says, 'No more questions, Your Honour,' before sitting down and glancing at her papers.

The defence are asked to pose any questions they may have and I feel every muscle in my body tighten. The barrister for the defence stands, a portly man in his mid-fifties. Old enough to be her father. I truly hope he does actually have a daughter the same age. I hope he can feel a smidgen of sympathy for this poor girl and treads carefully around her. She is fragile, and fragile people are easily broken but not so easy to put back together.

His wig is perched precariously on top of his head, his glasses resting crookedly at the end of his nose. He looks austere. Belligerent given the opportunity. I nibble at the inside of my mouth and wait, apprehension gnawing at my stomach. His voice is surprisingly smooth when he speaks, almost a whisper.

'You say your friend felt intimidated by this man? She was' – he checks his notes, somewhat deliberately, I feel, to add some gravitas to his question before continuing – 'looking over at you and widening her eyes. Is that correct?'

More tears spill out as she quickly turns to look at the judge. 'I'm sorry. I don't know what you mean? That word. I'm not sure...'

'Intimidated. That means, felt a bit scared of,' the judge replies softly, nodding at her, his smile genuine. I like this judge. He is trying to get the best out of the witness but I fear all is lost. She is a wreck. I just hope her child-like appearance and obvious terror evokes some sympathy from the rest of the jury.

'Yes,' she answers. 'I got the feeling she was scared of him. Not, like, terrified or anything, but there was something wrong.'

'But you didn't know that for sure, did you?' replies the barrister.

'I did. I've known her for, like, years and years, and I knew she wasn't happy being stuck over in the corner of the room with him.'

A ripple of satisfaction passes over my cold flesh. I see an inner strength emerging from this young lady. The gnawing sensation in my stomach begins to ease.

He rustles his papers and clears his throat. Another deliberate move, all designed to unnerve her. I hope she out-manoeuvres him. I hope she manages to remain strong and not crumple under the pressure. I hate this charade, all this play-acting and jockeying for control. A courtroom should be about telling the truth and nothing else. Trying to gain power over a vulnerable individual shouldn't play a part in these proceedings, and yet it does. I'm not so naïve as to believe that simply being honest will be enough to win over a jury, but what is happening here is dreadful. We are being made to watch as a young girl is pitted against an experienced middle-aged man who has worldly wisdom and a vast knowledge of the legal system on his side.

'And yet she didn't just walk away? Did you drink any alcohol that evening?'

'Objection!'

The defence barrister opens his palms wide, a sudden look of deference in his expression. He glances at the judge and speaks loudly, every word treacle coated. 'My Lord, I merely mean to ascertain whether the witness was in full control of her faculties. Whether she was under the influence of alcohol and able to clearly detect what was going on with her friend, or whether her judgement was blurred by the said alcohol and not altogether reliable.'

The judge smiles and replies, 'Yes, I think we need to hear the answer to this question. It is relevant to whether the witness was able to clearly recall her friend's reactions accurately.'

'I – I'd had a few drinks. I can't remember how many, but I wasn't falling down drunk or anything.'

She shifts about in her seat, eyes wide again. Like a cornered animal caught in a snare. My earlier rush of positivity dissipates.

'Please try. This is important. I'll ask once more – how many alcoholic drinks did you have that evening?'

A crimson flush creeps up her neck, resting on her cheeks and jawline. I want to scream that this is unfair, that she isn't on trial here. I can hear the dull hum of my pulse. It beats in my throat and reverberates in my ears, making me hot and dizzy. I run my fingers through my hair then clasp my hands together in my lap.

She begins to weep, her chest convulsing as she holds her fingers over her face in an attempt to stem the flow of tears.

'I'm only fifteen years old. I'm going to get in trouble for underage drinking, aren't I?'

The judge catches her eye and shakes his head, his face full of sympathy. 'No, absolutely not. You're not on trial here. Nobody is going to be angry with you. All we ask is that you try to cast your mind back and answer the question as best you can. We only want the truth. I promise you, you won't be in trouble.'

She sniffs and rubs at her eyes with the back of her hand before rummaging in her pocket for a tissue. 'I think that maybe I had four or five drinks.'

A murmur from the other jurors. A low gasp from somebody farther down the bench. A young girl doing her utmost to recall an incident as best she can is now being viewed as a drunken unreliable witness. Regardless of the judge's reassurances that her behaviour isn't under scrutiny, she is definitely the one on trial here. This is not good. I hoped she would elicit some sympathy from the other jurors, but she's been tangled up by her own naivety and words. She is on a downward trajectory. I can't see her coming back from this.

'And you still feel absolutely certain that your friend, Ms Albright, felt scared of the man, even though you had had four or five alcoholic drinks that night?'

Even from this distance, I can see that she is now shaking. I wait for her answer, the sinews in my neck stretched and taut like cat gut.

'Erm, I think so. I do remember her looking a bit frightened.'

'Frightened?'

'Well, maybe not frightened, but definitely not her usual self.'

'And can you possibly describe her usual self?'

She pulls herself together, sniffing and blowing her nose before crumpling the tissue into a tight ball in her closed fist.

'She's normally really outgoing and fun but that night she seemed a bit – I dunno, quiet, like something was wrong.'

'And you could see that even though you, by your own admission, had had four or five alcoholic drinks?'

She straightens up, a rush of bravery pushing her on. She shrugs and crinkles her brow defiantly. 'Yeah. Yeah, I could. I'd had a few drinks but like I already said, I wasn't falling down drunk or anything.'

He waits, using time for dramatic effect to allow us jurors to digest what we have just heard, then speaks before sitting down. 'No more questions, Your Honour.'

The walls close in around me, a wash of grey clouding my vision. I only hope there are more prosecution witnesses waiting to be called, stronger, less vulnerable people who can sway the jury, because if that was it, if that young inexperienced lady was the best they could find to help convict him, then this thing is over before it's even begun.

13

THE HOUSE

It was a never-ending din. Drills whining and whirring, hammers and chisels banging against plaster. And the dust. Dry, cloying, swirling clouds of dust. Tiny grey particles that hung in the air, clogging everyone's throats and coating their clothes and skin.

Connie's patience was wearing thin. And this was just the beginning, before they'd even begun knocking down walls and fitting new kitchens and bathrooms. Two truculent resentful teenagers thrown into the mix exacerbated the issue. Location of school uniforms and textbooks was impossible. They were living in a building site and Connie wasn't sure how much more of it she could take.

A knock at the door roused her, dragging her out of her dark musings. 'I'll get it.' Penny was up on her feet and heading down the hallway before Connie had a chance to shift out of her chair.

Things had been strained between her and her daughter after that incident in the early hours. That was last week and since then, conversation between them had been stilted, words passed back and forth with strained expressions and monosyllabic utterances. She had tried. God knows, Connie had tried. Despite being exhausted and under a great deal of strain, she had, on various occasions, sidled up to Penny and initiated conversation only to be met with a grunt or a sneer. Or worse still, complete silence. Until now.

'Mum, there's a man here asking for either you or Dad.'

Connie's stomach clenched, bony fingers curling tendril-like around her innards, squeezing and squeezing until she felt like she couldn't breathe properly. She knew then, by the tone of Penny's voice, that it was *him*. There was none of the usual hormone-fuelled bravado but a tone that was tinged with apprehension and possibly even fear. Her daughter wasn't a shrinking violet when it came to defending her rights, but even she knew her physical capabilities against a fully grown man, and she was sensible enough to stand aside.

Connie marched down the hallway, the sight before her further weakening her already failing posture and uncertain gait. There he stood, as tall as he was broad, his tweed jacket splattered with spots of crimson, streaks of it smeared on his hands and face. An injured lamb lay bleating in his arms. Connie swallowed down a shriek. Its eyes landed on her face, fluttering wildly before closing. She stole a glance at its chest, a rhythmic movement there that told her it was still alive. Barely. Her throat felt constricted, her breathing laboured as his voice cut through the silence.

'Care to explain?'

She blinked and took a ragged breath, trying to make sense of this nonsensical situation. Trying to keep her gaze averted from the twitching bleeding animal and the scarlet smears streaked across its white fur. It was a baby, its small face resting against his chest. Connie fought back a flood of tears. She considered saying nothing but sometimes a silence could be as damning as an admission of guilt.

'Sorry? Care to explain what?'

Caustic barking laughter echoed down the long hallway, his presence in their home incongruous and unwelcome. The guffawing stopped, a heavy silence following as they all waited. For something. For anything. Connie wasn't sure what, but she held her tongue, refusing to be browbeaten into saying something she might regret. Something he could twist and misconstrue.

'Oh, for fuck's sake,' he said after a few seconds, his voice cutting through the ominous atmosphere. 'Let's not play any more fucking stupid games here, shall we? This!' he said, holding the bleeding creature aloft. 'Would you like to explain who did this to my sheep?'

The thudding in Connie's temple made her wince, a pain shooting behind her eye. She stepped forward, pushing Penny behind her, away from this situation. Away from him, the hideous brute of a man on her doorstep. Despite her daughter's bravado, she was still a child and shouldn't be witness to such an awful spectacle.

'I have no idea who did this to your sheep. Now either get off my doorstep and off my land or I'll call the police and report you for harassment.' Her patience was wearing thin, anger at this situation riding roughshod over any fears she may have had.

'Your land?' He threw back his head and let out a shriek of laughter, his large teeth and sharp features heightening her hatred of him. 'It's my fucking land. It belongs to me and my children. The earth you're standing on has belonged to the Fairbridge family for centuries. You're the trespassers here. You and your family are no better than filthy squatters.'

Connie felt the air shift behind her and turned to see Penny move away. She could hear her voice in the background, an unintelligible murmur, distant and ethereal while he stood, mute and unmoving, menace radiating from him. Then the thud of footsteps as her daughter returned, her face pale and impassive.

'They're on their way. The police, that is. I've just called them.'

A small mewling sound rucked Connie's scalp, the hairs on her arms standing to attention as the injured animal let out a plaintive wail, its small tongue visible before its tiny head flopped back against Fairbridge's tweed jacket.

For the briefest of seconds, he stumbled, as if shocked into retreat, his chiselled expression slackening. 'I'm going to have to shoot this lamb now because of what you've done. Let's see what the police have to say about that, shall we? It's an offence to inflict unnecessary suffering on an animal.'

'And it's an offence to threaten people. Now get lost, you mad old bastard.'

Penny moved to shut the door but he was too fast for her, shoving his foot forward, jamming the big oak door in place despite her pushing at it with her splayed hand. A drip of blood fell from the lamb's face, landing on the doorstep. Connie watched as a large splat hit the stone, sending her stomach into a series of contractions. Revulsion swelled in her chest, sympathy for the distressed animal tugging at her with such ferocity she had to fight back yet more tears. It was only a few weeks old, helpless and frightened, and he was going to kill it. This was all his doing. He had maimed one of his own animals to provoke an argument. What sort of a man would do such a thing? The lump in her throat ballooned. She gulped it down, her face burning, eyes sore as if filled with sand. The urge to push him off her doorstep was so strong, it knocked her off balance, her head swimming with anger and despair. She leaned forward, clinging on to the doorframe, trying to stop the constant seesawing of the room.

'Oh, I'll hang around if it's all the same with you, because I don't actually believe a word you just said. The police aren't going to come all the way out here to sort out a dispute between a couple of irate neighbours. They've got better things to do with their time. We all know that it's a big fat fucking lie. You didn't make a call. You haven't got the guts.'

His sneer, the way he glared at Penny, set a fire raging in Connie's belly, a furnace that licked and scorched at the lining of her innards. She was a schoolkid, for Christ's sake. A child. He was a grown man who should know better. She hadn't moved her family here and made a seismic shift in their lives to be confronted with this kind of abuse. Enough was enough.

'Get out!' Her voice, an unexpected bellow, was enough to cause him to stumble backwards off the step.

Connie took the opportunity and grabbed at the handle, slamming the door shut before he could make another move and step inside. She turned the key and slid the bolt across, its definitive heavy clunk echoing around the house, then rushed from room to room, yanking curtains closed and shutting blinds.

If she could, she would have packed up their things and left there and then, vacating Hallshead Farmhouse, leaving it to the elements and their selfish psychotic neighbour, and yet there was a small part of her that felt compelled to stay and fight. Douglas Fairbridge was a bully and if there was one thing she detested with every fibre of her being, it was bullies. Entitled people who felt they had the right to trample over others as if they didn't count. So no, she wouldn't run. She would stay and she would fight this man. This wasn't her home. Not yet. She and Eric owned the building but it was still a shell of a house, rundown and uncared for. But not for much longer. She would work hard to make this place somewhere desirable. A lovely family abode. She would stay here and she and her family would thrive, showing the local landed gentry that they weren't about to be browbeaten into leaving.

'Did you actually call the police?'

It didn't matter either way. He was outside now with no way of getting back in.

'Of course I bloody well did. He's a psychopath.'

Connie stood, listening out for the sound of distant sirens, hearing nothing, until her legs buckled as the sharp crack of a gunshot rang out in the empty air. The wounded lamb. That man. That awful monstrous man.

Grabbing Penny's upper arm, she held her fast, guiding her back into the kitchen at the rear of the house. They stood, voiceless and immobile, disbelief and horror paralysing them.

'We need to tell Dad when he gets back.'

Connie could feel their earlier tension dissolving, the horror of this incident putting everything into perspective. She could sense her daughter watching her for a reaction. Penny stood, motionless, waiting for a reply. Connie's flesh burned, her daughter's scrutinous gaze making her hot and uncomfortable. She was the adult here. She had to do something, protect her children. Keep their family safe.

'I'll speak with him. We'll sort it.'

She had no idea how she was going to sort it but had to say something – *anything* to comfort her frightened teenage daughter.

'Maybe it was him.' Penny's voice was a whisper, her eyes sweeping the floor. Her hands were flexed into fists at her side.

'Maybe what was him?' The breath in her chest expanded, a sudden pain catching her off guard. She had fallen into Penny's trap and now there was no way out of it. She was a rabbit caught in a snare, the metal teeth of the trap holding her captive.

'The person who was outside my window. Maybe it was that mad weirdo who was standing out there staring up at me.'

A rumbling sigh erupted out of Connie's throat before she had time to stop it.

'You said it was the architect. You were convinced it was the architect and now it's our neighbour?' Her final words were a snort, carrying more aggression than intended. She was tired of this. She was tired of everything. 'Penny, this has got to stop. That man' – she pointed towards the shuttered window – 'is a vile individual. It's enough that we have to deal with him. The stress of him and this... this *house* is just about as much as I can bear. Please don't make things worse by throwing stupid unfounded allegations around every two minutes!' Connie raised her arms in desperation and glanced around at the crumbling plaster and the river of wires snaking out of the channels that were gouged out of every wall. Dust motes floated around them, thousands of tiny flecks dancing in front of her eyes, taunting her, reminding her of where she was and how much they still had to do to make the place habitable. Who knew that a sympathetic renovation could cause such turmoil and anxiety?

A wave of guilt pricked at her, washing away her anger as she watched Penny's eyes glisten with unshed tears. She stepped forward, arms outstretched to offer some comfort to her only daughter. Penny stumbled back, face stricken, before bolting out of the kitchen and disappearing down the hallway. Connie listened to the front door slam, a loud clunk signalling Penny's departure into the bleak vast landscape, her destination unknown.

'God almighty.' The chair creaked beneath Connie as she slumped into it and rested her head in her hands, wondering when all of this was ever going to end. There were times when she wondered if the journey to a better place, a better life, was really worth it.

14

PENNY

Day 2

We step out of the court, an unblemished sky lifting my mood. The earlier clouds have passed, leaving a canopy of blue. A soft breeze laps at my face. I take a deep breath, savouring the clean air and the stab of warmth from a distant setting sun, then pick up my pace, keen to get home. It's been a long day.

Behind, footsteps rush to catch up with me. I don't need to turn around to see who it is. It's her – Cheryl. The red-headed lady. Instinct told me to take a different route to the car park. I didn't, and now here I am, walking with her at my side as if we are old friends.

'So, what did you think of today's proceedings then?' She makes no attempt to keep her voice low, words and thoughts spewing out of her mouth, carried off by the breeze to unsuspecting passers-by.

The judge's strong remarks about not speaking anything of the trial until it is over ring in my ears. But then, this is what I want, isn't it? To convert everyone's opinion, align them with my own. This is my opportunity to dismantle any arguments she may have, to bend and shape her thinking and sow seeds of doubt where she has already planted firm ideas that are starting to take root.

I take a quick look over my shoulder. We appear to have left everybody else behind. I shrug and sigh.

'Well, I'm not too sure just yet. I don't quite know what to think. It's early days but like you, I already have some thoughts and opinions rumbling.'

I don't believe that she is remotely interested in my views. She proves me correct, her own thoughts spilling out before I have a chance to say anything else in return. A cascade of words she firmly believes to be the truth even though she has no evidence to back them up.

'Well, that witness was as much use as a chocolate teapot and quite frankly, I think the purported victim is making it all up.'

My skin puckers. A small spark of revulsion combusts in my gut. It's obvious Cheryl has little or no experience of suffering or trauma. I feel sure she has led an easy, effortless existence. No critical thinking required. No need or room for compassion. With suffering comes sorrow and sympathy. With endless unhappiness comes empathy and humanity. I don't believe Cheryl has any of those qualities.

I take a rattling breath and try to rein in those thoughts. I don't know her. I know of her type though, have come across the Cheryls of the world before now. A voice in my head is telling me to stop it, that maybe she has her own reasons for being the way she is. After all, we all have our own crosses to bear. It's just that some are weightier than others. And some people buckle under the strain while others stand straight and tall.

'What makes you so sure?' I soften my tone, smiling and choosing my words with as much precision as I can. It's like picking my way through the wreckage of a car crash, attempting to clamber over piles of protruding twisted metal and shards of broken glass to get to the soft bodies beneath. There has to be a thoughtful caring Cheryl in there somewhere. I just need to dig deep to find her. 'I mean, we've got a few days left yet. I suppose it depends what tomorrow and the rest of the week brings, doesn't it?'

'Nope. My mind is already made up. I'm a big believer in gut instinct and my gut tells me she's a liar.'

A pain takes hold in my jaw. I clamp my teeth together, focusing on the pulse that is beating in my neck. Maybe I was right to think badly of her. Maybe she is utterly heartless and trying to get her onside is a pointless endeavour. And yet there is a part of me that refuses to give up. I need all the help I can get. I want that man locked away and stripped of his liberties. And I need Cheryl if I am to succeed in doing just that.

I wait for a couple of seconds before speaking, my voice so low and quiet, I fear that the words I say will be carried away by the wind that whirls around us. It buffets our bodies as we wend our way around tall buildings that flank the multi-storey car park.

'But why would she do that, lie I mean? Why would anybody put themselves through this whole stressful situation?' I smile, tilt my head, keep my features soft and non-threatening. Hope she doesn't take umbrage and become defensive. All the while I am thinking of how soul-destroying it is to have people like Cheryl make snap judgements, assessing and deciding without knowing all the facts. Those girls in that courtroom did something I should have done many years ago. I'm here now to do what I can to defend them, to show the other jurors how terrifying it is to step into the light and have people like Cheryl delve inside your head and attempt to unpick your thoughts, to allow them to seek negativity and lies where there is only love and truth and all the while you are wracked with dread and fear and foreboding.

My smile stays glued in place. Despite disagreeing with her ethics and morals, I need to get this woman on my side, get her thinking aligned with mine, not have her as an enemy.

'Attention?'

I give a non-committal shrug. Another head tilt. Then, 'Maybe, but she hasn't appeared in court, has she? Her evidence is via a videolink. Also, her name won't be reported in any of the newspapers, so it's not as if the public is going to see any of it. So if it's attention she's after, it's not working, is it?'

Cheryl smiles and taps the side of her nose, a puerile act that puts even more distance between us. We are so very unalike, Cheryl and I. Completely different beasts.

'Ah, yes, but all her friends and family will know, won't they? She'll have garnered plenty of sympathy from them. I'm willing to bet her social media accounts will be full of it – friends texting her, family members telling her how awful things are for her, and all the while she will be sitting back, lapping it up while that poor man in the dock is having his name dragged through the mud.'

My bottom lip juts out so far, I fear it will detach itself from the rest of my face as I carefully consider her words and try to think of an appropriate reply. One that won't send her running in the opposite direction.

'Hmm. Maybe. But I think she'll have been told by the police not to mention any of it on social media. If she does, she runs the risk of the whole case collapsing around her so her bid for attention would soon grind to a halt.'

Cheryl turns to glare at me. 'Sounds like you're on her side?'

I force a laugh and shake my head. 'I'm just trying to be impartial and look at it objectively, playing devil's advocate and all that.'

The fact she is clearly on his side is of no importance to her. I keep my thoughts under wraps. Better to say nothing than utter something antagonistic and cause a further rift between us. We're already drifting in different directions, the gap between us widening with each passing second.

'Well, anyway, let's see what tomorrow brings, eh?' She laughs and shakes her head before sneaking a glance at me. 'I still think the defence barrister looks hilarious. At one point his glasses almost fell off his nose.'

I attempt another smile, my cordiality unable to stretch to actual laughter. Cheryl is about as funny as a nasty bout of diarrhoea. So I say nothing, refusing to become embroiled in making any disparaging remarks of my own. My focus today has been on what comes out of their mouths when all the while Cheryl has been homed in on his appearance, ridiculing his wig and spectacles while being deaf to their reasoned arguments.

'Right, well, I'm over in the far corner,' I say, nodding towards my vehicle as we make our way over to the car park. I ponder over her statement, wondering how effective our current legal system actually is; forcing twelve reluctant people into a room to decide the fate of another person hardly constitutes fairness and justice. All those diverse opinions, all those separate lives and experiences. They are the things that make us who we are. They dictate our decision making. Cheryl and I are living proof of how dissimilar people can be. Already she is flouting the rules and refusing to listen to evidence, preferring to follow her own instincts. There could be others like her, and if that is the case, then that man, in just a few days, is going to walk free. But then, Cheryl isn't the only one flouting the rules, is she? I am currently the leader of that particular pack, running the risk of ending up standing in the dock alongside him should anybody unearth my history and motives.

Acid burns at the base of my stomach.

I give her a wave and fish in my bag for my keys, then feel a hand on my upper arm, a set of strong fingers holding me in place.

'Is everything okay?' A furrow stretches the length of her forehead, her pale blue eyes fixed on mine.

I resist the urge to pull my arm free of her grasp. 'No, I'm fine. Just a bit tired. Once I get home and walk my dog, I'll be able to relax properly.' I shake myself free of her grip and manage a smile. 'See you in the morning.'

She lets out a sharp grunt of agreement, seemingly satisfied with my explanation, and marches off to the other side of the car park.

Relief wraps itself around me, the sensation of finally being on my own, away from Cheryl's inane chatter and her incompatible beliefs and sentiments, such a powerful feeling, I feel like weeping. It isn't just Cheryl, I know that. It's *him*. He's going to get away with it, and no matter how hard I try to influence those around me, if the evidence isn't there to convict, then I am fighting a losing battle. This was my chance, my one and only opportunity to right a terrible wrong, and I'm not clever enough to make it happen.

I run my fingers through my hair, griminess clinging to every inch of my flesh and scalp. Other people, the austerity of the courtroom, but mainly sitting opposite the man who all those years ago took my innocence from me have all left me feeling dirty and wrung out. I press the heel of my hands into my eye sockets, then slide the key into the ignition and head for home, thoughts of a long walk with Freda giving me the impetus to keep going, to press my foot down on the pedal and get as far away from the place as quickly as I can.

15

THE HOUSE

Even on the warmest of days, the bleak open landscape of North Yorkshire felt like winter, a biting brutal wind howling at her bare skin, its cold unforgiving fingers scratching at her eyes. Penny stood, hands bunched at her sides, the veins in her neck distended with unspent fury. In the distance, she could see the rooftop of Fairbridge Hall, its chimneys spiking the vast grey sky like huge ominous talons. She turned her thoughts to the injured sheep. And that gun, the sound of it still ricocheting in her head. She swallowed and stopped walking. What was the worst that could happen if she knocked at his door? It wasn't as if he would turn the weapon on her. He wasn't that stupid. Angry, pissed off and maybe even slightly unhinged, but he wasn't insane enough to shoot an innocent neighbour. That would mean a prison sentence. And people like him, wealthy privileged people, didn't take well to losing their liberties. Not that it mattered; regardless of his possible reactions to finding her standing on his doorstep, she had to do *something*. To do nothing was cowardly. And Penny prided herself on being courageous, refusing to shy away from bullies. People who thought they could ride roughshod over others.

Like a macabre fairy tale, a trail of blood led her to his sweeping driveway, the scarlet splashes petering to small droplets before disappearing round the back of the house out of view. Penny kept her gaze fixed on the front door, the sheer size of it, its imposing height and solidity squashing her bravery into a small compact box that sat somewhere deep within her chest. It was easy to speak of bravery and courage when cruelty wasn't present, but in the face of real barbarism, all those feelings shrank to nothing, vanishing into the ether like dandelion dust. Penny rubbed at her face with her sleeve. She could walk away, do this another day. Or not do it at all. She could go home and face her mother. That situation didn't appeal to her either. Still too much anger bubbling in her veins. She would have to simmer down first or risk saying things that were best left unsaid.

Gravel crunched beneath her feet as she marched up to the door and rapped on it. A dull pain lodged behind her eyes while she waited, the words she wanted to say running amok in her head, swirling and colliding like spinning tops. Words about how arrogant he was, how supercilious and breathtakingly rude he was, but once again she felt her resolve weaken when the door swung wide and she was greeted by a young man; his thick, dark hair swept back, a broad welcoming smile revealing a set of perfectly straight white teeth that gleamed like freshly fallen snow.

'Ah, sorry, I think that maybe I've got the wrong house?'

'No, no. It's perfectly okay. You've recently moved into Hallshead Farmhouse, is that right?' Another wide grin followed by an invitation to enter as he swept his arm behind him in a wide arc and bid for her to step inside. She was led into an impossibly large and ornate hallway that was as sparkly and clean as theirs was dirty and strewn with rubble.

'Yes, although it's not exactly a house any longer.' Penny felt her heart speed up. Sweat pricked at the back of her neck. 'More of a barn at the minute. Or a cave. No hot water and chunks of plaster and dust everywhere.'

'That's too bad. Please, come in and make yourself at home.'

Instinct told her to refuse, but she was tired and she was cold and generally pissed off. Just a few minutes, and she would leave. A few minutes of expelling the sour bile that was spinning and churning in her gut, and then she would thank him for his time and leave this place, never to return.

The shine and glare of the white tiled flooring, the sweeping staircase and sheer grandiosity of the place caught Penny in her solar plexus. She swallowed down a gasp, her eyes sweeping into as many rooms as possible as she searched for the older man. A noise from behind wrinkled her flesh, the hairs on her neck standing on end like tiny icicles. He was here. He was creeping up behind her. All her valour and bravado abruptly crumpled, concertinaing into a pebble-sized rock that sat somewhere deep in the bottom of her stomach. An image of the dead lamb ballooned in her mind, the older guy's grinning face and bloodied jacket as he stood with it in his arms like a prize kill, freezeframed in her brain.

'Shit!' Somebody brushed up against her legs, a warm pressure buckling her knees.

'Brandy! For God's sake. Come here, you dumb old dog.' The young man gave Penny another smile and shook his head, leaning down to stroke a large furry Afghan Hound that pushed its way between them. She glanced down. It was standing motionless, its head tipped up towards its master as if waiting for a command. Relief coursed through her veins, like a cold surge of water that cooled her hot flesh.

'I'm Cameron, by the way. Cameron Fairbridge. I believe you've already met my father?' Penny studied his face, mesmerised by his cheekbones and angular cut of his jaw. The way his hair fell over his eyes when he moved his head and laughed. His sigh as he uttered the last sentence told her everything she needed to know: that he, too, thought of the old man as a nuisance. Her skin tingled when he smiled at her, the light from the stained-glass window above the door catching his blue eyes, a vast ocean of promise in the tiniest of glances. Sweat bloomed under her arms. Penny swallowed and bit at the inside of her mouth until she felt sure she could taste blood.

'I'm Penny. Pleased to meet you.' Courtesy told her to shake his hand. Common sense kept it by her side. He seemed pleasant, and if she was being honest, extremely good looking and charming. But he was still a stranger. A handsome stranger but a stranger all the same. The sizzle of her skin gradually cooled the more she nipped and bit at the soft flesh of her mouth.

'Please, come through and have a drink. Tea, coffee?' He tipped his head to one side and once again Penny felt a rush of blood heat up her face. 'Or lemonade perhaps?'

All that biting and gnawing and she was still weak-kneed and hot in his presence. Stupid. She was being ridiculous. She took a shaky breath and replied, doing what she could to appear calm and unruffled.

'A lemonade would be good, thank you.' Her voice was reedy, a thin streak of nervousness and insecurity that betrayed her outward show of confidence. She had come here bristling with anger and now felt deflated, a wave of inertia bending her spine and weakening her resolve. All those magma-hot feelings of fury now disappeared like water trickling through her fingers.

She followed him into a large kitchen, her heartbeat a sudden gallop as she looked around at its size and sheer opulence. A large oak table stood in the middle, long enough to seat at least ten people.

'Please, sit down, make yourself comfortable.'

She lowered herself onto a chair, every movement she made, every scrape and creak, pounding and echoing in her ears. 'Where's your father?'

It was the briefest of moments, just two or three seconds, but his silence, his audible sigh, the slump of his shoulders; they said more than he ever could, his body language betraying his attempts at loyalty.

'Don't worry. He's out in the barn. It's where he spends most of his time.' Cameron spun round and handed Penny a glass of lemonade. 'It's where he belongs, if you ask me.' A wink. A smile. A small but noticeable moment of bonding. Butterflies fluttered in Penny's stomach. A dryness filled her throat. She gulped and took a long shuddering breath before taking two or three sips to alleviate the drought that had suddenly set up camp in her throat.

From the hallway came the dull tick tock of the grandfather clock. Fitting, she thought, for such a grand house. Each beat and tap accentuated the quietness of the room and exacerbated her anxiety. Questions scratched below the surface of her skin, but somehow, she couldn't bring herself to formulate them, to hear their clunkiness as they fell out of her mouth like boulders, hitting the floor and ruining the moment. Like how did they get all this money and what was wrong with his father? Why was he so angry and violent and cruel while his son, Cameron, seemed unerringly kind and affable?

The scrape of a chair close by dragged her back to the moment. 'I want to apologise for my father's behaviour. Sometimes, he can be rather – vexatious. It's just how he is, I'm afraid.'

Penny kept her silence, unsure how to react as he sat down next to her. Agreeing would feel just as vexatious. It was better to say nothing at all. Besides, she was embarrassed to open her mouth, her northern accent suddenly clumsy sounding and inappropriate in these luxurious surroundings. Her sloppy enunciation was in sharp contrast to Cameron's cut-glass diction, each word sliding from his mouth with such confidence and ease, it was hypnotic. Like being rocked to sleep or coated in warm honey. He shuffled his chair closer to hers. She could feel the heat pulsing from his body, a dry warmth that made her feel faint. A sudden flush of heat pricked at her torso. Perspiration dampened her waistband, causing her shirt to cling to her back.

'I won't ask how you're settling in. Moving house can be traumatic.' He laughed and shook his head. 'Not that I'd know. Lived in this old place all my life, but I can't imagine moving everything from here and transporting it elsewhere. It would kill me.' He looked around, his head shaking in mirth. 'My father and I and his father before him have simply accumulated too much stuff.'

'Is there just you and your father living here, then?' She whispered each word, keeping her voice soft and low, afraid he would think her rough and ungainly. She wiped at her top lip, shoving her hands back in her pocket to conceal her damp trembling fingers.

He nodded then glanced upwards, an abrupt scraping noise from above ending their dialogue. Penny tried to catch his eye for reassurance. They weren't alone. For some reason, she had assumed there was just the two of them in the house. Cameron's features morphed into something that sent a spike of confusion and discomfort through her. Voices too. Somebody was up there talking. Then a shout that was quickly silenced.

The distant shriek of a female. Goosebumps stippled Penny's flesh. She should go. What if it was the older man roving about up there, planning on doing something dreadful? Something unthinkable. And who was the woman?

Suddenly, the moment was over. A silence descended once more. Cameron blinked, rubbed at his eyes with the heel of his hand, and shook his head, his expression sombre.

'Sorry, I got a bit confused there. Mother lives here as well but she is very ill. Bedridden. The doctors have said it's terminal.'

Penny wanted to bite off her own tongue. She should have remained silent, said nothing and not asked any questions. Saying nothing was better than stirring up gloom and hurt, both of which left her feeling out of sorts. She never quite knew how to handle situations like this. After the death of her uncle and grandparents, she regularly salted herself away in her room, the desperation and low mood of the adults alien to her. It wasn't that she lacked pity, it was just that she felt awkward and had little or no experience of handling it correctly, the worry of saying or doing the wrong thing and causing more distress enough to send her scuttling away. Caught between childhood and adulthood, there were many things she felt unable to deal with, and illness and death, or imminent death, came at the top of that list.

'Sorry,' was all she could manage, before taking a silent sip of her lemonade, the bubbles catching and bursting in her throat, resulting in an undignified splutter.

'So, I gather you came here to introduce yourself or...?'

More perspiration gathered in an arc around her hairline. Why did looking at this man make her feel so hot and hopeless and inept? She was like an overgrown lumbering child in his presence. And why exactly had she come here? The reasons now seemed silly and pointless. It was easy to be brutally honest when she was alone in her own home, to yell and shout and demand that Douglas Fairbridge leave them alone and stop staring up at her bedroom window in the dead of night, and to never ever bring a bleeding animal to their doorstep again, blaming her and her mum for its horrific injuries when they all knew he had probably butchered it himself. In her head those words came easily, but sitting here in this man's kitchen, opposite his starkly different son who had made her feel welcome, and who smiled a lot and was personable, it was a totally different story. Word after word fell out of her mind, slipping through a sieve in her brain and scattering soundlessly at her feet.

'Yeah, kind of. Or maybe...'

Her words tailed off. He waited. The heat in the room grew, prickling her flesh, forcing her to shift in her seat. She was melting in his presence; his voice, his face, his probing questions and close proximity to her raising her temperature and lowering her confidence.

'Maybe...?' he said, an eyebrow raised at her, a smile playing at the corners of his mouth.

She thought of the noises from above, the sound of the female shriek still reverberating in her head. Why would a dying woman scream? Fear of those unexplained scrapes and shrieks and her lack of control in his presence propelled her out of her seat.

'Really sorry. I have to go. Thank you for the lemonade.'

The noise of her own chair, the banging of her feet as she stood up, the rustle of her clothing; they all crashed violently in her head, the hollow echo of it making her queasy and dizzy.

Cameron stood and headed to the doorway with Penny in close pursuit. His fingers were clasped around the door handle when she finally found the courage to speak, her words sounding disembodied and irrational. Why did this man have the ability to reduce her to a sweating nervous wreck?

'The gunshot earlier – did you hear it? You must have heard it?'

He nodded and lowered his head, a whispered apology escaping from his half open mouth as he swung the front door ajar and ushered her out. She could sense his welcoming manner dissipating, his patience with her decreasing. From somewhere behind him came another sound, an unearthly bellowing that frosted Penny's hot face, the back of her neck prickling with dread.

'I'm terribly sorry.' His voice was clipped, a sense of urgency creeping in. 'Mother needs me. I have to go.'

The echo of her heels on the stone step, the slam of the door, and the ensuing silence rang around the barren terrain as she found herself alone. Penny stood, shock rippling through her, the brevity of her sudden forced exit leaving her emotionally bruised and completely perplexed. Did she imagine the change in his demeanour? Or was he simply responding to her own change of mood? She did after all make a sudden bid to leave, embarrassed by her declining courage and lack of obvious wealth. She and Cameron Fairbridge were an unequal match. And he knew it too.

The scream of his mother, the dying woman upstairs, throbbed in her ears as she headed out of the courtyard and over the large gravelled driveway. Somewhere in the distance, the ethereal caw of a crow rang out into an empty sky. It jangled at her nerves, sending her scurrying home across the fields and over rocky paths to the safety of her own four walls where her mother was waiting for her.

16

PENNY

Day 2

Freda greets me at the door, all paws, tongue and fur.

'She's been fed and walked.' Damien strolls through to where I'm standing and plants a kiss on my cheek. His clothes and hair are crumpled and askew as if he has been wrestling with his latest graphic designs rather than simply drawing them. 'She's been really playful the last hour. A bit frantic actually. She's chased her ball all around the house and woofed and barked at every passer-by. I think she's missed you.'

When I'm working, Freda and I always have a lunchtime walk. I've missed her more than she will ever know. Dogs are such honest, trusting creatures. More so than many people. I think of Cheryl and some of the other jurors and suppress a shudder. Freda's big eyes and lolling mouth are a far cry from the starched environment of the courtroom. A welcome one. I bend down and tickle Freda's tummy, stroking her silk-like ears before kissing the end of her snout. 'Lovely Freda. What a good girl you are.' I sigh, feeling replenished. Cleansed of the dirt that clung to me while I sat in that place opposite *him*.

'I've cooked lasagne if you're hungry?'

At the mention of food, my stomach growls. All day, my appetite has been zero, suppressed by the thought of what lay ahead, squashed into oblivion by never knowing how things will pan out, but now I'm home, away from the courtroom and the other jurors, away from *him*, my usual level of hunger has returned with zeal.

Damien takes my coat and I hang up my bag, hooking it over the newel post, a wave of weariness hitting me square on. My legs are wobbly as I make my way into the kitchen, the beckoning aroma of garlic leading me towards the table. I drop into a chair and sigh.

'Your mum has had hers. I asked her if she wanted to come here to watch TV but she said she was fine. Today has been a good day. One of her better ones for a long while.'

I think of Cheryl and wonder what sort of a welcome she has gone home to, whether she is alone, or surrounded by a loving family. I suspect the former but have no evidence to back up my suspicions. Just my gut instinct; the exact thing she is using to help free a guilty man.

I push those thoughts aside. I can't let this thing rule my existence.

Just like it has for all your adult life.

Damien serves up the food and we eat in companionable silence, my thoughts now mired in what lies ahead for Mum. After a second helping, I lean back, my stomach fit to burst.

'That was amazing. Have I told you lately that I love you?' I lean forward and kiss his stubble-covered face.

'You haven't, but you could try singing it, Van Morrison style?'

I smile for what feels the first time in weeks. My face feels stretched and contorted, as if my teeth and tongue belong to somebody else.

'I'll clear the kitchen then I'll go round and see Mum. I might run her a bath and put her to bed. If she'll let me, that is.'

He smiles and lets out a lingering sigh. 'Yes, if she'll let you. You never know, she was really good earlier. It might have lasted.'

'Yes,' I say, my tone more than a little acerbic, 'and pigs might fly.'

* * *

I'm reluctant to mention Hallshead Farmhouse to Mum. After Dad's premature death from a heart attack not long after moving in there, as well as a whole host of other tragedies that befell us, not to mention Aaron's injuries from a horrific fire, our family was plunged into chaos, and almost every memory we have of that place is tainted and corrupted. It was a dark period in our lives and something I would rather not bring up in front of her, but I do need to know what Mum remembers. I feel compelled to get another perspective on that era. Opening this ancient can of worms may prove to be the most stupid and thoughtless thing I've ever done, and yet there is a part of me that has to know if Mum remembers any of it. I have no idea why. Perhaps it's because I feel alone with my trauma and need some form of backup, even if it does come from a confused woman who now, on a bad day, is barely able to remember her own name. Mum recounting that time could go either way but I take that chance all the same.

'Do you recall when I was a teenager, Mum, and we were living at the old farmhouse?' My words are slow and methodical, my voice smooth and non-threatening, a deliberate approach in the hope my question will have more impact. Stir up important recollections without unnerving her.

She nods and takes my hand, her skin dry and papery. Like parchment. Fine green veins snake just beneath the surface, a reminder of how frail she is. How damaged. There are times when my mother drives me insane with her unpredictable ways and flaring temper but every now and again, I stop and remind myself of what she has endured, how difficult life has been for her. How unutterably cruel. We lost everyone and everything in such a short space of time. And I lost my faith in humanity. Damien was the one who helped to restore my confidence and my belief in the good in many people. He helped me out of a deep dark hole, allowing me to step back into the light. And yet, even he doesn't know about that night. The rape. I say it only in my head, and rarely. It's like striking a match inside my skull, the friction and ensuing heat too much for me to bear. He thinks it was the other events that happened to us that damaged me – Dad's death and Hallshead Farmhouse going up in flames. And now after being married for over twenty-five years, it all feels too far down the line to have a sudden reveal, to let him know that I have more scars festering inside of me. Scars that are in desperate need of attention. I want to be healed. I just don't know how to do it, how to speak about it openly so I can start being me again.

She smiles at me and nods, then turns and watches the television, grinning at the presenter as if they are old friends.

'What do you remember about it, Mum?'

Her body is angled towards me, her head slowly turning. I can see a moment of clarity, as if she is about to speak openly, but then tears build and she stops and shakes her head.

'I can't. Not today. I just can't.'

My chest constricts. I lean forward and hug her, her lean frame always a shock to me. She was once a solidly built lady, her body strong and firm, but dementia has eaten away at her sturdiness and inner strength as well as her brain, leaving her a shadow of her former self.

I'm not even sure why I'm asking. It's as if I want some sort of affirmation, somebody who can confirm what a dreadful time it was back then. Not that I really need affirmation. The facts are the facts. It happened and there is no escaping it. Raking over a past I cannot change will solve nothing. All it will do is inflict more damage on my mother's already brittle state of mind. It was selfish of me to ask. Seeing parallels of my own past in that courtroom has left me exhausted, as if a great hand has reached in and scooped away my soul. What happened that night and the events leading up to it are a chapter of my life that I've worked hard to forget, and yet here they are, forcing themselves to the forefront of my mind, prodding and poking at me, making me remember. Mum is the only person who was with me at that time. Mum is the only one who knows. And now, all these years later, my need to speak to somebody about it is tearing me apart. Every time I try to broach the subject with Damien, the person I am closest to in the whole world, my brain freezes, going into shutdown. I want to tell him about the assault, I really do. It should be a simple thing to do; Damien is a caring, thoughtful man who would listen to my woes and comfort me, and yet it feels like the most difficult task in the world.

I let the subject rest and Mum and I sit and watch her favourite TV programmes for the next few hours until her eyes look heavy, her lids beginning to flutter and close.

'I think I'm ready for bed,' she says quietly.

'Come on then. Do you want me to help you?'

Some evenings she is more than capable, her routine an important factor in her life, but then there are other evenings when she forgets where her nightgown and slippers are kept. Tonight we will give the bath a miss. It would rupture the peace and quiet of the moment. Sailing on a calm sea is easier than sailing directly into a squall.

'I can manage, I think. I'd like a cup of tea, if you don't mind?'

'Of course. You go up and get ready and I'll bring it up.'

It takes only a few minutes to make the tea but by the time I get up there, her mind has drifted and she has mutated into another person. Not my mother at all. She is standing in the middle of the bedroom in her underwear, eyes glazed over, mouth trembling. I avoid looking at her directly, not wanting to gaze into her pale blue irises, afraid of the darkness that is there.

'I can't find it. Someone has stolen my nightie!'

'It's here. Don't worry, Mum, I've got it here.' I place the cup of tea on the bedside cabinet, then slowly and purposely, so it is obvious to her that it was always here, drape my fingers over the length of white cotton fabric that is hooked over the bedpost. I pick it up and hand it to her, helping to slip it over her head. We push her arms through the soft silky fabric and she stands sombrely, her chin lowered to her chest, eyes flickering in confusion, as if she is caught between two vastly differing places and is unsure which route to take.

'I keep thinking things,' she says quietly, the cadence of her voice soft and childlike. 'Stupid things that don't make any sense. And then they're gone. I saw some children playing in the living room yesterday, Penny. They were here. And then they weren't. Can that really happen? Can children come into my house and then just leave?'

I swallow down my sadness. We've avoided another of Mum's rages at least. Seeing her slightly distressed and bewildered, although heartbreaking, is still easier than enduring being scalded by one of her boiling cauldrons of fury. I heave a sigh of relief. She is chatty, an air of serenity about her, but I sense something else creeping in. Fear and confusion. And those emotions are just as disturbing as her bouts of anger. It's tragic to watch it unfold, to see how her features crumple when she realises what is happening to her. That her brain, her thoughts and memories are all disintegrating, everything she has learned, everything she has ever said and done, is crumbling and turning to dust.

'Oh, I'm not so sure. Let's get you sorted and into bed, shall we?' I reply, using the strategy given to me by the consultant who gave us the dementia diagnosis.

Don't encourage or deny whatever she says, just go with it and try to assist and defuse as much as possible to limit any further upset.

'Thank you,' she says softly, her voice full of trust, childlike in its inflection. 'I'm tired; really, really tired.'

She sighs as she slips between the sheets, her eyes closing the second her head rests back onto the pillow.

'Do you want your tea, Mum?'

Eyelids fluttering, she snaps them open and thinks for a second or two before replying. 'Ah, yes, thank you. A hot drink in bed. How lovely.'

I help her to sit up and she takes just a few sips before resting her head back again and speaking, the words she expresses sending a chill through me. 'It wasn't an accident, you know. They tried to get out and he just stood there and watched them as they died.'

I feel shaky and disorientated, her words drilling deep into my brain. I want to ask what she means, and yet at the same time, I don't, because I'm sure I already know. I remember after the fire, Mum claiming that Douglas Fairbridge was linked to Nan and Grandad's accident. I put it down to her lashing out and being angry, but maybe there was some truth to her words. Not that it matters now. Focusing on the rape case is about as much as I can handle. My gaze shifts to Mum's face, to her parchment-like skin and dry pursed lips. Already her eyelids are drooping, her lashes fluttering as exhaustion wins and she succumbs to its greedy clutches.

She lets out a snore, the harsh discordant noise reminding me of my father's death rattle, a sound that stayed with me for years after as we sat by his bedside praying for the best, but knowing deep down that the worst was about to happen.

I wait until she is in the soundest of slumbers before standing up and leaving her bedside, her words still rolling around my brain. I dismiss them, store them in a separate compartment in my head for another time. I have neither the time nor the energy to delve into the intricacies of it all. Even if I were to take on board her claims and do something about it, who would believe the ramblings of somebody like my mother? A woman whose brain is shrinking, her thoughts dull and fragmented. The best I can do is forget about what she has just said and pour all my efforts and energy into the present; concentrate on the trial and doing something positive about our damaged past.

Downstairs, I tidy up, closing blinds and curtains and plumping up cushions. I lay out the breakfast pots for the morning and dry a few cups and plates, the normality of it a cathartic experience. When I go home, I will give Freda her final walk of the evening and then I will climb into bed, knowing that Mum is safe and tucked up in her own home. I think then of Damien, my amazing supportive husband who has been beside me always, even when I didn't want him there, and how after spending the day working and caring for my mother, he will be at home waiting for me. I am so lucky to have him in my life, his kindness and patience anchoring me to reality. Reminding me that no matter how bad things get, there will always be light at the end of the longest and darkest of tunnels.

17

THE HOUSE

It had been almost a week since Douglas Fairbridge's visit. The cool atmosphere in the house had begun to thaw, a slow subdued warmth developing between Penny and her mother. Their iceberg-sized disagreement had shrunk to the tiniest of misunderstandings. A thin layer of frost that was beginning to thaw. They had a tacit agreement that the incident of the injured sheep wouldn't be spoken about. Many things about that day niggled Penny but sometimes it was easier to let them be. Her anger at the injustice of it all burned brightly in her thoughts, but with all that was happening in their lives and all that had happened, she knew that adding more drama and upset to their everyday existence would do no good. As far as she was aware, her father knew nothing of the visit. Her mother's initial decision to speak to him about it didn't transpire. If her father did actually know, then he was doing a fine job of ignoring it. Perhaps it was better that way. He was still grieving and was busy with his job and the repairs in the house, often chipping in with assisting plumbers and electricians when he got home from work on an evening. And meeting with the architect to discuss plans. The architect, who remained a thorn in Penny's side.

After switching her accusations to Douglas Fairbridge, she was aware of how flimsy and unreliable her narrative would look if she made any further complaints against the lecherous man who infiltrated her personal space. She felt tongue-tied in her own home, unable to voice her innermost thoughts and fears to her parents. And still he continued to look, glancing her way when he thought she wasn't watching, brushing past her, their bodies touching, the heat from his torso freezing her limbs and stilling her blood. His presence in the house filling her with dread. School became her respite, the lessons she once hated now a welcome reprieve from the mess and the noise. A welcome reprieve from him.

It was the early hours and she lay in bed, sleep evading her. The house was silent. Shadows crept across the ceiling, a crack in the curtains revealing a full moon that cast a silver line across the centre of her room, accentuating dark corners and crinkling her flesh. They forced her to pull the duvet up under her chin, her head lowered into the folds of soft fabric. It had been almost a week since her stalker had made an appearance. Either that or she had slept through it. That particular thought made her blood curdle; lying in bed while he stood outside. Watching. Waiting. Scheming.

Each time she closed her eyes, images filled her mind: bloodied dead animals, crouching shadows, ghastly towering silhouettes with long spider-like limbs that reached out to her, their fingers trailing over her body, coming to rest around her throat.

A noise from outside dragged her up, her feet brushing against the cold rough texture of the old rug beside her bed. Driven by fear and hatred, and sheer hot-blooded fury, she knelt next to the window and peered out, expecting her gaze to land upon something but all the while hoping for nothing. Her heartbeat pulsed in her ears, saliva pooling in her mouth like warm oil. She swallowed it down and waited, watching as clouds scudded past, cloaking the moon before shifting on, revealing once again its near-perfect circular shape and pale achromatic glow. Nothing. There was nothing there. Nobody to be seen. Still, she waited, crouching down on her haunches, her scalp tingling with anticipation and dread. Then it came again; another distant noise, a muffled movement and the dull creak of old wood, like the rocking of a galleon ship in a storm.

She knew what came next. Already, bitter experience had taught her what to expect after the faint sounds of movement outside. A film of tears marred her vision as a dark figure appeared at the edge of her line of sight, turning to stare in her direction. Her body folded in on itself, her limbs limp and rubbery as she wilted and dropped onto the floor like the stem of a broken flower. She lay for a few seconds, trying to still the thrashing of her heart. Her knees were pushed high into her abdomen, her fingers clasped tight around her shins. She stayed there, the whoosh of blood as it pounded through her veins a sonic boom in her head. The air around her grew thick, her breathing became heavy and laboured.

Only when the chill of the night nipped at her bare skin, goose-bumps raised in protest on her flesh, did she finally move. Panting, sweat coating her chest despite the drop in temperature, she slithered across the floor and crawled back into bed, her entire body pulsing, her limbs cold to the touch. She rubbed at her eyes and suppressed a low moan. The build, the outline, the stance – it could have been anybody. Too dark to see clearly. But it was certainly somebody. It was a male figure. And whoever it was, he was watching her. She wasn't imagining it. She wasn't an attention seeker. It was real. Somebody was standing outside her bedroom window staring up at her.

She mentally blocked out the possibilities, the reasons he was there too terrifying to contemplate. Pulling the bedsheets tight around her trembling body as if to ward off any incoming blows, Penny closed her eyes and tried to nap, but a labyrinth of dark thoughts continually snagged at her brain.

For hours, sleep evaded her. Sharp currents of dread shocked her into wakefulness every time she felt herself falling into a welcome balmy slumber. She had no idea how long she lay there for, but at some point, she must have finally succumbed, because she woke the next morning, her eyes still heavy with exhaustion as light permeated the room, fingers of pale sun filtering through the slightly parted curtains. Was it a school day or was it the weekend? Miniscule shards of glass scratched at her eyes, the savageness of it bringing a flood of tears. She had never known such tiredness. Such fear. Such frustration. It was a type of madness, living like this. Being alone with her terror; her parents, unable or unwilling to believe her. Her dad was busy with work, with the house, her mum despondent at how they were living, Hallshead Farmhouse still resembling a building site. The house. Everything was centred on *the house*. It took up every minute of their time, every ounce of energy. She thought about speaking to Aaron but could imagine his dismissals, his barking laughter, claiming she had an overactive imagination or was acting like a diva. Reminding her of the event at school. She was going to have to face this thing on her own.

The house was silent when she slipped out of bed and crept to the window, the cold light of day casting less of a ghostly glow over the landscape. Seeing him standing there last night had snatched all the air out of her lungs, but today the rolling hills and broken fence and the cool calm swathe of countryside filled her with a sense of peace. Anybody would think, glancing out there, that she had made it all up. Everything was tranquil as her gaze swept across the patchwork of green. It was hard to believe that something this unthreatening and picturesque could take on such a menacing edge once the sun dipped below the hills, but of course during the day it lacked one key component – *him*.

Sickness welled up in her stomach at the thought of him. She lay back on her bed, dread and frustration at her own ineptitude settling in her bones. She had two options – do nothing and continue with this frustration and horror, or be assertive and confront him, this man, whoever he was. The thought of going out there in the early hours and squaring up to him made her head throb. What if he lunged at her, attacking her with a weapon, leaving her for dead? What then? But to do nothing – the thought of that, being a victim, a fucking *spectator* in her own life – ratcheted up her anger and exasperation a hundredfold. She wasn't a warrior or an archetypal feminist who refused to be browbeaten by an intimidatory male figure; she knew her limits on that score, but at the same time, she wasn't a shy retiring young woman who buckled under the slightest strain. She was better than that, wasn't she? Gutsy. Bolder than most. And then she recalled how she had sagged in the middle when faced with Cameron Fairbridge, his wealth and breeding, his broad welcoming smile undoing her best intentions.

A noise came from somewhere in the house, the distant rattles and scrapes of other people rousing and moving about. The rest of her family were getting up, going about their day. She pressed the heels of her hands into her eyes, everything coming into focus, her brain finally able to work as it should. It was the weekend. No architect hanging around the house. And free time for her to go back to Fairbridge Hall and confront Douglas Fairbridge. The thought of it set in motion a rumble of discomfort in her stomach. The other option was to do nothing. Could she really do that? Continue to ignore the sound of that unexpected caterwauling that continually reverberated in her head? Maybe it had been Douglas Fairbridge upstairs dealing with his sick wife. And yet, Cameron had said that his father was out in the barn. Nothing seemed to fit; his changing behaviour, the story about his mother, telling Penny originally that he and his father were alone in the house. As charming as he was, his narrative was riddled with holes. Perhaps she should make another unexpected visit, catch him off guard? Maybe that old lady would benefit from somebody calling in and asking after her well-being. Penny didn't doubt that the Fairbridges had more than enough money to pay for carers, but what if Douglas Fairbridge was neglecting his wife's needs, leaving her alone upstairs, distressed and in pain? He had form when it came to intimidating women, that much she did know. She would wait for the right moment and ask her mum. There were no workmen in the house on a Saturday. No drilling, no noise. No added stress. As it turned out, Penny didn't need to say anything at all; her mother suggested a trip into town to pick out carpets and wardrobes for the bedrooms. For once, fortune was smiling down on her.

'We can make a girls' day of it,' her mother said half an hour later as they sat at the makeshift breakfast table that also served as a workbench for the builders. They nibbled at pieces of toast and sipped at glasses of fresh juice. The atmosphere, although not quite as relaxed and harmonious as it once was, had loosened. The band of tension that had had them all in its grip had slackened.

Aaron and her father nodded, their delight at being left alone and not having to endure the agony of trailing from shop to shop, poring over colour schemes and lengths of curtain fabric, obvious by the expressions.

'I'm off to see Luke anyway,' Aaron said, the depth of his voice taking

Penny by surprise. Puberty had had her brother in a stranglehold for the past six months, his skin a sporadic combination of wispy tufts of hair and bouts of acne that erupted out of nowhere, leaving his face an angry patchwork of bright red spots. 'Will probably be there for most of the day.'

'And I'm doing anything except shopping in town,' her dad said lightly. 'Had enough of hunting for wall tiles and flooring. I'll leave the soft furnishing choices to the ladies. You've both got far better taste than me.'

'I've also got the cheque book.' Her mother laughed, giving Penny a sly wink and a smile.

Suddenly, it felt as if the balance in Penny's little world had been recalibrated, the channels of communication finally opening up between her and her mum once more. Back to how they used to be.

Shafts of light shone through the gaps of grime on the window, bathing the table in an ochre hue, warming Penny's arms and neck. Soothing her. Soon, all the stress of this building work and the accompanying woes it brought would be a thing of the past. She needed to focus on that, give herself something to aim for. An end point. The thought of the figure that haunted her nights and made her fearful of the days continued to pulse at the base of her skull. She pushed that thought and those images away. She would wait to see what came next. Whoever it was, they couldn't get in the house. Bolts on downstairs windows and chains on all the doors made sure she was safe in her bed at night. Her mother had been determined on that score, threatening to call a locksmith if her dad didn't up their security after Douglas Fairbridge's first visit. An added fear of crying wolf often also lingered in Penny's brain. The school incident with Don McCarrick had shrunk her credibility, even though he had lied.

Penny finished eating and scooped up the remaining dishes and cutlery, carrying them to the sink with the notion that whoever was out there, at least they wouldn't ever be able to get in, and once they tired of their ridiculous game, they would leave and it would be as if they had never been there at all. It could even be some young lad from the nearest village who had heard somebody had moved into Hallshead and was sussing them out. Sussing *her* out. She shivered and plunged her hands in the lukewarm soapy water, shaking that notion from her mind.

'We'll set off in ten minutes, if that suits you?' Her mother's voice rang around the room, the gruff anxious edge it had taken on since living at Hallshead Farmhouse slowly ebbing away, revealing the real Connie, the softer genuine person beneath. She had been squashed and pushed out of sight by grief and shock and a sense of displacement after moving here, but Penny was now able to catch glimpses of who she used to be, and it gave her hope of a settled future for all of them.

Things would improve. She could feel it in her bones. She nodded and dried the dishes, the image of that man standing there outside her window last night already fading into obscurity. The person beneath her window who would soon tire of his little game. This time in a few weeks, she would look back and laugh, irritated at how worried and concerned she had been about a pathetic desperate loner who had nothing better to do with his time.

'Ten minutes works for me,' she replied, surprised at how contented and optimistic she sounded. Happy even. As if last night had never even happened.

18
PENNY

Day 3

An icy wind whistles around us, the noise muffling his words. 'I knew it was you. Fucking knew it, I did.' The voice behind me scratches at my brain, dredging up painful memories. Memories of a time in my life that continually haunts me.

I turn, aghast at the state of him. Horrified and heartbroken at what he has been reduced to. Aaron looks progressively worse for wear each time I see him. His face and body are stick thin, his flesh the colour of ash. Small flecks of dirt and decaying food hangs from his long straggly beard, the reek of alcohol, even though it's only 8.30 a.m., enough to make me take a step back to catch my breath. I want to rip off his filthy ragged jacket, take a look at the needle marks that are pitted all over his arms, and scream at him to stop trying to kill himself, but instead I find myself fighting back tears. The decline of my brother has been slow but steady. Seeing him standing there, an emaciated skeleton of a man, I fear that it's too late to pull him back from the brink.

'Where are you staying?'

Visions of him sleeping in shop doorways makes me want to weep. It wouldn't be the first time and if he is indeed spending his nights slumped there, it sure as hell won't be the last. The nights are cold, the weather more often than not inclement. I think of the rain that lashed at my bedroom window through the evening and tears burn at my eyes. How did it come to this? Why did I take one direction through life and my only sibling take another destructive route that has resulted in him looking as if he is one of the walking dead? We both suffered trauma. The only difference is that Aaron's was and still is visible whereas I kept mine hidden, telling nobody. Our mother was going through a nervous breakdown, her mind focused only on saving herself. I don't blame her for her initial reactions and denials when I approached her for help. Besides, what could she have done? The day I called the police after Douglas Fairbridge turned up on our doorstep with that injured animal, nobody arrived. The chances of them turning up to deal with shadows in the night would have been negligible. We were in the middle of the North Yorkshire countryside with nothing but cattle and the howling wind for company.

'I'm at Reed House over by the river.'

The tension in my body reduces slightly. He's staying at a halfway house in Middlesbrough and not sleeping rough at least. Perhaps he will get some sort of help while he's there, although judging by his appearance, it seems the assistance they are able to give only stretches so far. How can anybody help people who don't want to help themselves? For years, Aaron has batted away our offers, telling us he is fine and that his life is exactly how he wants it to be. I know he's lying. His drug and alcohol-addled brain still functions at some basic level. It's his pride that is preventing him from capitulating and agreeing to us stepping in and doing something – *anything* to stop him from doing these terrible things to himself.

'Aaron, I—' His eyes meet mine while he waits for me to continue.

My mouth dries up, the words I want to say shrivelling up and dying on my tongue, curling up like the brown crisp autumnal leaves that fall to the ground, trampled and crushed underfoot.

Still he waits, his face reminding me of our childhood, a time we thought was challenging, unaware that things would get a whole lot worse. Nervous breakdowns, premature deaths, the ruination of Hallshead Farmhouse; they were all waiting around the corner, ready to knock us off our feet and leave us floundering about, wondering what we had done to deserve such a terrible fate.

'Here.' I open my purse and press a twenty-pound note into his hands, hoping he spends it on a sandwich and a cup of tea, and yet knowing he will head off to a dealer for his latest fix, or somewhere he can buy cans of beer as soon as my back is turned.

He stares down at the money before shoving it in his pocket and hunching his shoulders, his eyes downcast, his pride damaged by the fact his younger sister is giving him handouts.

'I have to go,' I say, my voice thick with unshed tears. 'I'm doing jury service over there.' I point to the large granite building opposite, its dark framed windows and stone pillars an imposing sight.

Aaron nods knowingly, as if this was always going to be my vocation in life. I think of how he views me with my warm clean clothes and winter coat, my curled glossy hair, recently cut and styled by my usual hairdresser. I want to tell him that I still lose sleep over what we went through, that the nightmares come regularly, haunting me in the darkness, but instead, I lean forward and give him a hug. My fingers land upon bone, no flesh to be found beneath his dirty torn garments.

'You know where we live,' I say as I turn and start to walk away. 'Please come and see us. Anytime. Anytime at all. You're always welcome.'

'Penny?' His voice calls after me, and I feel a spark of hope ignite in my chest.

I turn, eager to see a flicker of recognition there, a silent plea for help that I would immediately act upon, but he shakes his head and strides away, his gait unsteady, his feet scurrying along the pavement until he rounds the corner and disappears out of sight.

* * *

Once again, I'm one of the first to arrive, the large room devoid of people save for a bored-looking desk clerk and a couple of older ladies sitting chatting at the far end of the waiting room. They continue with their conversation, my presence not important.

I try to push the image of Aaron out of my mind. I love my brother but only have a limited amount of energy and need to put what little I have into this case. I rummage in my bag and pluck out a bottle of water, taking small sips to alleviate the dryness that has taken hold in my mouth.

My eyes travel around the room. I am desperate to crush any rogue thoughts and avoid going through today's possible proceedings in my head. After yesterday's calamity, I can only hope things will improve, that a more reliable witness will be brought to the stand and the defendant's sneering stance and arrogant persona are finally dented, revealing the monster beneath. I want to hear from somebody who has irrefutable evidence that he raped that young woman. Because he did, except as far as I am aware, I'm the only one who knows it for certain. There are possibly other women out there he has assaulted but I'm the only one in this courtroom who truly knows *him*. What he is capable of. What he did and will continue to do if he isn't found guilty and locked away for the longest time.

With each passing day, my hatred for him grows. Prior to seeing him standing there, I didn't think it was possible to loathe that despicable creature any more than I already did, but it appears that there are vast chasms of resentment and disgust bubbling deep within me. As I lay there last night, listening to the growing storm, to the razor-sharp bullets of water that lashed at the window, robbing me of much-needed sleep, I considered waking Damien and telling him everything. But I didn't. Not because I couldn't or because it would have proven to be too traumatic, but simply because he would have insisted I do the right thing and step down as a juror. And I cannot do that. This happened for a reason, me being selected for this case. The chances of getting called for jury service are slim, but the odds of being faced with an aggressor whose actions caused such damage to me all those years ago must be so low that they barely register at all. I'm taking it as a sign that some things are meant to be. I don't necessarily believe in karma but I do believe in justice. He has evaded it for so long now, and it's time to readjust the scales, let him know how it feels to have your freedom ripped away from you, to have your life turned upside down and everything you thought you knew shaken about and almost obliterated by pain and fear.

It's wrong to feel this much hatred towards another person, and I know that it is very wrong of me to not speak up about my connection to that grotesque man, but my God, it feels good knowing I'm attempting to do something monumental, to put a dangerous individual behind bars and stopping him from doing this to anybody else. I'm not willingly breaking the law. I am just trying to do what is right, what should have been done many years ago.

'Morning.' One of the other jurors sits beside me. It's the lady with short blonde hair.

She is jumpy, her nails bitten to the quick, her movements sharp and repetitive. I watch as her knee jiggles up and down, the chronic look of tension and worry that is etched into her brow making me nervous.

'Morning,' I reply, trying to sound jovial and lacking in any apprehension at what might lay ahead.

'I just want this over with,' she whispers, her words and growing state of agitation acting like a virus, spreading and infecting me, making me feel even more fractious and out of sorts.

'I guess we all do, really. Only a few more days and it will all be over and we can go back to our normal lives.'

'Can't happen soon enough for me. It's already a bit of a farce, isn't it? No real evidence and a young kid who barely knows her arse from her elbow, saying stuff that sounds as flimsy as hell. The whole thing is a fucking joke.'

My stomach plummets. Another one. I'm surrounded by them. I'm fighting against a fast-flowing current this week, the other jurors blind to the defendant's other self, the monster that lurks beneath his charming façade. He hides it well, I'll give him that. I'm not sure what I can do to turn this tide. I can't do this on my own. It all feels so useless, my attempts at getting everyone to see him for the liar he actually is.

'I'm Penny, by the way.'

'Lisa.'

She doesn't look at me, her gaze firmly fixed on the floor as she continues to tap her feet, her knees still moving up and down in a rhythmic fashion.

A male voice cuts through the frosty atmosphere. 'Awful stinking weather, isn't it? Glad the rain's stopped but those clouds look like more could be on its way.'

I turn to the sound of the voice and am relieved to see Bob standing behind me. I have been given a reprieve from Lisa's nervous presence. A rush of contentment blooms in my chest. From what I have seen, he seems like a judicious man. Somebody who is prepared to listen to reason. Somebody who follows the rules and won't make decisions based on character. A man who won't be fooled by a sly wink and an enigmatic smile. I need him to be on my side more than ever now that Cheryl and this Lisa lady have both revealed their hand. They are strong characters. Feisty and determined. I feel certain their voices will be heard above others once we begin our deliberations.

'It's dreadful. More rain set in for the day by all accounts as well,' I reply, trying to sound breezy and contented when my innards are bound into a painful knot.

'It's fucking awful. Just like this place,' Lisa mutters, her eyes downcast.

'Not long to go,' Bob replies, his voice brimming with self-assurance, 'and we can all go home and get back to normal.'

He catches my eye and we both manage a wry smile, a pair of bonded souls in the presence of the embittered and disillusioned.

'So, what do we all get up to every day when we're not here?' Bob places his coat on the back of his chair and sits down, his voice just loud enough to drag Lisa out of her melancholic mood.

She looks up at us, her mouth twisted into a resentful sneer. 'I'm self-employed. Run my own beauty business.'

'I'm a counsellor and work from home,' I say in return. 'I'm also self-employed.'

I catch Lisa's eye, hoping to form a loose bond with her, but her mind is already elsewhere, her eyes fixed on somebody over my shoulder.

'What about you, Bob? What do you do when you're not deciding the fate of a perfect stranger?'

He laughs and shakes his head. 'Me? Nothing since I retired. I was a headteacher but I now spend my days reading the newspaper, building model aeroplanes and bouncing grandchildren on my knee.'

It slots into place – his calm peaceable manner, his confidence. His ability to take charge of a group of people. I was right to make a friend of this man. I just hope he sees sense and is able to change the minds of Lisa and Cheryl, get them to see how malevolent and destructive the defendant really is. So far, Bob has kept his opinions to himself, as have I. In just a few days, we will all be holed up together in the deliberation room, poring over the evidence, each of us keen to voice our opinions, and only then will I really discover how powerful he can be. How powerful *I* can be when forced into a corner by the ignorant and the unseeing eyes of certain jury members.

Around us, people slowly filter in, muttering about traffic, a lack of parking spaces and slow-moving public transport, and of course the weather. It's always the weather. We all simmer and settle, waiting for the call.

It only takes a few minutes until the voice comes over the loudspeaker for us to line up. The court clerk appears with his effervescent grin and jocular manner. I spot Cheryl in the distance. She gives me a smile and heads our way.

'Here we go again,' she mouths to me, as if our brief walk yesterday has bonded us. It hasn't, but in a desperate moment of panic, my need to control her thoughts overriding my principles, I return the smile and line up, ready for the proceedings. My stomach is already twisted with anxiety at what today will bring, whether new strong witnesses will appear to help my case or whether like yesterday, we will be faced with a fragile, frightened individual who helps to hammer the final nail into the coffin of poor Melanie Albright.

We file along the corridor and wait outside in our usual order, our voices mingling and growing in volume until the court clerk signals for us to be quiet. Seconds pass, my nerves jumping at every sound: the rustle of clothing, the distant screech of seagulls as they fly inland to escape the adverse weather conditions near the coast; they all scratch at me until eventually we are ushered back into the courtroom where the judge sits, greeting us with a fatherly smile. We sit in our respective seats, a silence descending until the barrister for the defence speaks, calling for their witness to be led inside.

I grit my teeth and pray that this witness is as weak as the young woman from the previous day, that their testimony and presence in the courtroom prove to be pointless and we are left feeling deflated and wondering who to believe. Then at least I'll be able to present my reasons in a balanced manner and not come across as somebody who is favouring the victim.

I watch as he appears in the doorway on the far side of the room and feel myself go faint. A rush of icy air billows through my empty veins as I attempt to clear my throat and sit up straight. Him. I should have known. After all these years, he is still here, hanging around like a toxic stench that refuses to leave, his residue permeating every inch of space, coating the flesh of those around him and sticking to it like glue. They were friends. Still *are* friends, it would seem. And now he is here to fight his corner. I know this man; I know how he thinks and operates. He will have no qualms about lying under oath. Just like his counterpart, he sees himself as untouchable. I take a deep breath and steel myself, my body as steady and solid as stone. I'm ready to listen to what he has to say, to unpick the lies that will pour forth as soon as he opens his mouth. I will dissect and analyse them in my head, ready for when we all gather together in that deliberation room to make our final decision after sifting through the evidence to try to come to a unanimous verdict.

The prosecution barrister stands as the witness is led into the dock. Their eyes meet and the witness turns to the jury and affords us a broad smile, his eyes sparkling with confidence as he straightens his tie and clears his throat, ready to speak.

19

THE HOUSE

'But what if she's being neglected?'

Connie felt the weight of her daughter's distress like a millstone around her neck. She couldn't take on any more responsibility beyond her own household. Besides, the Fairbridges had done little to endear themselves to her. Douglas Fairbridge was a rude callous man who didn't deserve her pity or assistance. He had money. They could afford the best care for his wife. A qualified nurse was better suited to intervening and providing help for an elderly lady than Connie could ever hope to be.

'Oh, love, it's great that you're concerned. I admire your compassion, but there's a few things we need to clear up. Firstly, please don't go there again on your own. We don't know them, and what we do know isn't pleasant. You saw what he did to that poor animal. Secondly, I'm not sure what we can do to help that lady. It really isn't any of our business. I think we have enough on our plate right now, don't you?'

Colour flared in Penny's cheeks, the flush enough to make Connie sigh, hoping their moment of friendship wouldn't be broken. It was weak, their current bond. As fragile and flimsy as gossamer. Bereavement, the stress of moving and renovating a house, and everything else that went with it, had done that to them, stretching their patience and attachment to breaking point. She had to tread carefully here, be mindful of her daughter's restricted grasp of how the world worked. Penny was bright, there was no doubt about that, but her life experiences were limited. She was proud of her intelligent compassionate daughter, but at the end of the day, Penny was still a child, a young teenager making the difficult transition into womanhood under the most trying of circumstances. She had made mistakes in the past, misinterpreted conversations and misconstrued innocuous comments, finding insults in badly worded compliments.

'I still think the least we can do is investigate. Imagine being bedbound and relying on that horrible old bastard for help every day.'

Connie raised an eyebrow at her daughter's casual use of profanity and smiled to soften her stern expression.

'Look, rather than be subjected to a barrage of abuse from Douglas Fairbridge, why don't we visit the shop in the next village and ask a few questions? I'm sure somebody will know something. Far easier than having to converse with a man who threatened us and killed one of his own livestock just for fun, don't you think?'

The weight that had been bearing down on Connie lifted as Penny smiled and nodded, a distant glow of happiness evident in the sudden sparkle in her eyes. It was a fine balancing act, conversing with her daughter. Like walking a tightrope without a safety net beneath. One wrong step and the distance they had managed to narrow would be ripped wide open again, the final thin strands of their delicately spun connection split and torn into tiny irreparable pieces.

'We'll take another look at the wardrobe furniture for your room and then call into the fruit and veg shop in Coldstone Village on the way back home, see what they have to say about Mrs Fairbridge and her illness.'

There was something else there too, another matter troubling Penny. Connie could see her enthusiasm rapidly fading as Penny's mouth opened and then snapped shut as if saying anything more would set them back, damaging the progress they had made. It could wait. Whatever it was, whether it was school or the Fairbridges or her daughter's fanciful imagination and absurd slurs about Duncan, the architect, it would have to be spoken about another day. They had limits. Scratch that; Connie had limits. One problem at a time. She would speak to Penny once they had more information on the ill lady in the Fairbridge household. It wasn't a task Connie particularly relished, delving into somebody else's business and personal information – God knows she had enough problems of her own to deal with – but she saw it as a hurdle; something to be leapt and conquered so they as a family could move on to the next pressing issue. It would also bring her closer to her only daughter, and that was more important than anything else. Her own patience had been stretched and bent out of shape just lately, her reactions not as helpful or positive as she would have liked. It was time to begin repairing the damage to her own little family unit, and if it meant poking around somebody else's family in order to pacify her daughter, then that was what she would do, no matter how uncomfortable it made her.

'Right,' she said, a sense of buoyancy in her voice, 'let's go and do some serious shopping and then we'll drive into Coldstone Village, see what's happening at the Fairbridge house. We're sure to put a few noses out of joint but what the hell. You can't make an omelette without breaking a few eggs.'

* * *

'Old lady? Which old lady?'

The female behind the counter wrinkled her brow, her displeasure at being asked such a question apparent in her expression: the way her lip curled up into a snarl, the darkness in her eyes. The line between her brows that was so deep, Connie felt sure she could fit her entire fist in it.

'At the Fairbridge house. Douglas Fairbridge's wife.'

'Ain't no wife at the Fairbridge house. Hasn't been for more than five years now.'

Connie felt the stiffness in Penny's arm as it pressed up against hers, the sudden chill of it as they both listened to those words. She had misheard the son that day at the house. That was the only explanation. Her daughter had been nervous, on edge. Had misunderstood his explanation.

'That'll be £5.99.'

Connie observed the woman behind the counter, was aware of how closely she was monitoring her and her daughter, her pupils sharp pinpricks that roved over them, taking in every little detail. Despite a heavy layer of makeup and a crude attempt at taming her wild wavy hair, the jowls gave away her real age, forcing her mouth into a downward slope that gave her a look of somebody in the clutches of permanent anger. She reminded Connie of a lion, with her dyed blonde mane and scowl. Her predatory stance. How she stood with hunched shoulders, both hands placed squarely on the counter as she waited for Connie to hand over the cash.

'Here you go. Lovely chatting to you,' she said, pressing a ten-pound note into her palm, hoping to kill this woman with kindness. They weren't exactly neighbours but it wouldn't do to make enemies of local folk. Word would undoubtedly spread fast in a place like Coldstone. Gossipmongers and haters she could do without.

The woman rummaged in the old till for change, dropping a mound of coins into Connie's hand.

'It'll be that nincompoop of a friend of his that you heard. Always at it, they are. Wandering around the place like a pair of schoolkids, hollering at folk, acting like they've never grown up. A load of village idiots if you ask me. Never been the same in that place since the old woman died. She was the one who kept them in line. Once she passed away, they became feral, doin' whatever the hell they liked. Just goes to show that being blessed with money don't necessarily equate to having manners and common decency.'

A burst of heat coloured Connie's cheeks, angry flames licking around her hairline. She stole a sideways glance at Penny, expecting to see a smug look, that defiant *I told you so* gaze that she had practised so well over the years, but instead she was met with something else. Something unexpected. Her daughter's eyes were brimming with tears, her chin quivering as she fought back the deluge that threatened to spill over.

'Thank you. For being so honest, that is. Having just moved here, it's good to know what we're dealing with.'

'Aye, well, just be careful. The Fairbridges make up their own rules, not like the rest of us. Judges and senior police officers are all friends of theirs. The old man might be eccentric but underneath it all, he's as sharp as a tack. Don't be fooled by his weird ways. He's always one step ahead.'

A serrated knife dug its way into the soft flesh of Connie's innards.

Judges and senior police officers.

The thought of Douglas Fairbridge and one of his powerful friends having the means to evict them from their home was like somebody taking a blade to her neck. Surely such things weren't possible? Even high-ranking police officers still had to abide by the laws of the land, didn't they?

'Thanks for the word of warning. We'll do our best to give them a wide berth.'

'Like I say, they're not particularly pleasant people. Mrs Fairbridge, the old lady, she was a gem. Put up with a lot, she did. Don't know how she stood it living in that house with him. Shame she died and her husband and that son of hers are still here. Sometimes life ain't fair.'

A wall of silence hung between Connie and her daughter on the walk back to the car, each of them too stunned to speak. It was as they arrived and slung the small bag of groceries onto the back seat that Penny finally broke the hush.

'I knew something was wrong. Why would anybody say their mother was alive when we could easily find out she had died years back?'

Connie shrugged and slipped into the driver's side, her hands resting on the steering wheel. The words of Douglas Fairbridge and thoughts of his powerful friends swarmed around her head. Maybe her gut instinct about Hallshead Farmhouse had been right all along. Maybe they should sell up now, move somewhere else. Somewhere far from this place and those people. She visualised Eric's face as she attempted to broach the subject, his creased features, his puckered mouth and rutted brow. The way he had of clamping his teeth together when he was agitated. The line he would use about sullying the memory of his parents and brother by rejecting their house. His childhood home. How he would paint Connie as cruel and uncaring. She didn't want to hurt him but neither did she want to live next door to a monster, somebody who it seemed would go to any lengths to get back what he claimed was his. Hallshead Farmhouse. Their only home. He had it in his sights, and from what Connie had just been told, woe betide anybody who stood in his way. He had the power to ruin them, both mentally and financially. He had power and money and influence. All they had was each other, and no amount of ingenuity and resilience could ever triumph against such giants.

* * *

Molly Wright slid the bolt across the door of her shop and flipped the *open* sign to *closed*. Perhaps she had said too much; the look on the older woman's face was enough to freeze fire as she'd spoken about the Fairbridges. But it had to be said. The new family deserved to know the truth. The truth as she saw it. No. It was the truth as *everyone* saw it. Most folk round these parts had all been burned by that family. The son was charming for sure, but a spoilt clownish imbecile. And as for the father, the less he lived inside her head the better. Their relationship had been a brief interlude in her life. A passing phase. A mistake. He was a lecherous individual with all the charm and morals of an alley cat. Widowed at thirty-five years of age, Molly had been lonely and in need of company when he'd strutted into her life, promising love, wealth and happiness, and instead he'd provided her with a whole load of heartache and near bankruptcy after attempting to take over her small business and shut her down so he could sell the land her property stood on. But that wasn't the worst of his sins. Fairbridge, unbeknownst to other villagers, had a penchant for younger females, catching him as she did, loitering outside the bedroom of her fourteen-year-old daughter when he thought Molly wasn't in the house.

She heaved a sigh as she pulled down the blinds with a sharp yank, relieved to be rid of him and his toxic abrasive ways. Better to live alone than be shackled to somebody like that for the rest of her days. The man was a disgrace to humanity and she hoped that one day he would die a painful death and rot in the flaming pit of hell.

20

THE HOUSE

The days bled into one another, Penny going through her usual routine of taking the long walk to the bus stop to get to school, then coming home to a house with an atmosphere so thick it could have been cut in half. Her mum had taken the words of the lady in the shop to heart and harangued Penny's dad to cut their losses and sell up before things deteriorated even further. He had turned on her and told her to stop exaggerating, that Fairbridge was simply a ridiculously eccentric old guy and the lady in the shop was a bored old gossip who spent her days spreading malicious lies about the locals. Voices were raised, arguments had. And still the building work continued. The architect made the odd appearance, bringing along an apprentice who seemed just as intent on staring Penny down whenever she caught his eye. Solitude became her only friend, the storm between her parents too loud, too great to bear, so she took refuge in her room with her textbooks and her music, moving only when everyone left on an evening and her parents had run out of insults to hurl at one other. Aaron kept his distance, the rift in the house a good enough reason for him to lie low, holing himself away in his newly painted bedroom with his Xbox and his music.

It still rankled Penny, the visit she had made to the Fairbridge house, her rapid departure from it. That noise from upstairs. It sounded like somebody crying. Time and distance began to play tricks with her memory, leaving her wondering if the noise she heard was animal rather than human. Old man Fairbridge had already killed one lamb; what if he was doing it to others? The thought of such a thing made her gag, her chest convulsing with disgust. Was that what happened when matriarchs died – the remaining family members all went to shit? Their behaviour suddenly deteriorating, resulting in them carrying out unthinkable acts of terror and debauchery? Perhaps the woman in the shop was right in what she said, that the old lady always kept them in check and once she left this world for another one, they were free to do whatever they wanted. The thought made Penny want to vomit, that two grown men were so dysfunctional, their desires and needs so perverse and depraved, that only one person had the ability to keep them on the straight and narrow. What were they, for Christ's sake – adults or psychotic schoolchildren?

A knock at her bedroom door sent an army of fire ants scurrying over her skin. Before she could stand up or call out, a sliver of light appeared, a shadow following. And there he stood, the architect. In her bedroom. With her. She shrank back on the bed, the urge to pull the covers over herself such a strong reflex action she had to press her hands down on the mattress to stop them from moving. Her school uniform widened the age gap between them, accentuating her rank in the world compared to his. She was still a child. He was a grown man. A professional. She hoped he could see that. Could see her apprehension and would back away. Except he didn't.

'Hi, sorry to barge in. Just need to take a few measurements. Not sure if you know but your room is getting an extension added onto it now. You can thank your dad for the extra space you'll have in here once it's finished.'

Without waiting for a reply, he pushed his way past and began writing in a small notebook, his eyes travelling over the ceiling and down walls, as if he was tracking an invisible insect. The way he held the small pencil between his bony fingers riled her, even the ridiculous fact that he was left-handed, his nails too clean and perfect as he scribbled down measurements and drawings. Small things. Inconsequential things. Things that irritated her to the point of wanting to scream.

Her dad had done this on purpose, changing the original plans, deliberately extending the building work to prove to her mum that they were staying here and a move was out of the question. Only a few weeks back he wanted everything kept the same as it was, and now this.

The architect pulled a tape measure out of his top pocket and held it against the far wall before stretching it to where she was sitting. She sucked in her breath. His body was almost touching hers. She could feel the heat pulsing from him. A dark patch was visible on his shirt under his armpit as he leaned farther forwards. Penny winced, the stale pungent smell of sweat forcing her to shift back against the wall, the sight of the dark wet fabric sickening her.

'I've got those other dimensions you asked for.' The apprentice stood in her doorway. Two of them invading her personal space, acting as if they had every right to be there, commandeering the room. Her room. It was difficult to interpret the possible smirk that passed between them; her reactions were dulled, her senses heightened. Everything felt twisted and bowed out of shape, her thoughts and limbs weak and useless as if she were wading through treacle.

Penny leaned back to try and open her curtains, the ones she kept permanently closed for fear of seeing her intruder, her *stalker*, standing there, but before she could reach them, the room was plunged into darkness, the air as still as death itself. Everywhere as dark as coal. And then she let out a shriek that clawed its way out of her throat as something touched her hand.

'It's just the trip switch.'

The architect's voice cut through the darkness. Or maybe it was his assistant or apprentice or whatever the fuck he called himself. Penny couldn't think straight, her mind a whirling snow globe, pieces of her brain floating around her cranium, her judgement skewed and off kilter.

A crackle above, and suddenly they were flooded with light again. Penny turned, her muscles as solid as tree roots when she saw the architect sitting next to her on the bed, his hand touching hers. Like a cat poised to attack, she raised her palms, raw instinct and self-preservation directing her movements. She scrambled back, her head knocking against the windowsill, before shuffling away to the other end of the bed, the look on his face sending a spike of ice up and down her spine. He was smiling, his mouth stretched into a near grimace.

'Sorry!' He placed his too-soft, slim hands in the air, the act of mock surrender cementing the idea in her head that it had been planned. Being plunged into darkness while he was sizing up her room. Sizing *her* up. His young friend continued to stand in the doorway, watching it all unfold. The whole thing was a ruse. She was certain of it. And she was the intended victim.

'Sorry, guys. Bloody oversensitive trip switch downstairs.' The electrician's voice hollered up the stairs, cutting through the moment, slicing through the deep feeling of sickness that twisted and turned like a whirling eddy in the pit of her stomach.

'Fucking hell, this just gets better and better.' Aaron appeared, standing outside her room on the landing. He pushed past the assistant into Penny's room, his eyes bulging with undisguised excitement. 'Come downstairs, see what they've found. It's fucking brilliant.' He made a swift exit, leaving Penny alone with the architects. 'I swear to God, this house just gets better and better, Pens. Come on,' he shouted from the top of the stairs. 'Come and have a look at what they've uncovered. This place is a bloody warren.'

* * *

'Surely Dad must know about this? He grew up here.' Penny's stomach clenched as she peered into the hole in the wall and beyond, her eyes peering into the dark hollow space that lay behind what was once a large ugly old fireplace. 'I mean, what the hell is it?'

'We just removed the big old hearth and wall of bricks above it and there it was.' A grimy-looking builder, his clothes pitted with brick dust, was standing next to Penny, his gaze drawn towards the seemingly endless cavity while Aaron dropped to his haunches and shone a torch inside the three-to-four-foot gap, the pale yellow beam of light highlighting a long forgotten room. Penny looked away. It scared her; it was a musty dank place that reeked of neglect. She shivered and wrapped her arms around herself.

'It's just a big old room,' Aaron said, standing up and looking around at the sea of startled expressions.

Penny wanted to laugh at the streak of grey dust that was clinging to his fledgling beard, but she couldn't muster up the energy or the enthusiasm. This house, its location, its neighbours, the people who invaded it day after day in a bid to improve it while inadvertently making it worse, made her want to scream and gnash her teeth together, to rip at her hair until it came out in clumps. She hated *it* and she hated them.

'Tell you what,' Aaron said, dropping back down onto the floor. 'Why don't I go in there and investigate?'

And before anybody could reply or stop him, he bent down and wriggled his narrow wiry body through the space, vanishing into the black void like a predator into the darkest depths of the night.

'Aaron! For God's sake, come back here.' Penny winced at the sound of her mother's voice behind her, the pitch of it so close to her ear, it caused her to stumble. The force and insistence behind it enough to shatter glass.

'S'all right. It's cool.' His face was illuminated by the flick of a switch as he turned on the torch, swinging it around before shining it back on himself, his smile manic, his teeth glinting like glass.

In another room, the phone rang. The air next to Penny shifted as her mother moved to answer it, leaving her alone with the builders and the architects, and Aaron, who was unexplainably and weirdly fascinated by the newly discovered cavernous pit. She could hear the shuffle of his feet as he wandered around in the faint hope of finding something he could shout about. Something bizarre and unique that would capture everybody's attention. And then came his voice, breaking with the excitement of his disclosure, saying words Penny didn't want to hear.

'Fucking hell, I've found some bones in here! And a door.'

He waved the torch about, the light spreading over the floor and a small collection of something unrecognisable that littered the area next to his feet.

Penny peered in then pulled back with a small shriek. The dining area in which she stood took on different dimensions, the walls closing in, the floor tilting violently. Penny's body was lead, her legs liquid. She fought the sensation, doing what she could to remain upright, trying her best to hold on to her dignity and decorum until she could do it no longer. A thousand stars burst and exploded behind her eyes, turning everything a murky shade of grey before absolute darkness set in.

21

PENNY

Day 3

Perhaps it's his smile that infuriates me. Or the way he tries time and time again to make eye contact with the female jurors, including me. Yet another misogynistic individual who doesn't recognise me from all those years back. Maybe it's because my hair is shorter, a different shade from when I was a teenager. Or maybe it's because I'm older, my face less rounded, and I am less inclined to smile and make eye contact with him. Or perhaps it's simply because I meant nothing to him then, my features immediately erased from his memory bank, and mean even less to him now. I'm inclined to go for the latter. He's a man of few morals, and I doubt he has changed all that much. People don't. We are who we are, our innate characteristics always lurking, controlling our behaviour. Who we are. How we treat others.

I think of my own brother and his propensity for impulsive behaviour that led him on the wrong path with the wrong people. Things could have been so very different for him. A clean and easier lifestyle. A healthy productive one despite what he went through. But only he can change that. My many attempts to contact him over the years to try and help him get his life back on track have failed time and time again. Mum sometimes asks after him, but as the dementia has progressed, her recollections of him and requests to see him have thinned out, becoming less and less frequent. The one time I did take her to see him was when he was living with a friend a few years back. I still had contact with him, albeit sporadically, and knew where he was living. I mentioned that Mum wasn't well and that it might be a good idea for her to visit him, to let her know that he was okay. He agreed and gave me a time and date, promising that he would clean himself up and be sober and amenable.

We arrived at the exact time given, to a house that was locked, all the curtains closed. I'm being kind. They weren't curtains at all – sheets hung up at the window is what they actually were. Dirty ragged sheets stretched across grimy panes of glass. Unwilling to give Aaron any leeway or any more of our precious time, I turned to leave, taking Mum with me, and was stopped by an unkempt half-dressed man who leaned out from the bedroom window and hollered down at us.

'He's just unlocking the door now. Give us a minute, yeah?'

Before I could protest, the door was swung open and Aaron stood there in the hallway, his clothes askew, his hair matted. With a look from beneath his furrowed brow, he beckoned us in and we followed. The stale smell of alcohol and tobacco combined with body odour wafted towards us, its sticky pungent fingers trailing over our clothes and hair as we trailed behind Aaron into the living room.

Mum and I perched on the sofa, a rash of cigarette burns peppering the arms while bottles rolled about the floor at our feet, clinking together with a dull chime.

'So, how ya doing, Mum?' He did his best to converse, his words slurred, his eyes half closed.

I wanted to leave, to stand and leave the place, taking Mum with me. She didn't belong in a house like that.

'Better than you by the looks of things,' she said in return, catching both me and Aaron off guard. 'For goodness' sake,' she said, shaking her head at him and surveying the room with a pained expression, 'what is going on with you?'

The atmosphere thickened, a heavy opaque veil putting a clear divide between us and him. My brother. My mother's only son.

I prayed Aaron would hold back, that he would think of our Mum's fragile mental health and say nothing. Instead, his voice rang out, loud and powerful enough to be heard in every house in the godawful slum of a street where he lived as he roared at us.

'Going on with me? Are you fucking kidding me?'

He stood up and began to pace the room, his movements jerky, his body a mass of twitches.

'You and your move to that desolate farmhouse is what went on with me! You took us away from a decent house to live in the middle of frigging nowhere. And look how that turned out.'

I expected tears from Mum and was surprised to see a shrug and an expression of nonchalance, her lip curling up at him in contempt.

'I didn't want to be there either. It was your dad's idea. His house, his parents. I just went along with it because we needed somewhere bigger to live.'

'And we ended up with nowhere to live because the stupid fucking place got burned down! Dozens of skin grafts and enough bullying at school to last me a fucking lifetime is what I had to put up with!'

Then Mum's weeping came, thick and fast. I sucked in a breath and fought back my own tears, the memory of that time too raw for me to give it any headspace, but Mum was beside herself, crying forcefully, her voice ragged with grief as she tried to reason with him.

'It wasn't my fault! I begged your dad to move somewhere else but he refused. I hated that house as much as you did. Still do. Besides,' she said, drying her eyes and straightening her back, 'we moved back to the old town in the end. So it wasn't all bad.'

The bald patch at the back of Aaron's head was, and is still, visible. The part where the flames licked at his neck as he ran from the house screaming, his hair on fire, the skin on the back of his skull melting like candle wax. He turned, as if to remind Mum of what he'd endured, the pinkness of his skin still catching me unawares, the rawness of it a reminder of that time.

'Not all bad?' he said, spinning round. 'For who, Mum? Not all bad for me, or do you mean for you and your favourite child?'

I winced at his words and stared down at my hands. If only he knew.

Mum sniffed, her tears quickly drying. 'You didn't always hate it there. And anyway, you had your toys to play with. And you both went to a nice school. The teachers were lovely. You got a teddy for coming top in the spelling test. Do you remember, Aaron? That grey fluffy teddy with a gold star?'

I caught his eye and shook my head. Her mind had quickly travelled to our distant past when we were very young and still in primary school. It signalled that the conversation was over. I knew at that point that we had lost Aaron and would probably never get him back. His scars were still noticeable whereas mine were hidden, buried so deep inside me they were almost embedded in the marrow of my bones.

I shiver, a chill passing over me at the memory, and pull myself back to the present, to the words being spoken in the courtroom. I have to listen to everything that is being said. Sometimes the smallest of details can bring about the biggest of changes.

'You were with the defendant on the night of the party, is that correct? The evening before the alleged assault took place.' The defence barrister smiles and glances down at his notes before looking up and meeting the gaze of his witness.

'Yes, that's correct. I was there at the party.' Another smirk.

I look down at my lap, at my interlaced fingers, ten rigid digits locked together, my skin tight and pale. When I raise my head, he is staring at me. I swallow and gasp, the fear that he has actually remembered me withering my skin. But I can see as I observe his dull expression that there is nothing there. No trace of anything that signifies a memory of me or that time from the past. His dark dead eyes move on and beyond me as if I don't exist. He scans the other jurors and then looks back at the barrister, who poses his next question.

'And can you tell me what you saw when the defendant was speaking to Ms Albright?'

'Sure. Everything looked fine.' He smiles and shakes his head, a small cackle erupting out of his throat. 'Better than fine actually.'

I cringe at his boorish behaviour, the way he has of assuming everyone acts and thinks as he does. The way he, without question, truly believes and assumes that everybody else is willing to scrape their bellies on the ground to think at his level. I hate him. Despise him. And the likes of him. I hope that he and his friend rot in the fires of hell forevermore.

'Better than fine? Can you please elaborate and expand your answer, telling us what you mean by that statement?'

Another unsavoury lopsided smile. He reminds me of a snake, slithering around the courtroom, searching for his prey, his hissing sibilant voice echoing around the silence of the room as we all wait for his reply.

'Well, let's just say, she looked and acted very friendly, if you know what I mean.' All that's missing from his performance is a sickening wink to accompany his full-blown chauvinistic display.

I suppress the howl of frustration I feel rising within me and focus instead on my breathing.

In through the nose, out through the mouth.

In through the nose, out through the mouth.

'Can you please speak plainly.' The judge glares at him, unimpressed by his childish displays of innuendo. 'We don't want inner thoughts or opinions. We only deal in facts in this courtroom.'

I let out a shaky breath, my respect for this judge growing by the minute. Thank God for his logic and presence of mind. He will help keep this man in line, dismissing his juvenile inferences with a wave of his hand and a stern telling off. I almost smile. Almost. But not quite. Perhaps later, when all of this is over, when the defendant is led from the courtroom in handcuffs.

'Okay. Sorry, Your Honour. What I can say is that I saw the pair of them kissing and it was most definitely consensual.'

A small shriek from somebody on the jurors' bench. Probably Cheryl or Lisa. He's opening up a chasm of doubt in their minds, one that is going to be almost impossible to bridge. I'll do my best but it isn't looking good.

'Can you please explain how you came to this conclusion?'

His earlier smirk and superior self-important expression have now been replaced by something less abrasive. More conducive to this clinical environment. Like his long-time twisted friend, he too knows how to play the game. The jury are being led and they don't even know it. Like lemmings to a cliff edge.

'Well, she made no attempt to push him away. And her leg was crossed over his like she was actually trying to pull him even closer.' He speaks reverently, his head dipped as if in prayer.

Dear God, I hate this. Has he no shame? I want to stand up and scream that he is a liar. I want to ask him if he thinks his friend would defend him if the tables were turned. I don't believe he would. His selfish streak runs too deep for him to ever do anything for anybody else and yet here is his close acquaintance, defending him to the hilt. Making sure he walks free while a young girl has had her dignity stripped away, her life put on hold. Her body defiled and beaten.

The prosecution declines to ask questions when requested. Wise move. The man is a liar so what is the point? How can a close friend be deemed a reliable witness anyway? His prejudice is plain for all to see. I just pray that Cheryl and Lisa are the only unobservant members on the bench and that everyone else is astute enough to see beyond this insulting ghastly charade.

The witness leaves the courtroom, a spring in his step, his mind empty of the damage he has caused to the victim in all of this. His thoughts are so crammed full of his own needs and wants, there isn't room for anybody or anything else. This was his moment to shine, his chance to show everybody how wonderfully damaged and depraved he is. He could have used this time in his life to do the right thing, to actually help someone who has suffered, but no – he chose instead to follow the well-trodden path of lying and being generally despicable because for people like him, it's easier. Easier than making a furrow down a less used route. One that people with integrity and compassion would always follow. Such a way would be beyond his comprehension.

I keep my eyes averted from the defendant, refusing to watch him as he stands there, proud and sure of our verdict. This thing isn't over till it's over. Things may not be going as I'd hoped but I'm not giving in until I've had my say.

22

THE HOUSE

It took a few seconds for everything to slot into place, for her senses and brain to start functioning properly. The bones. It was the mention of some bones. The thought of a dead body buried in a concealed room. And now he was kneeling next to her, the architect, his fingers placed on her wrist, his thumb feeling for a pulse. At every opportunity he was there. His touch, the heat of his body, the sour tang of his breath; they made her want to gag, to scramble to her feet and run as far as she could in the opposite direction. Except that wasn't possible. Her head swam; she was lethargic, her movements and thoughts sluggish, so instead she snatched her hand away and fought to sit upright, the room tilting and veering around her. His reaction to her brief fainting spell was disproportionate, stroking her wrist, leaning in so close their faces were practically touching. She had passed out for just a few seconds. She wasn't dying.

'I'm fine,' was all she could manage.

She didn't feel fine. The room continued to shift, a violence to its movements. Her stomach churned and roiled.

'Your head hit the floor when you went down,' the architect said, concern for her well-being evident in his narrowed eyes and wrinkled brow. He was still kneeling close to her. Too close. She pushed herself away and glanced around.

Her mum was still on the phone in another room speaking to builders, talking about extensions and costs and invoices. Aaron was still scrambling around in the dirt, his fascination with the newfound space too great to notice that his sister had passed out. She was alone with him. Them. The architect and his assistant.

'Here you go.' The architect handed her a glass of water, passed to him by his apprentice. He made a show of shuffling away, his head bowed with, what – a sense of compassion in the hope of restoring her dignity? Pity? His expression and body language was too complicated to fathom, Penny's brain still fogged up.

The cool liquid drenched her throat as she took sip after sip, her mouth dry, her tongue thick and furry. 'Thank you,' she said, handing it back after taking another final gulp to assuage the aridity in her mouth. A few seconds, that was all she had been out for, and yet her body and head felt mountain heavy, her limbs wiry like elastic.

His touch was gentle, hardly there at all, as he placed a cool palm around her elbow to help her up off the floor. He moved her slowly and deliberately like she was a rare delicate object in need of protection. She sat, the rigidity of the chair helping to stop the shooting pains that raced up and down her spine. She could sense him watching her, waiting for her to crumple, only stepping back and giving her a smile when it became obvious she was okay again. Her eyes found his. He blinked and looked away, staring at the floor. Something passed between them; a tacit moment of understanding.

Her resolve in that moment to keep on hating him weakened. Was this the same man? Was she the same person after the fall? She couldn't quite believe she was even entertaining such thoughts. Was her earlier judgement of this man completely wrong, her accusations unwarranted? It was so hard to tell, her mind in pieces, her ability to determine people's thoughts and intentions blurred and off balance after Aaron's forage in the darkness.

'I'll go and get your mum,' the architect said lightly, and before she could decline, he disappeared into the next room, leaving her alone with the apprentice who was closer in age to her than his boss.

Neither of them said anything as they waited, his eyes travelling around the room, darting into every corner, looking everywhere but at her. Penny almost laughed. Almost, but not quite. Hysteria was setting in, her fears and suspicions suddenly feeling unmerited. Distorted even. This apprentice was just a kid. Probably in his mid-twenties. And as for his boss, maybe she had overreacted to certain events and actions. Maybe, but she wasn't entirely certain. With no witnesses to either back up or dismiss her claims, she was left floundering in the dark. If the house had been in a better state of repair, closer to where they used to live, she would have had friends over to stay who could have assuaged her fears, but as it was, they were isolated with only the bleak landscape and psychotic neighbours for company. Maybe that was it. Maybe the Fairbridges had tainted her judgement of people, making her suspicious of everybody, not least of all strangers who wandered around the house with a sense of familiarity that disturbed her, their voices and movements echoing in every single room, while she showered and got dressed. There was no peace. No privacy or solitude.

'I'm Ryan, by the way.'

His introduction caught her by surprise. She sat up straight, running her fingers through her knotted hair. The ache in her head eased, the tight painful loops in her stomach gradually unfolding.

'I'm Penny.'

A laugh and a smile. 'Yeah, I know.'

She blinked and took a shaky breath, rubbing at her eyes with small tight fists to clear her vision.

'Don't worry, I'm not a stalker. Your parents told us your names when we first started this job.' He smiled, turned away from her and peered into the dark room behind the fireplace. 'Looks like we might have to readjust our initial drawings and plans now this other room has been exposed. I reckon your parents might want to use it for something.'

Penny thought of the extra hours they would spend in the house if new plans were drawn up and was surprised to feel no loathing or dread at the idea of it. She was beyond that, too weary for any more drama. Too weak to resist.

A shuffle of feet behind her, a sharp intake of breath. 'What on earth happened?' Her mother marched into the room and crouched at her daughter's side, grasping her hand and pressing a cool palm against Penny's forehead.

The weight that had been pressing down on her these past few weeks began to lift. A slow but steady untying of the tight ribbon of tension that had been wrapped around her skull. With her mother by her side, her concern a palpable force, everything in her world felt right again, as if a small recalibration had been made. One small adjustment – that was all it took. A show of attention, words of comfort. Penny's upper spine and shoulders, her head and limbs, were as light as air. She pressed her feet to the floor to stop herself from floating up to the ceiling.

Perhaps it was the bang on the head that had changed her thinking. She had read about things like that happening before – people passing out and thumping their skull then coming round and being able to play like a concert pianist or speak a different language. She didn't expect to suddenly become a genius, but being able to see through the fug of panic that had misted her thinking for so long felt like a step in the right direction. It was exhausting, being frightened and angry all the time. It shortened her temper and sapped her of all her strength. Being normal again felt good. Whatever normal was. But at least she could now see that her accusations may have been unfounded, her emotions and logic smudged away by their current living conditions and a sense of isolation. Thoughts of the figure outside her window still nagged at her. She blotted out those thoughts. It could be anybody. A local who enjoyed wandering in the middle of the night. She squashed down any remaining fears, refusing to give in to the negativity that knocked at her head, begging to be let in. Whoever it was outside her window, they couldn't get inside the house. She was safe here. Whether she liked it or not, this was her new home and nobody could enter uninvited.

The memory of Aaron's statement pierced her brain. Bones. There were bones in that old secret room. She should have felt terror at the thought of it. And yet she didn't. She felt a strange sense of calm wash over her until a bang at the door sent a dart of ice down her spine. The strength and power of the knock echoed around them like a death knell. It was aggressive. A pounding. Somebody demanding to be let in.

Aaron stepped out from his newfound hidey-hole and Connie slipped away into the hallway to answer it. Her small voice blended with a louder more masculine tone that grew closer until a shadow loomed over them and Penny felt her head begin to spin once more. She refused to pass out again. Such weakness was humiliating. She was stronger than that, more resilient. Nipping at a fold of skin on her forearm to stop herself from falling, and to keep the dizziness at bay, Penny turned around to see the handsome face of Cameron Fairbridge. He was standing holding a large bouquet of flowers and wearing a wide smile. Behind him was another man, smaller, his features not as striking, but undeniably suave all the same with his immaculate clothes and perfectly swept back hair.

'Me again. And a little token of my appreciation for putting up with my immense rudeness the other day,' he said, proffering the flowers to Penny. 'It was out of order.' He rolled his eyes and grimaced. 'Scratch that. *I* was out of order. I behaved like a buffoon. I hope you can forgive me?'

'And me,' the other man piped up. 'I apologise too.'

Penny's insides melted a little, her skin flashing hot and cold in Cameron Fairbridge's presence. Sweat coated her top lip. She rubbed at it and attempted a smile.

'Thank you. That's very kind of you,' chimed Connie.

Penny listened to her mother's words, a sudden muteness rendering her unable to form a coherent sentence of her own. She thought about the words of the shop assistant, about how Cameron Fairbridge was an idiot and a clown. Penny struggled to marry that notion to the man before her. Her heart pumped in her chest. She placed her fingers on her collarbone, tapping softly to counteract the pounding beneath her ribcage.

'I really am truly sorry. My friend Ivor and I had had a drink that day. I said some silly, unforgiveable things and he made some stupid noises. We embarrassed both you and ourselves. Anyway,' he said, glancing at the rubble and gaping hole where dust motes swirled in tiny pockets, 'thank you for not shouting at me and throwing me out of your house before I've had a chance to apologise.'

She tried to speak, to fill the awkward dead air between them, but everything refused to work properly, her tongue too thick for her mouth, her gums as dry as sandpaper. Even swallowing felt impossible, saliva gathering in the ridges of her teeth. She hated her ineptitude, her lack of grace and her inability to talk pleasantries when she was around people like Cameron Fairbridge. Wealthy people endowed with lots of charm and even more money.

'As you can see,' Aaron said triumphantly, breaching the stillness in the room, his face beaming as if he had broken records by being the first to step foot on an alien planet, 'we've just discovered another room in the house. It's even got a small door so it can be accessed from the outside.' He spun around, eyes bright as he addressed his waiting audience. 'I'm off to see where the door leads to. This house suddenly seems worth living in.' His face reminded Penny of a small child, his impulsivity and foolishness in stark contrast to his ripped dusty jeans and faded Slipknot T-shirt. 'Come on,' he said, lowering his head and stepping back inside. 'Anybody up for an adventure?'

23

THE HOUSE

They weren't bones. Certainly not human bones. Of course they weren't. Connie was well aware that her teenage son was prone to hyperbole in order to embellish a story. He emerged from behind the wall carrying a bag of old shells and fossils and the skeleton of a bird or two – she guessed at a crow or something similar. But he was right about one thing. There was a door in that room. She had ducked down and followed her son in through the hole in the wall to see what was in there. Turned out, not much at all. Aaron had shone his torch into a dark corner of the room, aiming it at an old wooden door that was not quite full size but still big enough to get through if you crouched a little. Connie had rattled at the handle, relieved to find it locked.

'If you think about the shape of this building,' Aaron had said, still fired up, his body practically vibrating with excitement, 'that door must lead into the old lean-to at the back of the house.'

Connie pursed her lips and thought about the perimeter of the farmhouse. He was right. The lean-to had been ignored and neglected for many years, unused by Eric's parents and almost ready to collapse. It had been an add-on to the original building, probably constructed in the 1940s or 1950s as some kind of storage area and gradually forgotten about, its flimsy structure not strong enough to withstand decades of harsh moorland winters.

Connie emerged from the newly discovered room after a few seconds and shielded her eyes, the dimmest of light cutting into her vision.

'Well, it looks like I've called at an exciting time.' Cameron gave her what appeared to be a genuine smile and Connie found herself doubting the word of the shopkeeper who, at the time, had seemed so convincing.

Maybe it wouldn't do to take anybody else's words as gospel when it came to judging people. Maybe she should reserve judgement and form her own opinions of this man. He seemed polite and thoughtful. Unlike his father. And those flowers must have cost a pretty penny. The way he smiled, bowing his head ever so slightly as he spoke to her daughter. And that sparkle in his eye; was it just a ruse? Connie didn't think so. Why would he need to do such a thing? And then there was the flush on Penny's cheeks as she sniffed at the spray, stroking the petals with pale trembling fingers. Either he was an award-winning actor or the lady in the shop was telling outright lies.

'Anyway, I'll leave you in peace.' He leaned down, peered into the hole and stood back up, his smile illuminating the room. 'Seems like you've got your work cut out. I'm sure Hallshead Farmhouse will look splendid once you've completed all the work.'

The rapid departure of the two men left a shattering silence, Cameron Fairbridge's larger than life presence creating a vacuum that was difficult to fill.

'Well, we're just about done here for now.' The architect's less-than-powerful voice rumbled in the background of Connie's thoughts, his movements behind her a dull rambling noise in direct contrast to Cameron's unexpected arrival in her home. The young Fairbridge lad had a vibrancy about him, his presence difficult to ignore.

Within seconds, she and Penny were left alone, Aaron already scrambling around the back of the house in search of the elusive door that would lead him into the newly discovered room.

'You should put those in some water,' Connie said, nodding at the explosion of colour and the array of silken petals that were nestled in her daughter's arms.

The sweet musky aroma of the flowers cut through the dry stale smell of brick dust and general decay, adding a certain warmth to the house. Giving it life.

Penny stood. Her legs were weak and spindly after the fainting episode. She hung on to the back of the chair, stretching and flexing until she found her rhythm before striding into the kitchen, arms flush with the flowers, her face deadpan. Connie could still see it in her daughter, however, the conflicting emotions that jostled for space in her head. The spread of colour on her cheeks and neck, the fluttering of her lashes and darting of her eyes. All signs of somebody who was secretly thrilled at being made the centre of attention whilst also feeling acutely uncomfortable, unused to being thrust in the spotlight by a man who arrived with a flourish, his voice and his aura as strong and vibrant as the roses and lilies and gardenia that he'd presented as a peace offering.

Connie left Penny to arrange the flowers, giving her the privacy she deserved. The space and time to still her pounding heart. She would ask later, see if Penny's attitude had changed. See if she had forgiven Cameron Fairbridge for his lies and brusque behaviour. For now, they had a house to sweep, rooms to scrub and clean, the dust left by the builders choking her. Her skin was coarse and gritty. It was as if the house itself was burrowing beneath her outer layers of flesh and funnelling its way into her organs. Cameron Fairbridge may have been the perfect gentleman but Connie's feelings regarding his father remained the same. He was an arrogant piece of shit and the thought of what he was capable of scared her witless. She would continue to be watchful and alert and not be fooled into thinking things were okay when they weren't. He and his son were clearly very different people and no matter how kind and effusive Cameron appeared to be, she knew better than to allow him into their home on a regular basis, acting as if things were peaceful and amicable between them. They most definitely were not.

'The architect,' Penny shouted over the gush of water as she filled a large jug and used it as a makeshift vase in which to place the flowers. 'Is that his assistant or some kind of apprentice with him?'

Connie sighed. It had been an eventful few hours and she still had much to do. 'Apprentice?' She suppressed a smile, surprised Penny hadn't spotted the likeness. 'Maybe he is his apprentice but Ryan is actually his son. He's working with his dad to gain some experience before going to university.'

Penny's hurried footsteps clattered in from the kitchen, kicking up dust and rubble in her wake. She stood next to Connie, her words spluttered in a hot stream of confusion. 'His dad? And university? I thought he was older than that?'

Connie shrugged. 'He took a couple of years out and has decided to go back. Why do you ask?' She thought of her daughter's previous accusations and hoped this piece of information would help quash any remaining doubts she had about the pair of them. Duncan, the architect, was married and had a daughter Penny's age. Connie hadn't seen anything untoward take place under her roof. She would have been the first to act if she had. Maybe this would put a stop to all of the nonsense. Connie had enough to deal with, her many pleas to Eric about selling up and moving on doing little to shift his opinion about Hallshead Farmhouse. It looked like they were here to stay whether she liked it or not. As long as Douglas Fairbridge kept his distance and left them to get on with their lives, she could just about bear it. Besides, it wasn't as if she had any say in the matter. She was stuck there whether she liked it or not.

24

PENNY

Day 3

'He seemed believable, didn't he?' Cheryl is seated next to me in the waiting area. She is attempting to whisper and failing. Her thoughts are blasted into my ear, a string of discordant sounds, each syllable, each word, a low screech, like a fingernail being dragged down a chalkboard.

I want to shift, to move away from her hot rancid breath and equally foul opinions, but we are all crammed together into the small space with nowhere else to go while we wait for the documents to be collected and handed out to us. I manage a smile, a tight grimace of sorts, my face feeling stretched and warped, but remain quiet, saying nothing in return. The eyes of the usher sweep over us and a flush creeps up my neck. I have done my utmost to keep my own feelings under wraps throughout this case but am now in danger of being tainted by association. Cheryl, like Lisa, sees her openness, and her voluble beliefs and estimations, as an asset, a facet of her personality of which she is immensely proud. A desire to scream at her that he, like his friend, is a liar, gets wedged in my throat. I swallow it down, frightened that if I speak, a whole torrent of abuse and truths that nobody wants to hear will pour out. Sometimes the quietest of people can have the loudest thoughts.

My eyes scan the other jurors, searching for Bob. He is a beacon of hope; my *only* hope. Things are beginning to look grim, my initial plans of swaying the other jurors swiftly disappearing into the ether. I spot him at the end of the room, surrounded by other people, their eyes lowered as they wait to be called back in. They all sit silently, gazes averted from one another. Unlike Cheryl. It would seem that she sees it is her duty to fill every microscopic pocket of airspace with each and every idea and notion that enters her head.

'They're ready for us now.' The usher opens the doors and we walk in. A piece of paper has been placed on our respective seats.

The tremble in my fingers feels noticeable as I scoop up the plans of the house where the rape took place. Air rattles in my ribcage when I scan the location and layout; my blood thickens, pounding in my ears like a volley of exploding bombs. I can barely bring myself to study it in detail, to be transported back there. The house in which the attack took place is the same but different. Homely yet not home. It was never home. Not to me. I steel myself and swallow to try and control the thump of the pulse that is gaining traction in my throat. My eyes scan the layout of Hallshead Farmhouse. I never revisited the place after it was decimated by the fire, but now here I am, absorbing these rudimentary plans and photographs, poring over every tiny detail. My vision blurs, a fine veil of tears stopping me from studying the drawing in any real depth. I blink repeatedly, a growl of resistance howling in my head while I try to regain some semblance of normality. I refuse to let anybody see the real me. The frightened, unconfident me. Deep inside I am still that teenage girl, my memories and thoughts stunted by the events of that night. Physically I might be here in this courtroom, but mentally I am still that young woman who hid under her own bed to try and escape her abuser. I have spent years trying to shake off that fear and now it's rising again. I won't let it. I had a right to be safe in my own home all those years ago and I have a right to be here, doing what I can to make sure that man is never able to harm another female. After Ivor Spencer's outright lies, me tweaking the truth a little and attempting to influence other jurors once we are in the deliberation process, barely registers on the scale of transgressions.

The defence barrister's description of the floorplan is a hushed noise in my head. It doesn't matter. I don't want to hear what he has to say anyway. I am focused on one thing and one thing only – getting Cameron Fairbridge locked up. I hope he is imprisoned with a cellmate who will make his life hell once they discover why he is there. Somebody who doesn't mind doling out violence should the need ever arise. My aim is a long way off but the image of him behind bars, slumped on a bare mattress in a tiny prison cell, augments in my mind. It's an image that will keep me going until the end of this trial. And if he is found not guilty – well, I will have to deal with that possibility once this is all over.

I glance down at the plans, if only to look like I am taking notice. The inside of Hallshead Farmhouse has changed drastically, interior walls now missing to form large open plan spaces. New fixtures and fittings. None of it looks familiar to me. Except for the bedroom, that is. My old bedroom is almost the same as it was. The damage caused by the fire didn't reach the back of the house. I escaped without any injuries, unlike Aaron, who was left with scars, both visible and internal. He never got over it. Still hasn't. I just wish he had used his anger and resentment at what happened and funnelled it into something productive instead of sliding into his current pit of hell. Back then, Aaron's nightmares were as regular as mine, each of us suffering in silence. I have managed to control the aftermath of that night but my poor brother has allowed it to control him.

It was horrific, the fire. We went to bed one evening and awoke to a veil of black smoke that had engulfed one half of the house. I remember hearing the creak of burning beams and the shattering of windows below us. I also recall choking and screaming, thinking I was going to die. But the most harrowing memory of that night is the one I have in my head of Aaron running from his room, the back of his hair alight, his expression stricken as he tried to bat out the flames while a hot river of tears coursed down his face. That's an image I will never forget. Ever. The fire took place just over a month after the assault. Trauma is a word that is spoken repeatedly and often overused, diminishing its real meaning, but in our case, trauma doesn't come close to what took place in that house. Rape. Heart attacks. Arson.

The police and fire service blamed workmen. They said that a heater used by the builders and plasterers had been left turned on and that a can of accelerant had fallen over and hit the heater. The circuit breaker for the new rewire didn't kick in on time and by the time it did, the fire had taken hold. I didn't believe that any of the workmen would be careless enough to do such a thing. Still don't. I blame the Fairbridges. They wanted us out of that place so they could possess it and that is exactly what they did, buying up the remains of Hallshead Farmhouse after our mother refused to move back in there. Our father would have stopped her, such was his attachment to his childhood home, but he wasn't around any more to get his way. I loved my dad but I was glad he wasn't there to put a halt to us moving out. The fire happened just two weeks after Dad passed away. Every two weeks. That was the space between each hideous event. First the rape, then my father's unexpected and premature death, and then the fire. Once the insurance paid out, we moved to a normal three-bedroomed house back in the suburbs. No more rolling landscape and bleak misty mornings. No more building work. And more importantly, no more of the Fairbridges. Until now.

I can't prove that they started the fire; if that were the case I would have reported them long ago, but the plasterers whose heater was found still plugged in claimed they had turned it off before leaving. I was and still am more inclined to believe them than the findings of the police report. The police were in awe of the Fairbridge family. Perhaps even a little frightened of them. Douglas Fairbridge was close friends with the chief constable and he and his son would have done anything to scare us out of Hallshead Farmhouse, including raping me, a teenage girl. I feel ashamed by my own lack of judgement, taking a liking to Cameron Fairbridge, curling up with desire at the slightest bit of attention he threw my way. I blamed myself for warming to him, my teenage blushes as deep as the reddest rose whenever I was in his presence. Cameron Fairbridge was and still is a master manipulator. He was there that day when we discovered the room. That was his way in and out of the house to get to me. Aaron had already played around with the door and the old handle, freeing them up, providing Fairbridge with a ready-made means of entry and escape. The route through the old lean-to required little or no effort, its crumbling state of disrepair no barrier to even the most inexperienced of intruders. We lived in the middle of nowhere and all the other doors and windows were secure. We were lax and we were horribly naïve. The Fairbridges were determined sociopaths. Our little family stood no chance against their unscrupulous ways and psychopathic prowess.

I inhale sharply, taking a juddering sigh. Even now, he is still pulling all the strings, captivating the other jurors with his simpering grin and charming ways. But I'm no longer that frightened impressionable young woman. I'm older. Wiser. I too can turn on the charm and be a sly old fox when required. And that is exactly what I plan on doing once we're behind closed doors in that deliberation room and I am able to speak freely.

We peruse the plans for the next few minutes, the judge explaining that it will help contextualise the case, give us a mental picture of where the alleged assault took place. The layout of Hallshead Farmhouse doesn't advance the case any. All it does is reinforce the belief of many of the jurors that Cameron Fairbridge is extremely wealthy and that wealthy people aren't capable of committing heinous crimes. I hear a few sighs of envy when they are told that Fairbridge owns two properties, the other one currently inhabited by his father in his senior years. After sitting listening for what feels like an age, we break for a very late lunch. Everybody filters off in different directions, some taking phone calls, others wandering into town to break the monotony of the day and seek a change from the bland environment of the main waiting area. By the time I finish my sandwich and coffee, we are called back and told that we can leave and that tomorrow the judge will do his summing up.

My heart sings like a bird freed from captivity the minute I step outside into the warmth of the autumnal sun. Somehow I have managed to shake off the company of Cheryl and walk unaccompanied to the car park, making sure I don't break my stride.

Perspiration has stippled my brow by the time I reach my vehicle. Visions of home with Damien and Freda waiting for me when I walk through the door glow brightly in my thoughts, the sight of their welcoming faces lightening the weight that has pressing down on me all day.

It's the sound of her breathing that catches my attention. Then the clip of her heels coming from somewhere close by as she approaches my car. I spin around, my guard already up, hackles raised. I am ready to deflect Cheryl's lame arguments and twisted reasoning, and I feel small bolts of electricity needle my scalp when I spin around and see a woman standing behind me. She is approximately the same age as me and is staring in my direction, her pupils dark and curious as they roam over my car, my clothes and shoes, stopping to study my face.

'Sorry,' she says breathlessly, her chin quivering as if tears are not far away. 'I followed you here. We need to speak. It's about him. Them. I need to speak with you about them.'

She swallows and runs slim manicured fingers through her long blonde hair. Her complexion is clear and blemish free. Her hair is long and glossy. She is the picture of health except for her eyes. Red-rimmed and bloodshot, she looks as if sleep has evaded her for the longest time. Tears well up when she speaks again, her voice cracking, her face suddenly creased with anxiety.

'Fairbridge and Spencer, I mean. I'm a journalist and...'

Limbs watery with dread, I begin to walk away. She shakes her head, freeing the tears. They spill down her cheeks, dripping off her jaw. A torrent of them, as if they have been held in place for an age and now that the dam has burst the ensuing flow is unstoppable. 'I'm not here to get a story,' she says, biting at her lip in a bid to halt the flow. 'I'm here to tell one.'

25

THE HOUSE

It happened on a Friday evening once all the builders, plasterers and electricians had left, the house unusually quiet after all the hammering and drilling. It was as if Hallshead Farmhouse knew that something dreadful was about to occur, a sense of pre-mourning radiating from the stone walls and ancient flagstones in readiness for Eric's collapse. Penny was the first to hear the crash, her footfall a clap of thunder as she galloped downstairs to find her father splayed out on the kitchen floor, his face pale, lips tinged blue. It was her scream that alerted Connie, her daughter's elongated shriek bringing her running in from outside where she had been stacking up bags of debris and rubble, doing what she could to clear the house and make it habitable for the weekend ahead.

He was still breathing when Connie reached him, the rattle from his chest enough to rouse the dead. Her fingers traced a line over his collarbone and throat, checking for a pulse, hoping it was strong enough to keep going until the medics arrived. She needed that reassurance that her husband wasn't about to die. Her fingers pressed at his neck. She could feel movement. Just. The slight throb beneath his skin gave her hope. Her own heart constricted in her chest. At least he was still alive, that was something. At least he was still alive...

The ambulance arrived in record time which, considering their remote location, was another thing to be thankful for, thought Connie as she sat with him in the back, clutching his cold hand, praying to God over and over for her husband to be saved. It had been many years since she had recited anything remotely resembling a prayer, but she was surprised how quickly it all came back to her, the Catholic upbringing she'd once hated giving her a modicum of optimism and comfort. It was three days later when the second heart attack happened and despite all the medical interventions, the drips and machines that invaded his ailing body, despite her constant prayers and recitals and mantras that he would one day be well again, despite her pleas that she whispered into his ear for him to stay with her, Eric couldn't be saved. He passed away in the early hours one chilly dark day, a scattering of stars peeking in through the large picture window as if to guide him through the darkness and the silence to his final resting place.

The following couple of weeks passed in a blur with visits to the undertakers to make arrangements for Eric's funeral. Nobody could have made a better husband or father. That was the thought that was foremost in Connie's mind as she sat down and wrote his eulogy. He was one of the best and now he was gone. A man not afraid of solid graft. A man not afraid to love wholeheartedly.

Work in the house continued albeit at a slower pace. Connie's brain was too fogged up to think clearly, her mind too full of sadness to cope with all the noise and confusion. She was weary, unable to do anything other than grieve. The nights were the worst; those long lonely hours as she lay in bed alone, shrouded by the dimness, afraid to sleep for fear of what would enter her head; those hideous torturous dreams that fooled her into thinking Eric was still alive, only for her to wake after finally succumbing to the briefest of slumbers, crippled by sorrow, the room dark and silent. The bed cold, sheets still taut and uncreased. Eric was their lynchpin, their keystone, and now he was gone. Her family was broken, their lives in freefall with nobody around to catch them.

Penny was the one who seemed to be taking it badly, even worse than Connie, her behaviour suddenly unpredictable with entire days spent locked away in her room. If she was being honest, it had started before Eric's death, as if a switch had been flicked in Penny's brain, all the lights dulling her usual movements. Connie had begun to make headway with her daughter, their previously frayed connection restored, but then things took a downward turn and Eric's death only served to heighten Penny's propensity for finding despondency in her life. She and her father were alike in so many ways and Connie knew that the shock of Eric's passing had rocked her daughter's world, but it seemed that there was also something else. Something bigger that she couldn't put her finger on. Penny spoke little and smiled even less. Her once vibrant and assertive child carried a certain darkness within her, the weight of it most days pressing down on her shoulders, dragging every last drop of happiness out of her until there was nothing left but a husk of a girl where her daughter had once been.

Seeing Penny's emotional struggles was hard, but of all the things that she had to work through – the clinical preparations and completion of documents that needed to be tackled after the death of a loved one, as well as the loneliness – it was the anger that engulfed her. The thing that raged in her head day after day, a vat of bubbling oil that sizzled and spat, threatening to spill over at the slightest provocation. The visit from Douglas Fairbridge was the thing that unleashed it. He arrived uninvited and unannounced one day, letting himself in through their unlocked kitchen door and striding through as if he lived there.

'I've come to offer my condolences,' he said, handing over a card.

Connie was standing at the sink. She turned, startled by his presence. Her initial instincts were screaming at her to tell him to leave, to simply fuck off and never come back. But manners and decorum forced a whispered 'Thank you' out of her mouth as she snatched the card from his large fat fingers, thinking she would tear it into a thousand tiny pieces and throw it away once he had left.

'Early days yet,' he said, his eyebrows hitched up, mouth twisted into a sneer, 'but I suppose you'll be selling this place and moving elsewhere now you're a widow?'

Stopping the vat of hot oil from spilling over took every ounce of strength she had, but she managed it, opening the back door instead and standing silently, eyes averted to the large oak tree in the distance, its shadow casting a wide web-like shape over the sprawling landscape.

'I'll be in touch,' he said with a sigh, and he marched out, with Connie shouting a loud 'Fuck off!' before slamming the door behind him.

The idea came to her later that evening as she lay in bed, the initial rush of it a heady alien sensation that knocked her off balance, making her feel drunk and giddy. Maybe it was the grief that was doing it, or the unfamiliarity of the situation in which she found herself, but after much thought, she was certain it was the anger she felt at being crudely pushed out of her own home by that man. Her shabby, dilapidated, freezing, rundown home. She may have hated Hallshead Farmhouse but she was damned if she was going to let Douglas Fairbridge get his way.

She rolled over and for the first time in over a week, she slept soundly, her previously jumbled thoughts now as clear and as strong as tempered glass.

26

PENNY

Day 3

Sitting with her in my car might be a terrible mistake, but we're here now and she seems harmless. Credible. Desperate actually, as if the thing she is about to tell me has eaten away at most of her soul, leaving her empty and hollowed out.

She is slim, her clothes fashionable and expensive looking. I spot a Gucci handbag at her feet, and wonder how much it cost. Her nails are long and free of nail polish and she is wearing only the lightest applications of makeup. I guess her to be about the same age as me. Same anxious expression and an infinite unfathomable darkness in her eyes.

'I remember seeing you all those years ago,' she says, her voice breaking.

'Seeing me? Where?'

She shakes her head and closes her eyes briefly as if to reassemble her thoughts, to put everything in order in her head before releasing what she is about to say.

'I'll start at the beginning, but first, you're one of the jurors on that case, right?'

I nod, a solid rock forming in my windpipe, making it difficult to swallow or breathe. The bottle of water in the centre console of my car is days old and probably teeming with bacteria. It's stale and warm but I greedily take a glug, the tepid liquid soothing the dryness in my gullet. It smells of a forest, the scent of old leaves and decaying foliage catching at the back of my throat. I screw the lid on, place it in the console again and lean my head against the cold vinyl headrest, ready to listen.

'Being a journalist allows me access to certain places. I saw the listing and his name and waited outside. That's when I saw you as you came out. I recognised you straightaway. You haven't changed that much.'

A thrumming takes hold in my chest. If she has recognised me, then surely Cameron Fairbridge and Ivor Spencer will have too. She could report me. This whole case could collapse.

'Don't worry,' she says quickly, her voice interjecting my thoughts, 'he won't have recognised you just as he doesn't remember me either. We were nobody to him. Dirt on his shoes, that's all we were. Pieces of rubbish to be discarded once he was done with us.'

'Sorry,' I say, rubbing at my eyes, a wave of fatigue suddenly overwhelming me. 'I'm really confused here. Who—'

'Who am I?' She smiles, revealing a row of perfectly white teeth.

A smile that belies a certain amount of sadness simmering just below the surface of her thoughts. We seek each other out, us lost desperate souls, magnetised to one another like a deadweight being pulled to earth.

'Right,' she says wearily, a slight slump to her shoulders, 'I did say I would start at the beginning, so here it is. My name is Nora Wright. I lived in Coldstone as a kid. Grew up there. My mum owned the little grocery shop in the village.' She stops and takes a juddering breath. Her fingers drum on her knee, her leg jiggling up and down while she waits. I smile, hoping my easy manner and patience will help her to relax, let her know that she is safe here in my vehicle. I can't see inside her head and don't know this woman, but I have a strong sensation that I know her story and can guess what she is about to say.

'My mum was an item for a while with old man Fairbridge, but they had a big fallout. Let's just say he was unscrupulous and tried to close down my mum's shop. He was, and still is from what I can gather, a ruthless old bastard. But anyway, that's a story for another time.

'I saw you a few times around the village after you moved in. We didn't get many new faces around the place and everyone was watching to see what would happen to Hallshead Farmhouse.'

A pulse bounces around my neck. I try to look impassive and say nothing, waiting for the next part. The part of the story I feel sure I can predict before she has even spoken.

'The old man was furious when your family moved in. Saw it as his duty to oust you at any cost. And then once you started the building work it became apparent that you weren't going anywhere, and that just riled him even more.'

I wait, none of this new information to me. It's as clear in my head as it was when it happened all those years ago. It's the next part I want to hear. And it's coming, I can feel it, the vibration of her revelation. This is just the build-up. The background to a dark tale that I've waited almost all my adult life to hear.

'Anyway, I was there, in the house that day when you called over. Fairbridge Hall. I was there.'

I think back, remembering my gumption, the bravery and anger I felt after Douglas Fairbridge killed that poor lamb. How I marched over to their big house, ready to do battle, and ended up sitting beside Cameron Fairbridge, my pulse racing, his wealth and the splendour and opulence of the house making me feel clumsy and out of my depth. And then that noise. Followed by Fairbridge's obvious lie about his mother. Except it wasn't his mother. It was this lady sitting here next to me. Nora.

'You were upstairs,' I say, the effort of voicing that memory making me exhausted and woozy. Hearing my own thoughts being spoken out loud after all these years is like unleashing a captive beast, its legs and body slowly wriggling out as it sniffs the air for predators before slinking away, relieved to finally have been freed.

She nods, a lone tear spilling out of her eye and travelling down her cheek. She bats it away with an angry fist and shakes her head as if to ward off any incoming blows. I want to lean over, to stroke her hand and tell her that the worst is over, that it's all behind us, but I'm frozen, my spine rigid as I wait for the next part of Nora's account of that day.

'They asked me if I wanted to see the house with a view to getting a part-time cleaning job. I'd just turned sixteen and liked the idea of having some money. So I went along, as trusting as the day is long. Ivor Spencer was there when I arrived. He'd hung on to Cameron's shirttails all his life, eager to be seen as landed gentry when in truth he was just a stable lad, desperate to get in with the people who had all the money. Problem was, it worked. Ivor and Cameron became quite an item around the area, going everywhere together, Ivor suddenly developing a cut-glass accent as if he had been raised like royalty when in actual fact he had been born and raised on a smallholding a few miles away by working-class parents.

'Anyway, I was given a guided tour of the house, my eyes out on stalks when I saw how big and luxurious the place was. Obviously I'd seen it from the outside but wasn't prepared for the size and lavishness of those rooms, and I'll admit, I got a little scared at the idea of cleaning in there all on my own.'

She stops and takes a quivering breath before starting again.

'But as it turned out, I needn't have worried because it was all a stunt. A horrible hoax to get me inside that house. There was never a job on offer.'

Her tears are rolling freely now. I rummage in my bag and hand her a tissue, then move forward and place my hand on her shoulder, unsure what else I can do to comfort her. Even after all these years, the memory is still raw. As if what took place happened only yesterday.

'They took turns, one watching while the other one raped me. When I heard you talking downstairs I tried to scream but a piece of fabric was shoved in my mouth while Ivor Spencer's hands were pressed around my neck.'

The howl in my head reverberates off every inch of my skull, bouncing and thudding until it hurts, a dull pain forcing me to wince and close my eyes.

'You have to tell somebody,' I say, my statement barely more than a whisper. 'You need to go to the police or speak to one of the barristers and appear as a witness for the prosecution.'

'No!' A wild expression contorts her features, her pupils as dark as night. 'No, I can't do that. I have a job now, a different life. And besides, my mother still lives in Coldstone. The Fairbridge family would make her life hell if I testified in court and got him put away. She has cancer and only a short while left to live. I'd like however much time she has left to be peaceful. That was why I didn't say anything when it actually happened. I was threatened with all sorts of dreadful scenarios if I opened my mouth. They said they would make my mum bankrupt and repossess her shop. It was all she had. So I remained silent.'

'So why are you here now, speaking to me?'

She shrugs and dries her eyes. 'Me speaking to you about this is illegal. I could end up in court myself, but as a member of the jury, I implore you to find him guilty. I only approached you because I know that you also know him. And that is also a conflict of interest. What you're doing is wrong. Because you did recognise him, didn't you?'

I can't breathe. This is the moment when everything comes undone, my neat orderly little life unspooling right in front of me. Before I can reply, she speaks again, her voice more of a plea than a threat.

'You have to do this. Please do what you can. And you know why? Because not only is Cameron Fairbridge a dangerous sexual predator, but he and his father are also a pair of cold-blooded murderers. This is a chance to put at least one of them away for good.'

27

THE HOUSE

'No alcohol, young man. I mean it.' Connie's voice rang around the room as Aaron hitched his haversack over his shoulders and strode from the kitchen into the hallway.

He turned, a hunk of dark hair hanging over one eye, his glare still evident from beneath his dark lashes.

'Yeah, whatever. Not like Dicko's parents are gonna be handing out gin and beer, is it?'

'Yeah, not like you two are not going to go hunting for it after they go to bed either. Just be careful is all I'm saying.'

The slam of the door confirmed Aaron's exit from the house, the two-mile walk to Paul Dickenson's house over fields and stiles just long enough for him to work the anger out of his system. Like Connie, since Eric's death, her son was a bubbling cauldron of fury. Getting out of the house would do him good, allow him some freedom and space to simply be himself. He could mourn properly later, when all of this was over, thought his mother as she swept the floor and tidied dishes in the vain hope of keeping herself busy, stopping her mind from straying to places she would rather not visit. Later she would sit and plan, get it just right. Because it had to be just right. No room for error. Douglas Fairbridge would soon discover exactly who and what he was dealing with. If he was thinking that she would prove to be a pushover, then he had better think again because Connie could dig deep when it came to keeping what was hers. She would sooner raze the place to the ground than hand it over to that hideous old shyster. She had reached a tipping point and woe betide anyone who was stupid enough to come along and give her that final fatal push.

'I think I'm going to sleep in the room next to yours tonight,' she said to Penny later that evening as they got ready for bed. 'With Aaron staying out, I don't like the idea of being stuck right at the other end of the house on my own.'

Penny shrugged, her expression blank, as if her mother hadn't actually spoken. That was something else she would need to sort at some point – her daughter's sullen moods and lack of interaction with the rest of the world in general. Something was definitely awry. But for now, she had enough on her mind. One thing at a time, was the thought that ran through her head as she climbed the stairs and turned off all the lights. One shitty problem at a time.

***

When it came down to it, Connie simply couldn't do it. She had had to wait almost two hours until she was certain Penny was asleep, having dozed off herself a few times, before heading back downstairs and out towards the unoccupied part of the house. Nobody would be injured. She thought she had it all worked out as she squatted there, petrol can in hand, matches at the ready, but it transpired that she didn't. It was too destructive. Too final an act. Just too damn terrifying to complete. It all seemed too easy and effortless in her head – strike the match, dash upstairs, grab Penny out of her bed and then head outside and wait while the fire took hold. But in the end, common sense won over, the haze of anger that had tightened around her flaking and crumbling away, like the decades-old paint that adorned the walls of Hallshead Farmhouse.

She left the can of fluid by the back door of the old lean-to and slipped the matches into her pocket, then headed back inside, the cold chill of the air biting at her exposed flesh. She would get up and move the petrol at first light, put it back in the barn. It was a stupid, dangerous idea to strike that match and she was ashamed for ever entertaining such thoughts.

Her head ached as she clambered back beneath the sheets, glad of the comfort. Glad that stupidity hadn't taken over completely and that she and her daughter were now safe in their beds.

* * *

He waited until he was sure she was sleeping. Not worth taking any chances. Not worth getting caught. Mind you, it would be his word against hers and he would win. She should have learned that lesson already. If she didn't know it by now, then she was about to have a rude awakening. Besides, it was her own fault. Fancy leaving a petrol can on the floor like that. Careless. The lid on the petrol container was loose. Another sloppy mistake. Proof that she was not his equal. A weak opponent, that was what she was. Weak and hapless. And about to lose her house.

He pulled his scarf tighter around his neck. The nights were closing in, cool air nipping at his flesh. Two hours he had been out here for. A lucky stroll, that was all it was, the hoots and screeches of the owls perched in the treetops of the sycamore tree waking him. That was when he spotted her, pacing and lurking. So he slid behind a tree and watched, amused when he saw what she had planned.

If I can't have it, nobody can.

He had met her type before, people whose thoughts centred around such a juvenile premise. A kneejerk reaction to his demands, that was all it was, but like most cowards, she was unable to see it through to the end. All he was doing by stepping in was helping, giving her that extra push when cowardice had forced her back inside. He was doing the old girl a favour, finishing the job for her.

Douglas Fairbridge bent down on his haunches, delight rippling through him when his fingers landed on a small heater that was stashed away beneath a pile of paint-splattered sheets. Fingerprints of plaster dust caked the exterior casing that he wiped away. She had even left the door of the old lean-to open and unsecured. Not that it would have mattered if she had locked it; the panes of glass were broken, the whole area easily accessed by anybody wishing to do harm.

It was all so effortless, so frighteningly easy, and at the same time, so damn rewarding. He didn't even need to knock the can over, to spill that wonderfully flammable liquid. Plugging in the heater and placing the sheets over the top would be enough. Once they caught on, the can would be close enough to add the finishing touches. And then he could stand back and watch as the fire took hold, before running back to the safety of his home at the top of the hill. He wasn't a complete monster though. Once inside, he would put his clothes away and change back into his pyjamas before calling the emergency services, the orange sky and the sound of shattering panes of glass dragging him out of his deep slumber. After all, he didn't want anybody to die; all he wanted was what was rightfully his. That said, if they died then they died. He wasn't God. He was just an ordinary man doing what he could to make sure his legacy and property was handed down to his children and their children. He was a Fairbridge after all, and standards and wealth had to be maintained at all costs.

* * *

Penny was dreaming about drowning, her lungs slowly filling with fluid as she gasped for breath. Somebody was pushing her underwater, their strong hands pressing down on the top of her skull, fingers entangled with her hair. Her head swam, her chest ballooned as, limbs flailing, she gasped and struggled and fought for breath.

Her spine clicked, her neck thudded; a deep pulse banged in her ears as she sat up in bed, eyes snapping open, the dream so real she could hardly breathe. There was darkness, but also something else. Something dry and acrid.

Smoke.

She could smell smoke, a trail of it filling her nostrils, clinging to her hair and nightclothes. Sticking to the back of her throat. Her movements rapid, she flew out of bed and flicked on the light, shrieking when she spotted the thin film of grey mist that was leaking under the thin line of light at the bottom of her bedroom door, grey tendrils of terror beckoning to be let in.

Opening the door would invite the fire in. Penny had seen it in films on the TV, and yet it was the only way out. She had no choice but to swing it open and run out into the hot grey mist with her sleeve over her mouth, eyes stinging, snot streaming.

She couldn't see any flames, just a pall of smoke that choked her, filling her airways. Impeding her ability to breathe properly, to think clearly. Legs trembling, she ran down the stairs and into the hallway before stopping and turning, suddenly remembering about Aaron and her mother. Panic had gripped her, her sense of self-preservation so strong, she had forgotten about them. She turned, her voice hoarse and powerless, its pitch drowned out by the roar of the flames as she screamed at Aaron to get up, for her mother to get out of bed and leave the house. Aaron's room was at the other end of the building. He probably wouldn't hear her but her mother was sleeping in the room next to hers, so where was she? Were they even still in their rooms? Or were they both standing outside, waiting for her in the darkness? Willing her to appear out of the burning wreck of a structure that was once their home and the home of her grandparents and great-grandparents.

'He's not here, remember?' Connie's voice came from somewhere behind her, the thick smoke impairing Penny's vision. 'He stayed out at his friend's house last night. Come on. We need to get out quickly!'

'No! Mum...'

Before she could say anything else about her brother being in the house, about how she had heard him stumble in and climb the stairs in the early hours, a barking cough erupted out of her throat. She stopped, her body bent over to try and catch her breath while her mother's hand pulled at hers. She could feel Connie's strong fingers as they wrapped around her forearm, propelling her forwards and dragging her out into the chill of the night. She resisted and gasped, unable to speak as she gulped in blasts of cold air, the iciness of it a welcome reprieve from the smoke while they staggered out of the door and onto the coarsely gravelled driveway. And then a sound from somewhere inside. A scream. An unearthly hollering that stilled Penny's blood. Her heart crashed around her chest as Aaron appeared at his bedroom window, flinging it open and leaning out, his shrieks cutting through the unearthly howl of the flames.

'Oh dear God!' The fingers that were clutching her arm loosened, her mother falling to the floor, knees hitting the ground with a sharp crack. 'Aaron. *Aaron!*'

'He came home late last night,' Penny shouted, despair and terror choking her. 'I tried to tell you. I heard him, Mum. I was still awake and got up to go to the bathroom when he came home. He's still in the house!'

More shattering of glass, the relentless pounding of flames that lit up the night sky. Then an ear-splitting scream that tore at her nerve endings and turned her insides to liquid as her brother came running out of Hallshead Farmhouse, arms pumping, a halo of orange blazing at the back of his head.

Penny ran at him, her own screams merging with his piercing cries for help. Instincts taking over, she pushed him to the ground, rolling him over and over onto the damp grass, doing what she could to put out the fire that blazed at the back of his head. Snot and tears streaked her face, a razorblade sliced at her throat when she tried to call out his name. Arms stretched, she ripped off her nightshirt and wrapped it around his head, batting at his face and hair until the flames eventually died down, leaving Aaron with patches of blackened raw skin that despite the chill and darkness of the night, despite her tears and stinging eyes, she could see as they lay slumped amidst the ruins of their house, would never properly heal.

Images punctured her brain, a brief glimpse into the future; her brother, alone, frightened and despondent, visions of him, a solitary figure walking through life unaccompanied. Sweat and a flood of salty tears mingled on her face, streaking over her cheeks and down her neck. In the distance, sirens wailed, a flash of blue visible in her peripheral vision. Beside her, her mother sobbed, rocking back and forth on her knees, blackened hands covering her face. This was it, thought Penny, her brain in overdrive, synapses firing off in all directions. They had hit rock bottom, their lives were in freefall. This was as bad as it would ever get. Threats, rape, heart attacks and death. Their home burning as they sat, helpless, unable to do anything except watch in horror while a wall of flames engulfed all that they owned. It was the end of everything as they knew it.

28

PENNY

Day 4

Sleep was fitful last night. Nora's words, her story, which almost mirrored mine, stayed in my head, bouncing around hour after hour. In the end I got up, too wide awake and too confused to sleep. Too tired to think straight. I made a cup of tea, sitting and sipping at it as I tried to go over everything in my mind. And now, only three hours later after just sixty minutes of undisturbed slumber, I am up and dressed and on my way to court for the judge's final summing up.

Cold-blooded murderers.

That was the phrase she used. I suspected she meant the fire at Hallshead Farmhouse and the attempts of the Fairbridges to oust us. It was never proven but deep down I had my suspicions. I think we all did. But that wasn't it at all. Nora was referring to an entirely different event, one that took place before we even moved in.

The death of my grandparents and my uncle.

'Your Uncle Sam was the most careful driver I have ever seen. There is no way he would hit that stone bridge and then drive into the water, no matter how high the river or how bad the weather was. As soon as we heard about it, we all said the same thing, that the Fairbridges had driven him off the road and into the water. There had been an altercation with Douglas Fairbridge a few days prior, so the timing was right. Your grandparents didn't usually let anything that grotesque guy said upset them, but from what we heard, it was a particularly nasty argument with Fairbridge threatening them with all kinds of trouble if they didn't agree to hand over the farmhouse.'

My heart freezes in my chest every time I think about it. Could it really be possible that the Fairbridges would do such a thing? I knew they were terrible people, but murder? It was a difficult notion for me to digest yesterday and even more so now, in the cold light of day. My befuddled sleep-deprived brain is struggling to comprehend them plummeting to such depths. Depravity and corruption yes, but murder? And then I think back to the blaze at Hallshead Farmhouse and how my first thoughts were given to Douglas and Cameron Fairbridge, wondering what lengths they would go to in order to get their hands on that place. Which, in the end, was exactly what they did. Mum sold it at a bargain price. Even Douglas Fairbridge knew that he couldn't simply take it from us, that a half-decent price had to be paid. So maybe Nora is right after all. Maybe the accident at the stone bridge wasn't an accident at all but foul play, although how it can be proven after all these years is anybody's guess. Maybe it can't and we will all go to our graves never knowing what really happened that awful afternoon when the river broke its banks and my uncle and grandparents tragically lost their lives in the watery aftermath.

I park up and head to the court, my walk brisk and efficient. Soon this will all be over. My physical presence in the court will be a dim and distant memory, but Douglas and Cameron Fairbridge will always be active in my head, what they did to me and my family an intense memory that will never diminish. I plan on working hard to push all thoughts of them away, not let them ruin the rest of my life, but they will never fade away completely. The scars caused by their wrongdoing will always remain.

It's a bright day, the wind bracing, the sky blue. I hope it's a portent of what's to come. Clear skies ahead once Cameron Fairbridge is found guilty and sentenced to a long spell in prison.

I'm still smiling as I stride into the waiting area, the sense of relief that this week is almost over a palpable force that expands deep in my abdomen, spreading through my veins, growing and blossoming like espaliered trees about to bear fruit. Green shoots of hope where there used to be tracts of desiccated barren land.

'Morning, Penny.' Cheryl appears out of nowhere, walking alongside me, grinning manically.

'Morning, Cheryl.' I try to appear bright and cheery but the sound of her voice has already poured cold water over my hopes and desires.

'So, just the judge's summing up to go and then we're all thrown together in that deliberation room. Exciting stuff, eh?'

I'm not a violent person, but I can't shake away the image that has implanted itself in my thoughts; an image of my fist as it slams into her face, then me smiling as she falls to the floor, blood-spattered and broken.

'Well, I'll be glad to leave this place and get on with my job next week, that's for sure.'

Cheryl shakes her head as if I am speaking a different language. She gives me a small wave and slinks away, her eyes scanning the small crowd for allies and those whose ears are closed to the truth.

This battle is going to be a long one. I'm going to have to dig deep and remain patient to try and win them round, but it's a battle I'm prepared to fight because good must always triumph over bad, no matter how small or seemingly insignificant the wrongdoing. If we as a society let the trivial things slide, it creates a gap wide enough for the larger misdemeanours to crawl in. Cameron Fairbridge thinks he is halfway through that gap. I will do what I can to make sure he doesn't make it to the other side.

We are called in first, our little huddle trudging down that long corridor to the courtroom like a line of ants. One more day and this will all be over. One more day and Fairbridge could be handcuffed and led into a police van and on his way to prison. My heart thuds at the thought of it, a tiny pulse of excitement at finally exacting revenge after all these years, thumping away in my neck.

The summing up is a long laborious event, the judge's words having a soporific effect on almost everyone present. Four days' worth of questions, statements and activity condensed into one long speech that even I, somebody who has everything invested in this case, am struggling to absorb.

We are told as he finishes that, for legal reasons he is unable to divulge, we must reach a unanimous verdict. I wince. This makes my job much more difficult. I have to convince eleven people that Cameron Fairbridge is a monster and I have to do that with only the flimsiest of evidence. I need to convince them that he is guilty of the rape of Melanie Albright. I say her name over and over in my head. I want her to know that I am on her side, that I have been with her throughout this whole trial, throughout every nightmare and every sleepless night she has had since the attack took place. Once upon a time, I was her. Still am in many ways. Despite trying to shed that time in my life, to stop being that scared young girl from Hallshead Farmhouse, she is still there, bubbling up to the surface, gasping for air. Praying Cameron Fairbridge receives his punishment for what he did to us. All of us. Me, Melanie, Nora and possibly countless others, all of them too frightened and in awe of his wealth and status to lodge any formal complaints.

We break for lunch and are shown the deliberation room where tomorrow we will sit and ponder over the evidence. It's an average-sized room with tea and coffee-making facilities and a small restroom next door. Once we are in there, we are not allowed to leave. It all sounds very formal and official, more so than the actual courtroom. Then we are dismissed and told to be back here for 9 a.m. tomorrow morning.

I leave feeling deflated and somewhat dazed. I take the route to the car park alone, relieved of the silence. Relieved to have some space to clear my head and prepare for tomorrow. It's what I have been waiting for. My stomach lurches at the thought of it. It's finally here and now I wish it wasn't.

I drive home, a sense of dread interspersed with flecks of exhilaration at the thought of what lies ahead.

* * *

A cool welcome silence greets me as I enter the house. I close the door with a quiet click and lock it, a reflex action that is the result of those short few months that we lived at Hallshead Farmhouse. Damien is in his office working and Freda is curled up in her basket.

The kettle hisses as it boils. I make us both a cup of coffee and take Damien's through to his study, knocking before entering in case he is busy in a meeting.

In the quiet of the room, the low squeak of his chair as he turns to smile at me, gives me a warm glow. It's the small things, the commonplace everyday things that I love. Things that are as familiar to me as my own skin. Things that mean I am home and I am safe.

'Nearly over. Just one more day,' he says as he takes the mug from me and sips at the steaming liquid.

My smile feels forced when I reply. 'Yes. It'll be good to be back to normal next week. How's Mum been?'

'She was asleep on the sofa last time I checked. That was an hour or so ago so she might be up by now.'

'I'll go and see her,' I say, backing out of the door and closing it with a muffled click.

Damien has an important project on the go and the deadlines are tight. I know he needs the space and the time to complete everything so I leave him alone for the rest of the day.

Mum is in good spirits, pottering around the kitchen when I arrive. I should feel buoyant and yet my insides are shrivelled into a tight knot.

'Now then,' she says when I sidle up next to her. 'Where have you been all glammed up in your high heels and tight clothes, eh?'

I glance down at my block-heeled court shoes and plain blue trousers, and laugh.

'I've been to the courts, Mum. Remember I told you I was doing jury service this week?'

She tuts and takes a clean mug out of the cupboard before washing it and putting it back. I leave her to do it. It makes her happy and I am in no mood to disrupt the moment. She continues to wash clean crockery, rinsing them one by one in the sink before drying her hands and turning to face me.

'There we are. All nice and clean now. Jury service you say? Tell you who's a bloody criminal and should be locked up – that Fairbridge man.'

My blood turns to sand. My face and limbs freeze. I'm made of solid stone, unable to move.

'What was his name again, Penny? Can you remember him? Came here once a few days ago all brassy and bold, thinking he was the big man.' She taps her finger against the worktop, the noise a deep thud in my ears. 'Desmond! That was it. Desmond Fairley.'

A pain shoots across my head, stopping behind my eyes. I can't decide whether I should correct her or change the subject. Already she is losing the thread, humming a tune and dancing around the kitchen like a child. What could possibly be gained from such a move?

'Douglas Fairbridge,' I say quietly. 'That was his name. And his son raped me.'

More singing and dancing, and then, 'I'm hungry. Can I have something to eat?'

It's as if I haven't even spoken, that period of our lives lost to her. Except of course it isn't, her mention of him proving that it's all still in there somewhere, but is it really worth teasing it out of her poor befuddled brain? There's nothing to be gained from it. All it will do if she does remember is bring heartache and anguish.

'What would you like, Mum? A cheese and ham sandwich okay?'

She smiles and clasps my hand, her cool fingers wrapped around mine, transporting me back to a time when the world held such promise. A time when we lived in our old home in Nunthorpe and my father was still alive. A time when my mother wasn't suffering with dementia and my brother wasn't a tormented drug addict. Hallshead Farmhouse ended up being the undoing of us. Our lives unspooled the minute we walked through that door. Tomorrow is when that all comes to an end, when I turn all that destruction and terror around and show the Fairbridges what we really think of them. What I can do when I am given enough power and the opportunity to wield it.

29

THE HOUSE

It was there always, the fear that she had somehow accidentally lit that match without realising, the fear that the police and fire service had got it wrong and it was all her fault. Aaron spent three weeks in hospital, bandages covering his head. Her son. Her lovely, damaged son, his skin burnt, his eyes full of fear. He would never be the same again. Various ongoing skin grafts did little to improve his appearance or dull the pain. The memory of that night would stay with them forever.

She never told anybody about her initial plans, too ashamed to discuss them with anyone. Too ashamed to even give them room in her own head. It was a moment of madness. She blamed the grief, the loneliness, the sheer weight of responsibility that was suddenly placed on her shoulders after Eric's death. But most of all, she blamed Douglas Fairbridge for adding to that strain, for his threats and instilling fear into her, making her think he had the power to evict her from her own home. She may not have wanted to be at Hallshead Farmhouse with its ancient fixtures and fittings, but it was all she had. To take that from her when she had recently been widowed would have proved a step too far. Douglas Fairbridge pushed her over a cliff edge, one she had been clinging on to, the perilous drop beneath too terrifying to consider, but still, she had managed to clamber back up before that final plunge.

They moved into a hotel while the insurance company assessed the damage. Douglas Fairbridge put in an offer and rather than add to their stresses, she accepted it, buying a smaller modern house close to where they used to live. It was easier for Aaron and Penny and it was easier for her. Surrounded by friends she could rely on, they lived there in relative happiness. As happy as any damaged, injured family could ever be.

Aaron and Penny had regular nightmares, waking up drenched in sweat while she comforted them, sitting by their bedsides until they fell back to sleep, their usual teenage resistance to acts of comfort and reassurance noticeably absent. She needed the closeness and warmth of their embraces as much as they needed hers.

They rarely spoke of Hallshead Farmhouse, each of them busy trying to forge a new life for themselves. But it never left, often rattling around in the back of Connie's mind, creeping up on her when she least expected it.

She could have sworn she once saw the Fairbridges, both the father and the son when she was shopping in Northallerton one day, their dark hair and old-fashioned tweed clothing marking them out as different among the crowd of shoppers. She tried to follow them, weaving through the hordes of people, but by the time she managed to push her way through to the front of the throng, they had disappeared. Just as well. She had no idea what she would have said, how she would face the man who did his utmost to ruin her life.

Gossips in Coldstone had spoken to her after the fire, tongues clacking about how it was the Fairbridges who had run Sam and her in-laws off the road, desperate to get their hands on Hallshead Farmhouse. Connie thought it was possibly true but was too exhausted by everything that had happened to take it any further. With no hard evidence, what options did she have? She did what Eric would have wanted her to do and simply got on with her life as best she could, caring for her children and keeping a roof over their heads. Douglas Fairbridge had to live with himself. If he had a conscience then she hoped it would prick him for the rest of his days. She hoped he tossed and turned at night, terrified that one day the police would turn up on his doorstep and charge him with murder. Connie firmly believed that justice and truth had a way of rising to the surface. She only hoped she was around to see it when it happened.

30

PENNY

Day 5

There is a fan in the corner of the room blowing a trickle of cool air our way. The collective heat from twelve agitated bodies has raised the ambient temperature, making everyone restless. Bob reaches down and turns up the switch, the constant low drone a welcome reprieve from the voices that have been ringing around the place. We have only been in here for an hour and already tempers are frayed.

'Let's look at the evidence again,' says a lady I vaguely recognise. She has been quiet throughout the whole thing and yet has suddenly sprung to life in the last few minutes, her words cutting through the sound of the others who are all chatting and vying for attention. 'The judge said we had to be absolutely sure that the defendant *knew* that consent hadn't been given. This is a really tricky one to work through.'

'Not for me it isn't,' says Lisa, the timbre of her voice doing little to disguise her contempt for the victim. 'He's innocent. She went there knowing what was going to happen. They had been kissing the night before at the party. Don't tell me she went there all sparkly-eyed and brimming with innocence. She is fifteen going on fifty. A proper little madam.'

I lower my gaze, worried my anger will tumble out. My contempt for her is evident in my expression every time I glance her way. I am trying to temper it and remain impassive but it's difficult when I'm surrounded with this level of ignorance and incompetence.

'Right,' says Bob. 'Let's not use gut instinct. We need to look for concrete evidence. We have to think about what has been said, and although it's tempting to jump to conclusions, we really shouldn't. People's lives are at stake here. We have to be meticulous and thoughtful. No room for error.'

I hide my smile, relief rippling through me. I say a silent thank you in my head. Now we can proceed properly with Bob at the helm guiding us.

'I'm with Lisa,' says Cheryl. 'We don't actually have any hard evidence so we're having to rely on gut instinct. And my gut instinct is telling me that she is lying.'

'What if he's the liar?' The deep voice takes me by surprise. The burly guy with tattoos is speaking. He is leaning forward, his arms resting on his thighs. 'What if, and hear me out here,' he says, glancing at each of us in turn, 'she had been groomed?'

A groan takes hold, spreading around the room like a Mexican wave. Burly tattoo guy and I catch one another's eye and surreptitiously shake our heads. This is an impossible task. We are fighting against an unstoppable tide of animosity and naivety. His idea is dismissed with sighs and objections. He sits back, shaking his head, a look of defeat creasing his face and darkening his eyes.

The next hour is spent debating, going over the evidence, or the lack of it, and we end up back where we started.

'If he did place his hands around her neck, why were there hardly any bruises?' says Lisa. 'I mean, come on! It's all a bit easy for her, isn't it? She sleeps with an older man, it all gets a bit rough and then she panics and cries rape. There is quite literally no evidence to convict him.'

'Yes,' replies Cheryl. 'And what about her attitude on that interview we watched? She was downright surly, as if she couldn't care less. What sort of young woman would act like that after they had been raped?'

'A frightened, angry one,' I say, my voice going up an octave to be heard above the hubbub.

'And with the greatest respect, how would you know?' she replies, her lip curled into a sneer.

'Because I was once her. I was raped at a young age. I know *exactly* what it feels like and can totally understand where she is coming from, why she appeared surly and petulant when she was asked questions about something that was so traumatic, so horribly life changing, it tears you apart.'

The room closes in around me, the ensuing silence deafening. My gaze sweeps around the group, everyone's mouths puckered as if all the air has been sucked out of the room. Their eyes are lowered, each of them looking at the floor, the walls, looking at everything and everyone except me. I've said it now. It's out there. There's no going back, no unsaying it. I hope it makes them think, stops them from being so judgemental towards that young woman. Melanie Albright. I say her name over and over in my head. She deserves that much, and more. She deserves to not be spoken about with such contempt by a group of strangers. Her name dragged through the mud when she isn't here to defend herself.

Bob breaks the silence, his voice a force to be reckoned with as he glances at each of them in turn. We are all seated in upright wooden chairs with a desk in front of us, the papers we have been given stacked on top.

'Let's go through the guidance the judge gave us. That's the only way I can see to break this deadlock.'

'Before we do that,' Lisa says, confidence and irritation oozing from her, 'why don't we have an initial vote to see who thinks he's guilty?'

I do nothing. At least half a dozen people nod. My words have been ignored, my heartfelt admission that I spent all night rehearsing has been torn up and scattered to the four winds.

'Okay,' she says triumphantly. 'Raise your hand if you think he is not guilty.'

Bob and I glance at one another, our eyes locking briefly before we look away and stare down at our desks. I eventually glance up and count nine hands raised. Only me, the tattoo guy and Bob have voted against.

'Well,' says Cheryl, 'Houston, it looks like we have a problem.'

A few titters. I make a point of doing nothing, saying nothing, my features fixed in place by annoyance and fear. Icy fingers clutch at my heart.

'The judge said we need to be unanimous,' says Cheryl as she nibbles at a fingernail.

I feel the heat of everyone's stares as their eyes bore into me and Bob and the tattoo guy. We are the difficult ones, the people who refuse to go along with the majority. I want to stand up and yell that being in the majority doesn't necessarily make the rest of them right. The hardest path is often the coldest and longest route of them all. Especially if you're travelling it alone.

'We could be here forever at this rate,' says the older lady who sat next to me throughout the trial. 'I'm looking after my grandchildren next week. We can't be here till then.'

I feel the desperation leaking from her. We all want to go home but we need to do the right thing and not let a guilty man walk free.

'Better to free a guilty person than to imprison an innocent one.' The voice comes from the other side of the room. 'If there isn't any evidence then we have to let him go.'

'Except we can't because we need to have a unanimous vote!' Lisa's voice is dangerously close to a shriek.

'Well, if we can—'

The door swings open and the lady who showed us into the room stands there, her head cocked to one side. 'I've been sent to ask if you have reached a unanimous verdict yet? And also to tell you that you need to elect a spokesperson. Somebody who can take charge and isn't afraid to stand up and read out the verdict.'

'Bob?' I say enthusiastically. 'How do you feel about doing it?'

A few murmurs from around the room. Then Cheryl pipes up. 'I don't mind doing it?'

Bob sits quietly while the other jurors agree to let her take charge. It feels like a reversal of hierarchy, as if the animals are suddenly running the zoo.

'We haven't reached a unanimous verdict yet,' Cheryl barks, her new role clearly very important to her, 'but we're working on it.'

'I'll just go and let the judge know that you haven't decided yet,' the woman says and disappears, returning just a few seconds later.

'The judge would like you all to return to the courtroom for a few moments.'

I wonder what wrongdoing we are about to be accused of and am surprised when we are gathered back inside to hear him tell us that the rules have changed.

'For reasons I am unable to divulge, I can now inform you that a unanimous verdict is no longer necessary. We can proceed with a verdict of ten votes to two.'

We head back to the deliberation room, the footfall of the other jurors light and airy, mine heavy and full of dread. I've lost. I have blown the only chance I had to punish Cameron Fairbridge for what he did to me. I am a failure. Discontent rumbles in my gut.

We spend the next hour going round in circles, discussing how the evidence simply isn't there to convict, even Bob edging towards finding him not guilty. The words I want to say dance about on the tip of my tongue. Forbidden words that could see me prosecuted if voiced out loud. Words about how he is a serial rapist, how he has no conscience and will continue to attack other females if he isn't brought to justice.

I pitch in, giving it my final shot. I either say what I need to say now or keep the guilt of doing nothing tucked deep inside my soul for the remainder of my days. 'What if Melanie Albright was too nervous to say anything? What if she froze? Are we honestly saying here that a frightened young woman deserves to be raped and the attacker will get away with it because she was too scared to say or do anything? Too fucking intimidated and terrified to move or say *no*? Are we saying that even if she shouts at him to stop and he doesn't hear her, then everything is okay? Because it isn't okay. It is *far* from okay. What was she supposed to do – scream at him until he got the message that she didn't want him to attack her? Are we saying that it is up to the victim to make sure he knew she hadn't consented? Because if the law states that that is the case then quite frankly, the law is an ass!'

A sea of shocked faces stare at me. My heart bashes against my ribs. I am so very close to revealing the truth about Cameron Fairbridge. So close to telling them about my ordeal and the ordeal of Nora Wright. But I don't. I am not stupid enough to implicate myself and not cruel enough to implicate poor Nora, who was brave enough to approach me and open up about what happened to her when she was no more than a child. The best I can hope for is that she makes an historical accusation and gets him back in the dock along with Ivor Spencer, and makes a better job of convincing the jury of his guilt than I have. But she will have to do it alone, because after sitting as part of this jury, I cannot do it. I know now that I've given this thing everything I've got. My offerings and interjections may not have amounted to much, but most of these people had already made up their minds before we even got to this point. And I'm tired. Aside from cracking open my ribs and holding aloft my beating damaged heart, I have done everything I can. I have revealed more to these strangers about my past than I have to my own husband, and I am now at an end with it all. With *them* all. This group of individuals with their preconceived notions and skewed judgements can all go to hell.

'And what about those bruises on her neck? He actually admitted that he was rough with her! Do they not count for anything?'

I have no idea why I am still trying to convince them of his guilt. Their shocked expressions have now morphed into something less malleable – anger and impatience. I'm keeping them from their families, their jobs, their homes. Those things are more important than the truth. More important than making sure Cameron Fairbridge is punished for what he did to Melanie Albright.

The vibration inside my skull as I shake my head makes me dizzy. I bite at my lip and half turn away to display my disgust.

'I say we have one more vote,' says Lisa, her voice a whisper, her breathing a shallow rasp. 'Otherwise we're going to be here all day and the rest of next week if we don't get a bloody move on.'

'And like I said,' the older woman pitches in, 'I can't be here next week. I've got my grandchildren to look after. I can't let my daughter down. She's already struggled this week with me being stuck here.'

I want to scream at her that I don't give a flying fuck about her daughter and her stupid grandchildren, that this is important and if we don't do this properly and send him away for a very long time, he will rape again and again and again because it's what he does. What he is. It is etched deep into his DNA, carved into the very essence of his character like his eye colour and the cut of his jaw. But I don't. Because there seems little point. These people weren't moved by my own revelation. What chance do I have of changing the course of this decision if I can't puncture the tough veneer of these heartless ignorant people? I hate myself for giving up so readily but what choice do I have? I lower my head and watch as ten people raise their hands when asked if they think he is not guilty while me and tattoo guy sit half slumped in our chairs. Bob too. Even he has let me down, turning his back on me and siding with the others.

Cheryl stands and knocks on the door, smiling broadly like an overexcited child at the chance of taking centre stage. The woman peers in, her head curling around the door jamb, her expression eager and relieved. She also wants this thing to be over. At the end of the day, all everyone ever wants is to go home. Truth and justice apparently pale into insignificance beside comfort and routine.

'We've got our verdict,' Cheryl announces triumphantly as she stands up and clutches the piece of paper in her hand. This is her moment of glory. Her time to shine. She is light-headed at the prospect of all eyes in the courtroom being focused on her as she tells the judge that Cameron Fairbridge has been found not guilty and is free to go home.

31

PENNY

Day 5

I watch him leave the dock, the usual sparkle gleaming in his eye. That monster has got away with it. Again. So fucking arrogant. That's all I can think as we leave the courtroom and head back to the main waiting area. He is a haughty, odious man who isn't capable of compassion or contrition. A sense of gloom hangs over me. The other jurors are delighted. They can all leave this place having done their civic duty. I wish I could start the week all over again, be more persuasive and dynamic, but it's too late now. Cameron Fairbridge is free to do whatever he wants. The not guilty verdict will embolden him. He will be even more daring, take greater risks. He believes that nobody can stop him. And the problem is – he is right. I know of three attacks on vulnerable females that he committed. How many more are there that haven't been reported? Part of me is glad I never had children. I wouldn't want any daughter of mine having to live in a world with the likes of Fairbridge and Spencer in it. Their particular brand of toxic masculinity is something that is hard to avoid.

'Penny?' I hear Bob's voice behind me as I shrug on my coat and head for the door.

I don't slow down. If he wants a conversation, he will have to catch up. I'm not in the mood for idle chit-chat and polite exchanges.

'I'm really sorry to hear what you went through when you were younger. It must have been traumatic.' He is striding alongside me, his face angled towards mine.

'You could say that,' I murmur, tears welling up in my eyes.

I blink them away, refusing to allow Cameron Fairbridge to continue ruining my life. Enough is enough. I have my husband and my mother. And Freda, my dog. I have more than he will ever have. The Fairbridges of the world don't understand what true love feels like. They are lonely creatures, constantly prowling, searching for prey. I actually pity them. They die never knowing how it feels to have a loving family around them. We all depart this world alone but some of us have people we care about with us at the end. He will have nobody. He will gasp his last in an empty room, and that is what will get me through this difficult time. Knowing he will never experience true tenderness.

'Take care, Penny. I just wish we could have come to a different conclusion but sometimes the law works against the innocent while the guilty walk free.'

And with that he is gone, walking off in the opposite direction, a mere speck in the distance. I stand and watch until he rounds the corner and vanishes out of sight.

* * *

She is standing next to my car when I get there, her eyes downcast as she scans her phone.

'I take it you're waiting for me?' My voice is brusque. Harsh and unwelcoming even.

I can't help it. I'm tired, my mood is low and I fear I am about to take a verbal battering for not persuading the other jurors to convict him. As a journalist, she will already know the result.

'He's free.'

'He's free,' I reply, my voice sore, my pitch and modulation weak and gravelly.

'Well, I don't suppose you could get them all on board. Only a tiny percentage of rape cases ever make it to court and out of that tiny percentage even fewer are found guilty. You were fighting a losing battle from the start, but it was worth a try.'

She slips her phone into her pocket and stares at me.

'So now what?' I say, feeling suddenly clumsy and inept.

'Now you get to go home and relax. Spend time with your family. Forget about this whole sordid business.'

I sigh and chew at a loose nail. 'I'm not sure I can. Forget about it, that is.'

'So what are you going to do? If it's retribution you've got planned, remember he has high-powered friends. Cameron Fairbridge always comes out on top. It's just how it is – how *he* is. The Fairbridges are used to winning.'

In truth, I have no idea what I'm going to do, but doing nothing feels wrong. Limp and weak-willed. Right now he will be driving back to Hallshead Farmhouse feeling victorious and untouchable. And that's because he is. Frustration is like a flamethrower in my head, scorching my cranium, making me itchy and restless.

'Not sure. I need time to think. I might go there tonight in the early hours, to Hallshead Farmhouse, just sit in my car and watch him from a distance. No idea why. That's what us little people do. We're powerless, all of us trying to balance and find space on the bottom rung of the ladder while the Fairbridges sneer down at us from the top.'

Nora shakes her head and sighs. 'Can I respectfully suggest you just go home, crack open a bottle of wine and drink yourself senseless, then get up in the morning and erase all of this from your memory? It's the only way the likes of you and I can survive. Anxiety and stress are like acid, eating at our internal organs, nibbling away until they reach solid bone, by which time we're almost dead. Don't let him win, Penny. Don't let that horrible arrogant shit of a man win.'

She leans forwards and hugs me then turns to leave before stopping and whispering, 'Don't sit outside his house, Penny. It's a bad idea. Please, forget he even exists and just go home.'

And then she too is gone, her heels clipping the pavement as Nora, my only ally, the only other person who fully understands my plight, disappears, leaving me alone and marginally bereft.

* * *

Freda runs ahead of me, her gait steady, her limbs as light and nimble as air. She doesn't walk or run. Freda dances, her paws navigating their way through a pile of leaves and over tree roots. My own feet are heavy as I trudge after her. This is our favourite route, the path through the woods next to the old railway line. I often think we could do it blindfolded. I know every bump on the ground, every fallen trunk that teems with insects. The rush of the breeze through the treetops is a reassuring sound, the familiarity of it something I can cling on to in times of uncertainty. And now feels like a very uncertain time indeed.

I think back to who I was all those years ago, how I was perceived by others when I was a teenager. An inexperienced frightened young girl who masked her insecurities with anger and brusqueness. I considered myself pithy and expressive when in truth I was rude and abrasive. The memory of the architect is like a lance to my vital organs, how I treated him, the accusations I made when all the while my ire should have been directed at the man who had me tongue-tied. The man who showered me with expensive flowers and acted like a perfect gentleman. I can only blame my behaviour back then on fear and naivety, my surliness and petulance a cover for how scared I was. There had been so many changes in our lives. More than I could handle. Hindsight is such a wonderful thing, time and space allowing us the room to breathe and grow and learn. I often wish I could meet the architect or his son so I could apologise profusely. Because that's what decent people do.

'Good girl. What a clever girl you are.' Freda comes running back to me, a stick between her teeth, her tail wagging wildly.

She drops it at my feet, her tongue lolling while she waits. I throw it again and she pads off, disappearing into the dense woodland, giving me time to think, to work out what to do next. Doing nothing feels wrong. Impotent. And yet I don't know what I actually can do to alleviate this feeling, to rid myself of the weight that is still bearing down on me, pushing me further and further into the ground. I will be subterranean if I don't relieve myself of this anger, my face pressed deep into the earth, suffocating beneath the clumps of wet soil that fill my throat and lungs.

We walk for another half hour or so and by the time we get home, I have hatched my plan. It's not so much a plan as a roughly hewn idea, rudimentary in its layout, lacking in any kind of finesse. But it's all I've got.

The evening passes without event, Damien showering and having an early night after a hectic week. I call round and put Mum to bed. She too is tired and gets undressed and into her nightie without any fuss or drama. I pray this is a sign of what is to come later on. It's not too much to ask, is it? That after years of torment and rage I am finally allowed a brief spell of freedom, a small interlude of happiness when everything goes my way and I can rebalance the scales of justice that have been tipped against me for so long.

I lock Mum's door and head home, peeking in at Damien, who is already in a deep sleep. The conditions are perfect. This is it; this is my time. The moment I have waited for. The moment when the stars are all aligned and the universe is smiling down on me. If I don't do this now, I will never do it. It's as good a time as any.

32

PENNY

The verdict has already made the local newspapers. He has been named and that makes me happy even if it is a not guilty result. His name being published will hopefully make any past victims sit up and take notice, the story gathering enough mud that some of it might just stick. Melanie's name has been withheld so at least that is something. On a whim, I look her up on social media and spot her straightaway, a link to the story on her post where she claims that every word she said was true.

Not enough evidence, but that man definitely raped me.

I hope she shares it far and wide. I hope a thousand or more people see it and read the story. It will sow seeds of doubt in everyone's minds, his name, even if only for a short while, dragged through the dirt; his character briefly lower than a snake's belly. Right where he belongs. Already I can see her post has been shared half a dozen times. It's a small victory but a worthy one.

I am sitting in my car on the driveway of my house, waiting to make sure all the lights in the neighbourhood are out. The occupants of just one house six doors down are still awake. We live on a hill. I could release the handbrake and sail soundlessly off the drive and onto the main road, but I'm not about to take any unnecessary risks. I have plenty of time. I can wait.

My phone vibrates in my pocket. I lift it out and stare at the message sent from an unknown number.

> Please don't do anything stupid, Penny. He really isn't worth it.

My hackles rise. I think I know who it is but send the question anyway.

> Who is this and how did you get my number?

The reply comes straight back, flashing up on my screen.

> It's Nora. How do you think I got your number? I'm a journalist. It's my job to find things out.

Before I can type a reply, another message flashes up.

> I looked up your married surname on the local BMD site and then googled you. You're a counsellor. The number is on your website. These things are relatively easy when you know how.

My fingers hover over my phone while my brain rummages for something to say.

> I'm fine. Tucked up in bed.

> And yet still awake and on your phone?

I consider typing up something witty but instead turn off my phone and slip it back in my pocket, putting all thoughts of Nora out of my mind. I know what I am about to do and that is my focus. Everything else is just detritus that will clutter my thinking.

It's another ten minutes before darkness descends completely and I am able to leave, keeping my revs low until I exit the road and the houses are a speck in my rear-view mirror.

The journey to Hallshead Farmhouse takes over an hour. I travel on winding country lanes, keen to avoid any CCTV. As I pull up on the main track that runs past Hallshead Farmhouse, I can see even from this distance that it is in complete darkness. My heart is a gallop as I sit, watching for any signs of movement. I concentrated only on the road on the drive to this place, keeping my anger and fear locked away, but now I am back here, I can feel a certain amount of terror rising. My roughly thought-out plan just got even more ragged, its edges twisted and torn. I push back my shoulders and tell myself to not be so stupid and cowardly, to grab this opportunity and do what needs to be done. I don't even know if Cameron Fairbridge is inside the house. He might be sleeping in the big place on the hill. If that's the case, I will visit there too.

A chill nips at my face when I open the car door and step out into the night. Stars twinkle above me, the clear sky lowering both the temperature and my ability to think straight. It's always colder up here in the hills of North Yorkshire. The warmth of the day soon slips away once dusk sets in, leaving behind a blanket of icy air that wraps itself around the unprepared. Fortunately I brought my thick coat. Thick enough to stave off the cold but not so heavy that it is cumbersome, stopping me from doing what I came here to do.

I clamber over a fence and take a furrowed muddy path across the surrounding fields to the back of the farmhouse, trying to recall the various doors in and out of the house. They will be locked for sure, and the layout of the building has changed somewhat. Cameron Fairbridge isn't an idiot. He might be dangerous and he is without doubt a psychopath, but he is intelligent enough to understand that people often do hazardous, unpredictable things and therefore must protect himself. He of all people should know that. He is one of the unpredictable ones. A terrifying predator.

I try the doors anyway, not surprised to find them locked. No alarm or security, however. Not that scared then. He must feel sure that this remote location will save him from any intruders. If he thinks that then he is wrong.

The old lean-to has been demolished and in its place is a large conservatory. Using my phone for light, I peer through the panes of glass to the furniture inside. A large white leather sofa fills almost half of the living space, with brightly coloured cushions scattered over it. Next to the sofa is a glass coffee table with ornate brass legs, and taking pride of place next to that is a large animal-shaped pink standard lamp. Plenty of money but very little taste. This place is very different to the mansion where he once lived. No antique furniture. No original fixtures and fittings. It resembles a brothel. Visions of young women being lured here with ill intent fill my mind. A sickly sensation rises in my gut. I swallow and tiptoe around to the other side of the glass, hoping to find an open window. That's when I hear it – the snap of twigs underfoot. I spin around, my heart bouncing around my chest like a jack-in-the-box, and I see nothing but a veil of darkness. Probably an animal. Maybe a deer or a fox. It isn't a person. It can't be. This place is too remote. Our time spent living at Hallshead Farmhouse didn't last long but the eeriness of the solitude is something that has stayed with me.

I continue with my tour of the perimeter of the house, looking for a way in. There will be one. I just haven't found it yet. No property is completely secure. I of all people, should know that fact. All I need is a pane of glass that isn't double glazed or a wooden door that can be jemmied open. And then a memory comes to me, hurtling into my brain like shrapnel. The barn. It's connected. There is a small high window in there that leads to the house. It's tiny, probably only big enough for a child, but if my memory serves me correctly, it's just wide enough for me to slide through, my small frame suddenly a benefit.

Feet twisting beneath me on the dewy grass, I pad around the other side of the house, tiptoeing over the gravel and into the crumbling old barn that still has the same large wooden doors which pull apart with the greatest of ease. Using my phone to illuminate the way, I pick my way through a carpet of old farming implements that are scattered across the ground. A particularly heavy shovel catches my eye. I could use it for protection if required. Problem is, it could be used to kill me as well. Cameron Fairbridge is a big strong man and would fell me as easily as blowing over a feather. The memory of him lying on top of me all those years ago enters my brain, the sheer heft of him making me shudder and giving me enough nerve to do what I have planned.

I spin around then glance up at the window at the side of the house.

It's not open, but it is made of wood. Not double glazed and therefore easily broken. A steady rhythm thrums in my neck. Am I really ready to do this? Am I brave enough to break the law and run the risk of being arrested?

I swallow and rub at my eyes with cold fingers, anger and resentment and a whole host of other unmentionable emotions consuming me. Yes. Yes, I am ready to do this. I've been ready for this moment all of my adult life. It's been a long, slow build-up to this but I am driven by the cracks in our justice system. If I don't stop Cameron Fairbridge, who will?

No tools or implements are needed to get inside. I grab a large crate, drag it over to the window, then step up and, using my elbow, I knock my bent arm against the glass. I can feel movement, the pane shifting in the old frame. All that's needed is a little more muscle behind the push. Trying again, I hit my elbow against the window and hear a satisfying fracturing sound as it gives way. Covering my hand with my sleeve, I punch at the window, knocking shards of glass aside. I pick them out of the wooden surround until it is clear of any remaining pieces and there is enough room for me to wiggle through. My thick coat acts as protection against any cuts or bruises from any protruding edges and in seconds I am inside, standing in the old boot room of Hallshead Farmhouse. An iron fist twists at my guts. We rarely came in here as kids. It was a forgotten part of the house. Unused and unloved. Still is by the looks of things. While the rest of the building has had a huge makeover, this particular room still smells dank and musty, the stench of it evoking unwanted recollections and catapulting me back to my teenage years.

I swing my phone around, the torch lighting the entire area. A couple of old coats hang on pegs on the far wall but apart from that it's empty. The sound of my feet on the concrete floor is the only thing to be heard, the ghostly echo of my footfall a dull shuffle that pounds in my ears. I tiptoe to the old wooden door and turn the handle, a staccato beat filling my chest. It opens. I stop and take a deep breath, steeling myself for what comes next, preparing myself physically and mentally before stepping over the threshold and, like a thief in the night, entering the main part of Hallshead Farmhouse. My chest tightens with anticipation as I glance around. This is it. I'm here now. There's no turning back.

33

PENNY

I'm engulfed by the darkness, the torch on my phone barely casting any light in the shadowy corners of each room. The hallway is bigger than I remember. Wider and longer. The living room and kitchen are also completely different, their new layout making me disorientated. I continue moving until I reach the stairs, my footfall as silent as the grave. My heart continues to climb up my neck as I pad across the landing. Pushing each door ajar and peering in, I swing my phone across immaculately made beds. Room after room and each of them empty.

I continue, my breathing a demonic roar in my head, my heartbeat accentuated by the surrounding silence. Pictures adorn the walls of the landing area, one of them a large canvas print of Cameron Fairbridge and his father. Bile rises in my throat at the sight of their sour conceited expressions. I swallow and hang on to the handrail for balance then step forward and wait. Just one more room to go. The master bedroom. The final part of the house. I touch the handle and slowly push open the door, sweeping my phone over the bed. A loud buzzing pounds in my ears. It's empty.

I flick on the landing switch and flood the place with light. Then on impulse, I go from room to room, dragging quilts off beds, knocking items to the floor, pulling down curtains and blinds, an inner rage taking over. Years and years of pent-up anger finds its way out. He deserves this and more. What he really deserves is to be sitting in a prison cell next to a six-foot-eight monster who has designs on ripping his throat open with a shard of broken glass or a jagged knife, but that didn't happen, so here I am, exacting my own revenge. My trail of destruction in his luxuriously renovated farmhouse-cum-penthouse will be but a slight inconvenience in his orderly protected little life.

Driven by fury, hatred and frustration, I head downstairs where I empty kitchen cupboards, sweeping items onto the floor and kicking over chairs. I throw large precious ornaments at the wall, smiling as they shatter into tiny pieces, then I spot a bottle of bleach. I grab at it and squirt liberal amounts onto an expensive-looking rug, the colour immediately leaching out. I stop, panting and gasping for breath, amazed at how destructive I can be given the chance. My eyes roam around the place. It's a mess. I've done enough here. I would love to wreak more havoc, to break and ruin everything he owns, but it's time to go. Just before leaving, I push over the large television in the living room, the crack of it as it hits the wooden floor a gratifying sound. The Fairbridges have more than enough cash to repair this place, but it was never about the money. Causing this damage and knowing I have inconvenienced them has already helped to unburden me of the hatred and resentment that has been bearing down on me for decades. I was buckling under the strain and already I feel lighter. Happier, as if the weight of my troubles is slowly ebbing away.

I step back, a hoarse gasp rattling in my neck, my eyes roving over the carnage. Something doesn't feel right. I try to still my heavy breathing and swallow, a dry feeling catching at the back of my throat. A familiar smell creeps past, curling its way into the room, stinging my eyes and making it hard to breathe.

Smoke.

That dry, acrid stench and the coarse scratching sensation on the soft tissue of my throat and nose transports me back to this place. To that time. That night when everything irrevocably fell apart; me and my mother, watching as Aaron stumbled from the house, his body burning, his face melting. Our time in this place finally at an end.

I have to get back to the old boot room. The sharp choking odour is growing stronger with each passing second. Navigating my way past the clutter and overturned pieces of furniture on the floor, I find my way there, slamming the door behind me and resting on it to catch my breath. By the time I manage to climb up and reach the broken window I can hardly breathe. My eyes are streaming, my vision blurry. I rub at my face and hoist myself up to the empty frame but my limbs are already weakened. I feel sapped of all strength, my body continually sliding back down every time I try to clamber up. I am tired, so very tired. It's difficult to think straight. A powerful hand is clutched around my windpipe, stopping any air from getting in. Maybe this is my punishment for what I've just done. Maybe there is a God up there and he does actually look out for the wealthy and the privileged whilst ignoring the rest of us. If that is indeed the case, then I'm doomed. I have just wrecked a large house, ruining everything I could find. I was simply readjusting the scales, making a small reconfiguration to the mechanism so the perpetrator knows how it feels to have his home invaded, to feel scared and threatened in the one place where he should feel safe.

My breathing is ragged. My nose and throat feel scorched, as if a fire is raging in my head.

I don't want to die. Not in this place. Not here where it all began.

With a sudden surge of strength, I throw myself at the wall, my fingers gripping the window frame. I can feel small shards of protruding glass as they pierce my fingertips, but I ignore the pain, concentrating only on using my upper body strength to haul myself through the small space where the window once was. I have to leave this place, to get back home to my husband, to my mother and my dog. That's where I belong. Not here in this godforsaken building. This was never my home. None of us ever really belonged here. We were inadvertently hurled into Hallshead Farmhouse, a place that didn't want us. And now we are finally free of it.

I pull myself up and slither through the gap, the sheer effort making my body tremble and vibrate. My lungs feel ready to combust and my head is pounding. The damp grass outside breaks my fall, my body curled into a foetal position when I emerge into the darkness, gasping for air. Screaming is impossible. I barely have the strength to walk. And yet I must. I have to get away from this area. No time to hang around. No time to think about the fire and how it started. I need to reach my car and just drive. Except I can't. Standing and staying upright is a struggle, my limbs rubbery. I'm as floppy and as weak as a newborn foal.

Behind me, in the distance, I hear cracking, then a sudden boom. Crawling on all fours, I spin around, my eyes narrowed as I stare at the top of the hill, a cloud of orange billowing into the night sky. Fairbridge Hall is on fire. Hallshead Farmhouse is also smouldering, the flames slowly taking hold.

Then hands are lifting me up off the ground, strong fingers clasped around my upper arms and guiding me back to my car, my legs scrambling for purchase on the damp slippery ground.

'You need to get away from here. Leave. Just leave!'

The voice is a throaty whisper close to my ear. Almost a growl. I don't recognise it. Through a film of tears I turn to see a face I don't recognise. Or maybe I do. It's hazy, the memory, her features pulling me back many decades. I try to think clearly, to sift through years of memories and images, but it's so difficult, my brain a befuddled mess.

'Now they really are burning in hell,' she says. 'Exactly what they deserve.'

I stare at her until she pushes me forward, telling me to go, to get in my car and go home before anybody arrives.

'I'm guilty as charged,' she says, her words clearly enunciated, her face still familiar yet at the same time alien to me. 'I'm dying anyway. By the time they come to arrest me, I'll be on my way to the big man in the sky. Or maybe not after this, eh?' She glances over at the flames that are now taking hold in Hallshead Farmhouse, streaks of orange leaping out of smashed windows and billowing high into the dark cloudless sky. 'Who knows, I might just meet those two bastards down in hell.'

I stare at her face; the shape of her eyes, the angle of her jaw, her expression. It slowly slots into place, the final piece of the jigsaw to complete the full picture.

'He raped my daughter. He's getting exactly what he deserves. The courts might not have found him guilty but I know him for what he is. A lowlife predator with no conscience. His father is the same. Both pieces of shit. The world will be a better place without them.'

'Nora,' I manage to splutter. 'You're Molly Wright, Nora's mother. You're the lady who worked in the village shop.' I think of my earlier conversation with her daughter. I think of Nora's revelation, her tears and the hurt that had built inside her for all of these years. I am Nora. I comprehend her pain. I have lived her life. A life filled with fear and foreboding. And I also know why Molly is here. Why she is doing what she is doing.

She doesn't reply, grabbing my car keys out of my hand instead and opening the door to push me inside.

'Go on,' she says, leaning down and staring in at me. 'Go home. None of this ever happened. You weren't here. Go home to your family and live the rest of your life knowing that justice has finally been done.'

'But I—'

She taps my hand and smiles. 'Don't worry. I know who you are and why you are at this place. Like I said, none of this happened. I didn't see you. You were never here.'

And with that, she turns and walks over the field, her silhouette swallowed up by the darkness.

* * *

The neighbourhood is still sleeping as I let myself back into my house and creep upstairs. I take off my clothes and dispose of them in a binbag, tying it up and putting it at the bottom of the wheelie bin outside. Then I come back inside, take a shower and wash my hair and climb back into bed, the small cuts on my fingertips still tingling and throbbing. At twelve years of age, Freda is too tired to fret, sleeping peacefully in her basket, unaware of my movements. Damien is also still out for the count, his limbs like solid stone when I cuddle up next to him and attempt to snuggle beneath his arm.

Outside, the world is silent, everyone slumbering in their beds while only an hour's drive away, two houses are burning. Two people hopefully choking to death, the fumes poisoning their bodies. I should feel pity, some small stirring of sympathy for them, but I don't. I can't begin to imagine how many lives they have ruined. Perhaps my lack of concern makes me as bad as them. Or perhaps the fact I tried to do the right thing and deliver justice in the proper manner and failed has left me bitter and full of hatred. Even if I had done the moral thing and called the emergency services, it would have been too late. Both buildings were already alight. And my doing such a thing would have implicated me. Have I not been punished enough? I have lived in the shadow of fear for many decades now. It's time to bid it all goodbye.

I think of Ivor Spencer and how he will cope without his connection to wealth and entitlement. I have no knowledge of his address and know nothing about his current life, but I do hope that one day he will pay for what he did to Nora. That's a battle for another time. I've done what I can to reset the damage Cameron Fairbridge inflicted on me. Perhaps Ivor Spencer will wither and die like an uncared-for plant if his friend Fairbridge perishes in the fire.

I close my eyes and feel a curtain of contentment begin to descend, the heaviness I feel in my limbs borne out of a sense of relief that at long last, it is all over. Tomorrow I will wake and smile because it will be the beginning of the rest of my life.

34

PENNY

'I fell. Couldn't sleep so went for a wander in the garden in the early hours to clear my head and tripped over a plant pot.'

Damien is staring at my hands, at the pinprick scarlet cuts that litter my fingertips. He shakes his head and smiles.

'I know,' I say, smiling back at him. 'What an idiot, eh?' It appears my propensity for lying knows no bounds. I've become quite the master at it. It's time now to put a stop to it, to start living a more truthful existence.

He places a cup of coffee in front of me and sits down at the kitchen table. 'Bet you're glad it's all over, eh?'

'God, yes. It was all-consuming. I can't wait to get back to work, to get some normality back in my life.'

He leans forward and kisses me, the heat from his body warming me. 'You've done your civic duty. Well done, you.'

I shiver and pull my cardigan tighter around my shoulders. 'Your turn next,' I say and smile.

We finish our coffee, the urge to check the news on my phone so strong, I have to press my fingers against the surface of the table. They practically twitch in resistance. I'll wait until Damien is occupied elsewhere. I don't want my expression observed as I read about the decimation of Hallshead Farmhouse and Fairbridge Hall, and the death of its occupants. I want that episode of my life to be over. Reading about it will be the final chapter in a long, seemingly never-ending tale of tragedy, and then I will move on with my life. As if none of it ever happened.

'I was going to do a bit of work this morning then we can go into town for lunch if you fancy it? Maybe Stokesley or Yarm?'

I like that idea a lot. Normality. I welcome it.

'Sounds perfect.' My voice sounds and feels disembodied. The voice of somebody who has lived a hundred lives.

I'm still operating on another level. I won't be my usual self until I've checked the news and read about the deaths of two people and see the smouldering remains of those buildings. Only then can I move on.

Damien heads upstairs to his study and I grapple with my phone, my co-ordination limited. I'm all fingers and thumbs as I load up the local news and scan the headlines. It's not the main story but it's there, farther down the page.

Fire ravages stately home

Police are investigating a blaze that tore through Fairbridge Hall and a nearby farmhouse in North Yorkshire. A 69-year-old woman has been questioned in connection with the incident. One man has died and another is believed to be in a critical condition.

More on this story later.

My heart crawls up my neck. One of them is still alive.

Shit.

I will have to keep checking the updates. Wait for names to be released. But for now, I'm going to have to live my life, act as if nothing untoward is happening when in reality, my past, present and future all hang in the balance. I have to trust Molly Wright, to believe her when she said she wouldn't name me, because if she does, then this brief respite from hell is over.

My chest expands when I suck in a lungful of air. I rub at my eyes, a strange fusion of weariness and elation expanding inside of me. Also relief. Somehow, I know that she will keep her silence. I don't know how I know that, but right now, that belief is all I have to cling on to.

I tidy the kitchen and pop next door to see Mum, who is surprisingly sprightly. We sit and flick through the old photo album, a favourite pastime of hers.

'Where's that?' she asks as we turn the page to a picture of me and Dad taken at Hallshead Farmhouse. 'And who is that man and young girl?'

I try to explain but it proves too difficult a task, Mum claiming she doesn't have a husband and that she doesn't know any young teenage girls, asking repeatedly why I was showing her pictures of complete strangers.

'Mum, that was me. Do you remember?'

Her eyes scrutinise my face, a possible flash of recognition there. 'Maybe. Is she your little girl?'

I shake my head and blink back tears. We've looked at enough old photographs for one day. I am placing the album back in the box when she suddenly speaks up, her voice crisp and clear, taking me by surprise.

'I remember that man, though. The one with the bouquet. Do you remember the flowers, Penny? He gave that young girl some lovely expensive flowers.'

My body is limp, as if all the energy has been drained out of me. Cold air charges through my veins. The flowers. How could I have forgotten? That was part of his grooming technique, a way of slowly and insidiously edging his way into my affections. And the awful thing is, it was working. I was actually being lured into his sickly little trap, but of course there was never any need because in the end he used brute force, getting what he wanted and in the process, ruining my life.

I put everything back in its place and make Mum a cup of tea, waiting in the kitchen while the memory ebbs away.

'I'll call round later this evening, get you ready for bed, Mum.'

She is already busy watching the TV, her eyes focused on the screen, my words lost to her. But then I stop, my blood freezing as the newsreader says the words I don't want to hear.

It is believed that an elderly man perished in the fire at Fairbridge Hall while a younger man, thought to be his son, is in hospital in a critical condition. A local woman is still being held in police custody in connection with the incident. We'll bring you more information on this later. Meanwhile, Sharon is here to tell us whether we can expect an Indian summer. How's the weekend looking, Sharon...?

My fingers are clasped around the doorframe, the room spinning around me. He's still alive. Cameron Fairbridge is still alive. I should have known he would cling on to life, his ego too big a force to ever be destroyed.

'I'm going to lock your door, Mum, and like I said, I'll be back later this afternoon. We'll have some tea and then after supper I'll run you a bath and tuck you up in bed.'

I leave, stepping outside into the fresh air before she can disagree and throw a huge tantrum. My face burns, the cool air soothing my hot flesh. I close my eyes and shiver. He has evaded justice and is now still hanging on in there, breathing the same air as me. Does that man not know when to give up?

My thoughts turn to Molly Wright. Did she wait around and admit to what she had done, or was there some incriminating piece of evidence that led the police to her? I pray that the fire has burnt away all traces of me ever being there and that she keeps her word, telling the police she was alone at Hallshead Farmhouse.

My phone rings before I enter the back gate, its shrill pitch an unsettling noise. I pull it out of my pocket, an unknown caller flashing up on the screen. Nora. It has to be Nora. I try to keep the tremor out of my voice and steady myself as I answer.

'Hello?'

'Were you there?' she whispers. 'Last night, were you there with her?'

'Nora? Sorry, I'm not sure what you mean. There with who?'

I can hear her breathing down the other end of the phone, her gasps heavy and erratic.

'God, I'm sorry. I shouldn't have rung you. It's Mum. She – she has been arrested for starting the fire at both of the Fairbridge houses. And I'm...'

She stops and I say nothing. Better to remain silent than say the wrong thing and incriminate myself. I didn't start the fire. I am certainly innocent of that crime. I did, however, break into the house and wreck it. I sit down on the small bench next to the gate that separates our gardens.

'I don't know what to say, Nora,' I eventually stammer. 'I'm so sorry. I honestly and truly don't know what to say.'

Her sigh is low and protracted. 'Her cancer is advanced. She's admitted to arson. She was there when the fire engines and the police arrived and told them she was the one who started it.' Nora begins to cry, her voice breaking. 'This is all so horrendous. I have no idea what to do, Penny. I'm a purported hard-nosed journalist and for once I'm lost for bloody words.'

It feels as if she is sitting right next to me. I try to keep my attention fixed on her words but my brain is screaming at me that a neighbour may have seen my car leave the driveway. All I have is Molly's promise that she made to me, that she will take all the blame.

* * *

She is sitting in the window staring out at passing traffic when I arrive. It's been two days since I spoke to Nora on the phone, a tense two days with every phone call and every knock on the door jangling my nerves. It looks like Molly Wright has kept her promise and I am not about to be arrested.

'I took a wild guess and got you a latte. You look like a latte kind of person.' She smiles, the radiant curve of her mouth in stark contrast to the tiredness in her eyes.

'Good guess,' I reply, wondering how she knew. Wondering if every habit I have is really that obvious to those around me.

I slide into the chair and on instinct, reach over to place a reassuring hand on Nora's shoulder.

'I should have expected something like this, really,' she says, her eyelashes fluttering as she speaks. 'Mum has always been feisty. Never been one to go down without a fight.'

I nod, still reticent to speak for fear of inadvertently saying something I shouldn't.

'She was furious about the verdict. Said he had managed to wriggle out of being held to account and that she kind of expected it really.'

'Where is she now?'

I imagine Molly sitting in a cell, her small body crying out for painkillers as the cancer eats away at her internal organs.

'She's been bailed. With her advanced illness, she needs hospital care and isn't considered a risk.'

My chest inflates as I sigh and bite at my lip, relief flooding through me.

'I'm fine with that, Penny. I really am. It was a shock at the time but the cancer will get to her before the courts will. She has weeks left, not months.'

We sit in silence for a few seconds, sipping at our coffee and staring outside. Splatters of rain hit the window, slow at first before increasing in speed and strength. A heavy downpour to match our mood.

'I thought you might want to know that Cameron Fairbridge is currently in James Cook Hospital but is going to be transferred to a private hospital in York.'

I widen my eyes. 'Really? And you know this how?'

'I'm a journalist. It's my job to find out things. And no, I won't divulge my source, but believe me when I say, he is definitely being transferred. You didn't expect one of the Fairbridges to stay in an NHS hospital with all the other plebs, did you?' She pulls out a piece of paper and quickly shoves it in my palm, curling my fingers around it as if it's a nugget of pure gold. 'This is the address. If ever you feel like visiting, that is. It might be worth it just to see how he will live the rest of his life.' A silvery tear traces its way down her cheek. She sniffs and pulls out a tissue, dabbing at her face. 'Ivor Spencer has got away with what he did to me, but at least we got the main man, eh?'

Nora stands and is gone before I can respond. I glance up to catch one more glimpse of her, but Nora Wright has vanished into the deluge of rain.

35

PENNY

She didn't make it to the end of the month. Molly Wright passed away just three weeks after her arrest. She died at home with Nora at her side. It was peaceful in the end. After the turmoil of the previous few weeks, Molly drew her final dying breath in her own bed surrounded by her family. I didn't attend the funeral, keen to remain anonymous and not be seen by the other attendees. The police were there and it felt like the sensible option to keep a low profile. I sent Nora a text explaining that I couldn't cancel a particularly important client and sent flowers and a card instead. She understood and we said we would keep in touch at some point in the future. Whether or not we will keep our promise is anybody's guess. It's been a difficult time and we both need some space to heal after having old wounds reopened by the trial and subsequent not guilty verdict.

Douglas Fairbridge's funeral was, by all accounts, a quiet, modest affair, his high-ranking friends abandoning him and his son too ill to attend. Ivor Spencer stood by the graveside tossing handfuls of wet soil onto the coffin while muttering a short prayer. Some people get the send-off they deserve.

I am sitting in the car park of the hospital, an iron fist squeezing at my stomach. A breath is trapped in my gullet. I have my story ready, should anybody ask who I am. Cameron and I were neighbours long ago. We grew up in the same village. He was close friends with my brother. We cared deeply about one another. I even have a photograph should anybody ask, a photoshopped picture that was far easier to concoct than I ever thought possible. In it Cameron is leaning his head on my shoulder while I am smiling and holding a drink aloft. I just need to see him one final time, to observe his suffering and make sure he will never leave that hospital bed. To make sure he will never again be able to attack another woman. I need to do this to feel safe. Not just for me but for females everywhere.

My phone call to make this visit was relatively easy with few probing questions. If anything, they seemed grateful that somebody was making an effort to come and see him. Ivor has been conspicuous by his absence according to Nora's sources, his access to status and wealth now severed. Who would want to be saddled with a series of hospital visits, sitting by somebody's side and talking about the latest television programmes and the weather? It's what any normal caring person would do, but Ivor Spencer is no normal caring person. He is a leech. A hanger-on. A parasite. He and Cameron were well matched.

I lock the car and head towards the main doors. Damien thinks I'm in York to see a client. I don't like lying to him; in fact, I hate it, and once this is over I have made a vow to myself that I will tell him everything. Almost everything. I am not going to reveal that the man who raped me is the one who was on trial last month. The one who walked free and is now lying incapacitated in a hospital bed. Revealing all the nasty grizzly facts will do nobody any good. Some things are best left undisturbed. Why poke a sleeping bear?

A waft of warm air billows over me as I step inside the building, the receptionist greeting me with a broad smile.

'Cameron Fairbridge? Ah yes, he's in room thirty-six on floor two. There is a lift or, if you're feeling energetic, the stairs are just to the right through those double doors.'

It's quiet, the sound of my movements accentuated by the surrounding hush. I take the stairs to give myself even more thinking time. To prepare myself for sitting at the bedside of the man who raped me. To prepare myself for seeing his features, feeling the heat of his body. I know nothing of his injuries but have been warned that he will drift in and out of consciousness. This will be my first and final visit. It's all I need to settle my inner turmoil. I have to be witness to his wounds, to see him suffer and squirm, and if that makes me a terrible person then so be it. Sometimes good people do bad things and sometimes bad people do good things. I'm somewhere in the middle, about to step over that dividing line so I can move on with the rest of my life.

The corridor is empty save for a nurse at a desk down the bottom. Her head is lowered as she studies a computer screen. I stop outside room thirty-six and wait for a few seconds. My palms are clammy. I rub them at my sides and press my hand onto the doorplate, pushing it open before stepping inside.

I don't know what I expected, but it isn't this – this disfigured faceless man who is lying in the bed. His skin is mottled and shiny, his mouth not a mouth but a hole in his face. Bandages cover his hands and head, and he has only one eye, the other one sunken into his skull. I swallow down my shriek, a small gasp escaping instead. Not a gasp of horror. A gasp of relief. His remaining eye is initially closed and flutters open as I sit down next to his bed and speak.

'Hello, Cameron. Not feeling so good, eh?'

His eye is dull as he stares at me. It's hard to say given his current state of health, but I don't believe he knows me. I don't need him to recognise me. He will find out soon enough who I am and why I'm here.

He doesn't respond. No blinking. No attempt to move his bandaged hands. He just lies there, watching me. Waiting.

'I'd have brought you some grapes or chocolates but I can see that would have been pointless.' I stop and take a couple of short stuttering breaths before continuing. 'I haven't come here to gloat, although it is doing my heart good to see you so incapacitated. I've actually come here to tell you a few things.'

I glance out of the window at the world that continues to spin while we are in here, trapped in our own little void of hell. The sun makes a brief appearance before a cloud scuds across the sky, a swathe of grey matching the mood in the room.

'You don't remember me, do you? Cast your mind back a couple of decades to the family that moved into Hallshead Farmhouse after those unfortunate deaths of the family who drowned in the river. You remember Sam and his parents, don't you? Lovely people who would never have harmed a fly.'

I wait, hoping to observe a spark of recognition, but all I see is that dead-eyed stare and that gaping hole in his face that churns my guts.

'Anyway, Eric and Connie moved in with their children. Two teenagers. Am I getting somewhere now, Mr Fairbridge? Are you starting to remember? Or was I so unimportant and insignificant that once you had broken into our home and raped me, I was obliterated from your mind?'

I may be imagining it, but I could swear his breathing has become laboured, the bandages across his chest rising and falling in rapid succession. I hope he is panicking, the fear of what I am about to say or do looming large in his mind.

'I'm just here to tell you that you didn't break me. I'm here and I'm fully intact. See?' I dramatically tap at my limbs, standing up, doing a little twirl. 'No long-term damage. Your sick little games weren't worth the effort.'

I am not going to let him know how difficult things have been for me. I won't give him that pleasure. He is now the broken one while I am able to rise out of my chair and leave this place, as free as the birds that dance in the branches of the large oak tree next to the window in his room.

'My husband is at home waiting for me, so I'm not going to take up too much of your time. I hear you've not had many visitors. What a shame, eh? In pain and all alone. Never mind, some people get the life they deserve. I suppose once you're discharged from here, you'll need round-the-clock care. Somebody who will wash and dress you and wipe your shitty arse every day.'

My heart is hammering. I stand up and lean over him, the stench of his infected sores an assault on my olfactory system. We are close; so close I could reach down and touch his face with mine. So close I could place my palm over his disfigured mouth and broken nose and press hard until he stops breathing.

'Goodbye, Cameron. I hope the rest of your life is miserable. I'd like to say I forgive you, but after that show of amateur dramatics in court last month, I definitely don't. You are a depraved, spoilt, egotistical maniac who has ruined too many lives.'

I want to say more, but I can hear footsteps outside so instead I straighten up and give him a wide smile and a wave, my voice deliberately saccharine sweet for the ears of any passing doctors or nurses. 'Bye, Cameron. Take care and look after yourself.'

The sun has made another appearance when I leave the hospital and head back to my car. My mother always used to say that it shines on the righteous. I glance at my watch and throw my jacket over my shoulder, a sudden lightness lifting me. I shield my eyes from the glare and smile, thinking that today is definitely going to be a good day.

36

ONE MONTH LATER

He looks better. Slightly improved. Still rake thin but a brief spell in hospital has helped improve his complexion, put some meat on his bones. I lean forwards to hug him and inhale the scent of Aaron's freshly laundered pyjamas and recently washed hair. Part of me expects him to shy away from contact and I'm pleasantly surprised and pleased when he embraces me and plants a dry kiss on my cheek.

Aaron was found slumped and unconscious in a doorway of a large local supermarket. The manager was kind enough to call for an ambulance and since that time, his demeanour has improved and he's agreed to attend sessions to try and get clean. He was so emaciated that his vital organs were close to shutting down. It's been a long road but recovery is in sight and we are all behind him, doing what we can to ensure he gets all the help he clearly needs.

Mum is coming to see him tomorrow. I have told her about how ill Aaron has been and although she didn't quite understand all of the details, there was a flicker of recognition whenever I said his name. Sometimes the past can be as terrifying as an uncertain future, each of us not knowing what tomorrow will bring, but as long as we face it together, we can't go wrong. Better together than apart.

'Bye, buddy. We'll catch up with you tomorrow. Take care of yourself,

Aaron.' Damien shakes his hand then shrugs and smiles and gives him a strong, affectionate hug.

'Bye, Damien,' says Aaron, his once dead eyes showing signs of light and contentment. 'And thanks for everything.'

'No bother, bud. That's what families are for.' Damien winks and purses his lips. 'Don't suppose you fancy swapping places with your sister, do you? We're off shopping for holiday clothes after we leave here and I'm not sure my wallet can stand the strain.'

Aaron lets out a dry cackle that erupts into a bout of coughing. He rubs at his chest and sits up in bed. 'Sorry, too many cigarettes. Those bloody Woodbines'll be the death of me.'

I manage a smile and wave goodbye as we exit the ward and wind our way through countless corridors and lifts to get to the ground floor, a once impossible sense of completeness now within my grasp. Aaron is being cared for. He has a bed to sleep in every night and although I am not so naïve as to believe that the road ahead is going to be smooth and without problems, at least we are making headway. I can't ask for more than that.

There is only one more thing that I need to do, one more loose end that I have to tie up. If I don't do it, at some point in the future, it may unravel and whirl me up in the fabric of its ragged edges.

Damien and I climb in the car and head into town where the sun is shining and the atmosphere is peaceful and unchallenging. We stop for coffee in one of our favourite cafes and choose a table outside in a secluded corner of the courtyard.

It's here. The moment is right and I am ready. Ready to tell him about what happened to me in Hallshead Farmhouse. I will start at the beginning, long before we even moved there. I will start with the incident in school, show Damien how being unsupported left me feeling vulnerable, frightened of male attention, unsure how to interpret their words and body language. I will tell him how after moving to the farmhouse, I saw somebody outside my bedroom window, how I was frightened and confused and turned my anger on an innocent man, imagining the touching, blaming the poor architect when all the while the real monster was hiding in plain sight, his deviance and warped intentions masked by wealth and a charming smile.

We place our order. I then lean forward and take my husband's hand in mine, the words I have held in place since I was a child about to pour out of me like an overfilled cup. A river of secrets and tears that will run unchecked and pool at our feet.

'Damien, I have something to tell you. This isn't easy for me to say. I've spent all of my adult life with this thing curled up inside of me, but the time is right for me to start opening up to you and telling the truth.'

He watches me, his expression open and non-judgemental, his mouth curved into a gentle lift that shows neither happiness nor anger.

'When I was no more than a kid, as you know we moved into Hallshead Farmhouse, but I haven't told you the full story. It's time now,' I say, tears threatening to fall, 'to tell you the whole chapter and verse of what happened to me when I was just fourteen years old…' I take a juddering breath and hand over my heart and my deepest fears and emotions to a man I trust and love more than life itself. And then I begin.

* * *

MORE FROM J. A. BAKER

Another book from J. A. Baker, *Hush Little Baby*, is available to order now here:

www.mybook.to/HushBabyBackAd

ACKNOWLEDGEMENTS

As always, there are lots of people to thank for helping this book make it out into the big wide world. First and foremost, thank you to my husband, Richard, for his support which is endless and unerring. Countless visits cancelled or postponed, me sitting slumped and stony-faced at my laptop, desperate pleas for new ideas as I cry that I will never have enough energy or impetus to write any more books – he accepts them all without question, knowing I have deadlines to meet and plot holes to fix. So thank you, my love. You are my muse and support without which, I would collapse sobbing, in a red-faced, snotty-nosed heap. Your promises of coffee and cake at our favourite haunts in Yarm and other towns across Teesside is the thing that keeps me going. That and the hope that one day, one of my books will be a massive bestseller that gets turned into a blockbuster film and we can buy a huge villa somewhere warm for our ever-extending family to visit. We can but dream, eh?

The staff at Boldwood Books have shown me nothing but kindness and support and so my thanks go to them, especially my editor, Emily Ruston, who helps lick my rough-edged novels into shape and never complains when I turn my nose up at possible titles and covers. Also thanks to Jennifer Davies who did a thorough line edit of this book. Your wise suggestions have helped fine-tune my book.

Thank you also to Rachel Sargeant, my proofreader who has the thankless task of searching for those elusive missing words that despite various edits and re-reads, mange to sneak past even the most eagle-eyed of people, and also to the marketing team who work tirelessly to help promote and sell my books.

My ARC team are the absolute best, so I could not fire off a volley of thank yous without giving them a mention, so thank you, thank you a thousand times over for reading and reviewing my books. You guys are the absolute best.

Dawn Cottingham, my friend of over fifty-five years (are we really that old?), you are a treasure, reading every book that I write and singing my praises to anybody who will listen. Never change, you wonderful witty woman. Here's to the next few decades of fun and laughter! We have so many adventures ahead of us.

Valerie Keogh and Anita Waller, I probably would have hung up my quill long ago were it not for you two wonderfully supportive ladies. You keep me sane and never complain when I come to you full of woe, so my gratitude to you is immeasurable.

A thank you to my family for simply being there and being who you are. With four children and their partners, and five grandchildren and a dog, our lives are busy and full and I wouldn't ever swap it for the world. My writing would be nothing more than a pile of shallow ramblings were it not for the richness and fullness of my life.

Before I send to you all to sleep with my mad musings, I would like to let you know that I am on social media and welcome conversations with readers, so if you fancy a chat and a virtual coffee, I can be found at:

www.facebook.com/thewriterjude
www.instagram.com/jabakerauthor
bsky.app/profile/thewriterjude.bsky.social
www.threads.net/@jabakerauthor

Best Wishes
Judith

ABOUT THE AUTHOR

J. A. Baker is a successful writer of numerous psychological thrillers. Born and brought up in Middlesbrough, she still lives in the North East, which inspires the settings for her books.

Sign up to J. A. Baker's mailing list here for news, competitions and updates on future books.

Follow J. A. Baker on social media:

- facebook.com/thewriterjude
- x.com/thewriterjude
- instagram.com/jabakerauthor
- tiktok.com/@jabaker41
- bookbub.com/authors/JABaker

ALSO BY J. A. BAKER

Local Girl Missing

The Last Wife

The Woman at Number 19

The Other Mother

The Toxic Friend

The Retreat

The Woman in the Woods

The Stranger

The Intruder

The Girl In The Water

The Quiet One

The Passenger

Little Boy, Gone

When She Sleeps

The Widower's Lie

The Guilty Teacher

Hush Little Baby

The Good Daughter

THE Murder LIST

THE MURDER LIST IS A NEWSLETTER DEDICATED TO ALL THINGS CRIME AND THRILLER FICTION!

SIGN UP TO MAKE SURE YOU'RE ON OUR HIT LIST FOR GRIPPING PAGE-TURNERS AND HEARTSTOPPING READS.

SIGN UP TO OUR NEWSLETTER

BIT.LY/THEMURDERLISTNEWS

Boldwood

Boldwood Books is an award-winning fiction publishing company seeking out the best stories from around the world.

Find out more at www.boldwoodbooks.com

Join our reader community for brilliant books, competitions and offers!

Follow us
@BoldwoodBooks
@TheBoldBookClub

Sign up to our weekly deals newsletter

https://bit.ly/BoldwoodBNewsletter